Tangela didn't have the strength to turn away from his touch. The truth was she craved him. Like wine. Like chocolate. Like sensuous lovemaking.

Caressing her cheeks with the back of his fingers, he weakened her resolve. Then, the unthinkable. Their lips came together in a passion-filled reunion. His kiss—his sweet, gentle kiss, was like balm on her wounded heart and soothed away her deepest pain.

Desire gripped her, filled her, swallowed her whole. His lips moved beautifully, expertly over her mouth. Tangela didn't feel as if any of this was real. They were enemies. Bitter, angry exes who couldn't stand each other. They'd had a volatile breakup, and before last month they hadn't laid eyes on each other in two years.

But when she felt his tongue inside her mouth, seeking her own, Tangela slanted her head to the right, hungry for more.

Books by Pamela Yaye

Kimani Romance

Other People's Business
The Trouble with Luv'
Her Kind of Man
Love T.K.O.
Games of the Heart
Passion Overtime
Love on the Rocks

PAMELA YAYE

has a bachelor's degree in Christian education and has been writing short stories since elementary school. Her love for African-American fiction and literature prompted her to actively pursue a career in writing romance. When she's not reading or working on her latest novel, she's watching basketball, cooking or planning her next vacation. Pamela lives in Calgary, Canada, with her handsome husband and adorable daughter.

Love on the
ROCKS

Pamela Yaye

KIMANI
ROMANCE

Baby Justice,
I miss you and think about you every single day.

KIMANI PRESS™

ISBN-13: 978-0-373-86150-7

Recycling programs
for this product may
not exist in your area.

LOVE ON THE ROCKS

Copyright © 2010 by Pamela Sadadi

www.kimanipress.com

Printed in U.S.A.

Dear Reader,

Destiny can be delayed, but never denied....

Love is a powerful drug. It can make a sister break out in song, or cause a perfectly sane man to lose his mind. And that's exactly what happens to Warrick Carver when he spots his ex-girlfriend, Tangela Howard, at a Las Vegas costume party. Not only has she lost weight, colored her hair and squeezed into a skintight Catwoman costume, she's sashaying around the room on the arm of another man. So what's a rich, successful architect to do? Scheme his way back into her life, that's what!

I hope you enjoy Tangela and Warrick's story in *Love on the Rocks,* and getting the chance to catch up with Sage and Marshall from *Games of the Heart.* Don't worry, you'll be seeing other cameos from your favorite characters in the near future. I've revamped my Web site, and I'm running a Valentine's Day contest, so please come visit me at www.pamelayaye.com.

Stay tuned for my next Kimani Romance, *Pleasure for Two,* coming out in November 2010.

Until next time,

Pamela Yaye

Acknowledgments

I dedicate this book to all of the people I love: my darling
husband, Jean-Claude, and my daughter, Aysiah.
My amazing parents, Daniel and Gwendolyn Odidison.
My super-cool siblings, Kenneth and Bettey Odidison.
And all my friends and relatives near and far.

Love on the Rocks is my seventh Kimani Press romance
novel, and I'm proud to be part of such a supportive,
hardworking team. Sha-Shana Crichton and Kelli Martin
continue to help me create strong, engaging stories, and
I'm thankful to have two fabulous *sistas* in my corner.
May God bless you both.

Chapter One

Warrick Carver strode off the elevator onto the twentieth floor of Truman Enterprises. He radiated success, and his brisk gait suggested he was a man of purpose. Walking tall, he pushed open the glass door, nodding to the robust security guard keeping watch over the suites of luxury offices. Polished-looking in a wool suit and an azure tie, he approached the reception area, wearing a wide smile that crippled every woman within a one-mile radius.

Energized by the pungent aroma of Colombian coffee, he mentally reviewed his morning schedule. A budget meeting, a visit to one of the construction sites and an afternoon conference call to Japan. His head throbbed just thinking about it.

Peals of girlish laughter punctured the air. His personal assistant, Payton Ellis, and three female associates were gathered around her desk in a tight circle clucking like a band of chickens. Warrick couldn't see what they were looking at, but it incited nods, murmurs and shrieks of delight. On any other day, he'd overlook their impromptu coffee break and make a beeline for his office, but the Human Resources manager was due any minute, and he didn't want the overbearing warlord to catch anyone slacking off.

"Back to work, ladies." No sense antagonizing his employees, he decided, keeping his tone light. "You can finish up your discussion at lunch."

"Guess who's on the cover of *People* magazine?" Payton asked, wearing a cheeky grin.

Shrugging nonchalantly, Warrick joked, "I don't know. J-Lo and the twins?" Celebrity gossip didn't interest him, but Payton made it her business to know what was happening in the lives of the rich and famous. It didn't matter how many times he told her he didn't care where Bono ate lunch or who Naomi Campbell had bitch-slapped, she chattered incessantly about her favorite stars as if they were her closest friends.

"You'll never guess who it is." Before he could even begin to think of an answer, she screamed, "It's Tangela!"

"*My* Tangela?" Warrick didn't catch his mistake until he noticed the amused expressions on the women's faces. Coughing to hide his discomfort, he helped himself to a disposable cup and filled it with water from the cooler positioned against the wall. "Isn't that something?" His smile was superficial. No teeth, no shine, no light. "Good for her. That's great."

"I'd say. She's lost almost eighty pounds!"

"What!" Water sloshed over his cup and splashed onto the tiled floor. "That's impossible. Tangela was never fat, she was thick and curvy and…" Images of her supple breasts, wide hips and mile-long legs flashed in his mind, derailing his thoughts. "It can't be," he managed, coming to. "Maybe the woman just *looks* like Tangela."

Payton grunted. "You guys dated for seven years. I know what she looks like."

Warrick considered her words. He wasn't questioning his assistant's intelligence, but he knew his ex-girlfriend wasn't on the cover of some cheap tabloid. Losing eighty pounds in two years was an impossible feat. No way she'd subject herself to a strict, point-counting diet. Tangela loved food. Buying it, cooking it, eating it. Despite what health gurus and nutritionists said, she wasn't addicted to food and would tell friends and family, "I'm not an emotional eater. I just love fried chicken!"

It's not her, he decided, convinced his assistant had downed one too many mojitos last night during happy hour. Besides, Tangela didn't need to lose weight. Not a single pound. She was perfect from the top of her pretty little head to the bottom of her dainty size-seven feet. "There's no way she'd go on one of those extreme diets or—"

"Oh, it's her, all right. But don't take my word for it," she said, dangling the magazine in front of his face. "See for yourself."

Holy shit! Eyes bright, jaw slack, Warrick stared mutely at his ex-girlfriend's image. Blood stopped flowing to his brain and he felt as though his mouth was packed with salt. A harsh acerbic foam coated his tongue. He'd hoped she'd gained weight, gotten her nose pierced—which he'd been firmly against—or chopped off her hair. But she hadn't. Not only was she a shadow of her former self, she'd grown her hair long, wore natural-looking makeup and had milky-white teeth. Warrick didn't think it was possible, but Tangela was even more striking.

"I'd kill to look like that," one of the women announced.

"I think she's too thin," criticized another. "Tangela's always been pretty—she didn't need to lose all that weight."

Warrick agreed. Two years ago, Tangela had been curvy and voluptuous, like his favorite American Idol, Jennifer Hudson, and now she was a stick figure. Since he could remember, he'd always had a thing for "healthy" women. Broomstick-thin types who graced movie screens and magazine covers didn't impress him. He appreciated an athletic physique as much as the next man, but he loved hips and thighs and butt and his ex-fiancée used to have it all.

Dropping his empty cup in the wastebasket, he leaned against his desk for support. Colors and images and objects collided in his brain and his chest inflated as though he was holding his breath underwater. With much difficulty, he focused his eyes on the cover. The words *Amazing Weight-Loss Stories* were splashed across the page in thick bold letters and Tangela stood proudly in a skimpy, lime-green bikini. *We dated for seven years and I never saw her in anything but a boring one-piece!* Her smile was bold, suggesting a wild, playful side and stirred repressed memories in him. Emotions he didn't have a name for rose to the surface at the mere sight of her.

Senses sharper than a comic-book character, he examined the *People* magazine cover in acute detail. Everything about Tangela was gorgeous. The ultrastraight auburn hair, the shiny lipstick, the hoop earrings. Hands propped audaciously on her hips, shoulders thrown back, chin tilted in supreme confidence, she radiated an inner beauty that literally took his breath away. Warrick didn't need to peek inside Tangela's head to know what she was thinking. Her eyes shone with mischief, her cleavage was blinding and he'd never seen her skin look more vibrant. Tangela knew she was hot and she wanted the world to know. "I think she's… I mean…" He trailed off. "I don't know what to say."

"Doesn't she look incredible?" Payton watched him intently for several seconds. "I already finished reading the article. Go on," she ordered, "take it."

Warrick stepped back. "I can't. I have work to do." As he turned away, he made a point of saying, "And so do you."

At five o'clock that afternoon, Warrick emerged from the conference room feeling tired and spent. Preoccupied in his thoughts, he continued down the hall, reviewing in his mind the conversation he'd had with the group of Japanese investors. As he passed his assistant's desk, he noticed the *People* magazine sitting on a stack of manila files. No longer safely tucked away in the side drawer with the other tabloids, it sat on the middle of Payton's desk, mocking him, teasing him, a painful reminder of the woman he'd loved and lost.

Glancing around, he flipped it open and scanned the table of contents. "Amazing Weight-Loss Stories," Page 87. But before he could locate the article, Payton appeared out of nowhere. "Looking for something?" she asked innocently.

"No." Sliding his hands into his pockets, he jangled the loose coins. "I need to clear my head. I'll be back in fifteen minutes."

"The Web conference went that bad, huh?"

"Worse. They're threatening to find another firm." He stood there quietly, a reflective expression on his face. "But I'll think of something."

Drumming her manicured nails on the desk, she looked carefully around the office. "Is there anything you need before I go?"

"No, I'll see you tomorrow. Have a good night."

"I will. Jerell's taking me to see *Lord, Why Me Again?* at the Arts Center."

"Poor guy." He chuckled heartily. "Your husband has my deepest sympathies."

Payton giggled. "It's fun, the acting is great and the audience really gets into the show."

"I bet," he deadpanned, a miserable expression on his face. "Sorry, but it's just not my thing. Tangela forced me to watch one on DVD and I hated it."

"Relationships are about give and take. Jerell goes with me to the plays, and I leave him alone when he's watching football. It's called compromise. You—" she patted his back "—should try it sometime."

"That's why I'm single. I can work as much as I want without anyone getting on my case." He made sure to add, "And that's how I like it."

"Sounds lonely."

Sensing she wanted to say more, he said goodbye and strolled toward the bank of elevators. Outside, Warrick was swept up in the hustle and bustle of the Las Vegas business district. Men in tailored suits strode down Fremont Street, tourists snapped pictures of everything and nothing and evening traffic moved at a snail's pace.

Deciding against flagging down a taxi, he pulled up the collar on his suit jacket and stepped around a group of high-school students in ghoulish face masks. If not for their costumes, he would have forgotten it was Halloween. As he passed a row of cafés and convenience stores, he caught a glimpse of Tangela. Or rather, of her picture on a stack of *People* magazines. Was there no escaping this woman?

His eyes narrowed. How many more times would she intrude on his thoughts today? Last he'd heard, Tangela was living in Mexico studying Spanish, something she'd always wanted to do, but never did because she hated the thought of them being apart.

Warrick grunted. Funny, she'd professed her love with more conviction than a Keyshia Cole song, but didn't have a problem sneaking out in the middle of the night in the car *he'd* bought her. No, she wasn't the loving, devoted, fiancée she'd pretended to be. Tangela had been out for herself from day one, but he'd been too stupid to realize it.

Without thinking, he stopped at a convenience store, counted out the exact change and requested a bag for his purchase. He couldn't risk someone seeing him with the magazine. They might think he was still carrying a torch for his ex. Or worse, that he wanted her back.

An hour later, behind the privacy of his office door, Warrick stared disbelievingly at one of the November issues of *People* magazine. He scarcely remembered what he'd eaten at the Third Street Grill or the ten-minute walk back to his office. But now that Payton and her posse had left for the day, he could read in peace.

Appraising the cover, he emitted a low, hollow sound from the back of his throat. Tangela Howard. The small-town girl with the big heart. Raised by a drug-addicted mother, she'd relocated to Las Vegas at seventeen and worked two full-time jobs to pay for university. A year after earning a degree in employment relations, she'd applied to American Airlines in hopes of working her way up from flight attendant to operations manager. Warrick admired the way she'd coped with all the misfortunes in life and had made it his job to give Tangela her heart's desire. His efforts had all been in vain.

Warrick held the magazine so close to his face he could see her clear nail polish. This was the first day since Tangela had walked out on him that he hadn't woken up thinking about her, and as he searched inside for the cover story, he wondered how seven years of love, companionship and earth-shaking sex could have flatlined so quickly.

Shifting on his high-backed leather chair, he released a quick, inaudible sigh. Seeing Tangela again unnerved him. Made him think about things he had no business thinking about. Like how she used to kiss him the second he came through the door. Or how she'd gently caress his face when he was nestled deep inside her.

To keep from taking another trip down memory lane, he studied her picture intently, as if she was a stranger. And she was. This woman with the slender face, toned arms and lissome shape bore no resemblance to his ex-girlfriend. Her eyes were slightly tinted at the corners and had a hint of gray. Definitely contacts, he decided, continuing his appraisal. Gone were her short, springy curls. In their place a high ponytail that grazed her bare shoulders. The ruffled halter bikini made a strong statement: she was a bold, sexy woman who was thirsty for adventure.

Warrick flipped through the magazine and stopped when he saw another full-length picture of Tangela. A small, passport-size photograph was on the corner of the page. Above the snap was the word *Before*. Tangela was in her navy American Airlines uniform, smiling directly into the camera. Warrick recognized the photo. He'd taken it the night she'd aced her final exam. Almost two years to that day, she'd left him.

Feelings of nostalgia assailed him, but he refused to think about what they'd done on the kitchen counter that afternoon. Face pinched in concentration, he pored over the interview as if he was studying for the Nevada bar exam.

According to the article, Tangela had lost the weight through diet, exercise and nutritional supplements. *Why?* circled in and out of his mind. Why would she put herself on such a stringent diet? Warrick found the answer at the end of the first paragraph.

"I didn't set out to lose a lot of weight, but when doctors diagnosed a blood clot in my right leg, a friend sat me down and told me to get my act together. I took his words to heart and that was the beginning of my transformation. Walking, exercising, eating well… Now I'm fit and healthy and ready to begin the next chapter of my life."

His? The word was more painful than a slap shot between the eyes. And, as if it were a real-life blow, he needed time to gather his thoughts. Tangela had a boyfriend? It had only been two years since they—correction, she—had broken off their engagement. Not enough time for him to heal, but obviously enough time for her. He continued reading, his frown growing deeper with each fatuous sentence.

Warrick snorted. *Emotional eating is the driving force behind weight gain.* "Who wrote this crap?" he wondered aloud. "There was nothing wrong with her!" He'd dated Tangela for seven years. If she'd had a food addiction he'd know. Fast food had always been her weakness, but everyone had their vice. He liked beer, she liked cheeseburgers and for others gambling, porn or alcohol did them in. Who was this *People* magazine reporter to judge?

Warrick was so engrossed in reading the article he didn't notice his sister in the doorway until she cleared her throat. "Is this a bad time?"

Startled, he stared up at his sister. "Rachael, what brings you by?" he asked, sliding the magazine into his top drawer and coming around the desk. "I wasn't expecting to see you today."

"Do I need an excuse to visit my little brother?" She gave him a one-armed hug. "My Pilates class just finished and since the studio is only a few blocks over, I decided to swing by. What are you up to?"

Scratching his cheek, he shrugged with an affected air of boredom. "You know, this and that. Working hard to keep our clients happy. In fact, I was just reviewing contracts when you walked in."

"Liar! You were checking out Tangela's spread in *People,*" she announced, plopping down on the padded chair in front of his desk. "And you were slobbering all over yourself, too!"

Unzipping her leather handbag, she retrieved her copy of the magazine. Shaking her head, she gestured to the cover with her hands. "I still can't believe it's her! The last time I saw Tangela, she was a mess. Wailing, crying, rambling about how much she loved you. It was awful. She was a pitiful sight back then, but now look at her." Her voice was a mixture of awe and respect. "Tangela's one bad-ass chick!"

"Why didn't you tell me she was upset over the breakup?"

"Would it have made a difference? You didn't want to marry her and there was no getting around that." Abandoning the magazine, she wore a fond smile. "You're a good man, Warrick, and one day you're going to make some woman very happy. But Tangela's not the one. You know it, I know it, and so does she." Rachael softened the blow by saying, "Don't look so glum, bro. The breakup was the best thing ever to happen to you. You said so yourself."

Tongue-tied, he listened to his sister say he was too immature for a commitment as enormous as marriage. Warrick started to defend himself, but the words didn't come. What could he say? Rachael was right. He wasn't ready. And at thirty-one he didn't have to be. He had his whole life ahead of him. Why would he want to ruin it by giving up his freedom? A ball and chain held as much appeal as taking a spin in the electric chair.

"I don't mean to be harsh, but you get an A in business and an F in relationships. You're just not the settle-down type and that's okay. It's not like Dad has been a good role model." Eyes soft with sympathy, she crossed her legs and waited a half second before she continued. "Since I'm here," she began, straightening, "there's a situation we really need to discuss."

Notorious for being overdramatic, his sister used the word *situation* so regularly he never knew what to expect. Was the maintenance light on in her Land Rover? Had his brother-in-law forgotten their anniversary? Or was her poodle, Fefe, sick again?

"I want you to promise me you won't trip when you see Tangela."

"Fat chance of that," he scoffed. "I won't be in Guadalajara anytime soon. But if I ever make it down there, I'll be sure to look her up."

Staring at him, her forehead wrinkled in confusion, she asked what he was talking about. "Tangela got back from Mexico weeks ago."

"What!" The force of his tone shook the windows. "Are you serious?"

"Yeah, she lives in a swanky new singles complex in Canyon Gate."

"I had no clue. Why didn't you say anything?"

"You didn't ask." Rachael rushed along. "Tangela doesn't want to go to the Hawthorne party because you'll be there, but I assured her it wouldn't be a problem."

"What are you, the middleman now?"

"No, just a concerned friend. Tangela's dating a new guy and you've got…" She paused, as if waiting for divine intervention. "And you've got work. You're both happy, thriving even."

Sneering, he gripped the arms of his chair. So, that's what this was about. Tangela had moved on and didn't want him getting in the way. Wasn't it bad enough she'd walked out on him? To stick it to him, she'd lost weight, sexed-up her look and lured their friends over to *her* side. Back in town less than a month and she was already turning his life upside down. Typical Tangela. She might look like an angel, but she was a barracuda in heels.

But as her image passed through his mind, his anger deflated, leaving him feeling empty inside. Learning she was someone else's girl pissed him off. Stroking his chin, he told himself he didn't care. But deep down, he did. Who was this guy she was dating? Tangela had always had a thing for men in uniform. Buff, muscular types who made females swoon. Curious about her new boyfriend but worried his interest would be misconstrued, he decided not to interrogate his sister.

"Rachael, I'm not going to cause a scene. Like I told you before, I'm over her."

Looking hopeful, she said, "You've put the past behind you and you're going to be cordial and friendly when you see her, right, Warrick?"

Warrick nodded absently. He'd planned to skip the party and spend the evening evaluating the New Orleans development project budget, but if Tangela was going, he was going. But where was he going to find a costume at the last minute? As he searched for a solution, another thought came to mind. *I don't have a date.* There would be lots of other couples, and Tangela would be there, prancing around the room on the arm of some hunky beefcake.

Second thoughts surfaced. With everything going on at the office, he didn't have four hours to waste schmoozing with the Las Vegas elite, even if it was for the Hawthornes. Every year, the powerhouse couple threw a Halloween party at their lavish home, and although Warrick enjoyed partying with his friends, he couldn't muster up the energy this time.

"You made the trip for nothing. I'm not going. I have too much to do around here." Anxious to get back to work, Warrick thanked Rachael for coming and hustled her out of his office. "Tell the boys their uncle is taking them toy-shopping on Sunday."

Rachael groaned. "I don't have any more room in the house for trucks and GameCubes, so keep the new toys at *your* house," she suggested, stopping in front of the elevators.

"What will my lady friend think if she trips over an action figure?" Warrick shook his head, a roguish twinkle in his eyes. "Can't have her thinking I'm one of those soft mushy types who loves children, now can I?"

"Oh, so you're seeing someone." Her eyes were bright, round stars and her voice was infused with enthusiasm. "That's terrific! I've been really worried about you," she confessed. "You haven't been yourself ever since Tangela left. The old Warrick was fun and outgoing and loved to have a good time." She added, "I miss him."

"I wish everybody would quit saying that. I'm not dead, I'm busy. I have a lot going on right now." The elevator chimed and the doors slid open. *Saved by the bell,* he thought, ushering Rachael inside. "Have a good time and give my regards to Mr. and Mrs. Hawthorne."

"I will. See ya!"

Alone now, he thought back over what his sister had said. Tangela had some nerve sending Rachael over here to talk to him. He had as much right to be at the Hawthorne party as she did. Hell, more. The couple were friends of *his* family. Tangela had met them through him, and even though she saw them regularly, it didn't mean they liked her more. Screw her and her stupid magazine cover. Tangela might think she was all that, but she wasn't.

Warrick's gaze fell on the clock hanging across the room. Six-oh-nine. If he hauled ass, he could make a quick stop at a costume store and still arrive at the party on time. Half walking, half running, Warrick sped back down the hall. All he needed now was a date. Names and faces swirled in his mind. Janet?

No, she was in San Francisco on business. Maliyah wouldn't be able to find a babysitter on such short notice, and although Claire was an accomplished pianist, she couldn't hold a candle to Tangela in the looks department.

Head bent, Warrick considered every woman he knew. He couldn't invite just anyone to the party. Not when Tangela looked like a million bucks. His date had to be gorgeous, sexy, hot. Someone who'd make the men drool and the women jealous. That was the only criteria and by the time Warrick reached his office he knew just who to call.

Chapter Two

"**W**here is she?" Warrick asked, his gaze combing the darkened living room. An hour ago, he'd been greeted by Mrs. Hawthorne, ushered over to the bar and offered a variety of cocktails and appetizers. "Are you sure the woman you saw was Tangela?"

The question must have sounded like a desperate plea and Warrick's friend, Quinten Harris, dressed as one of Nevada's finest, gave him a scathing look under his fake cop glasses. "Let it go, dog. You guys are all wrong for each other. You're like a ticking time bomb. You're good for a couple of months then—" he threw his hands in the air "—ka-boom!"

Quinten laughed, but Warrick didn't, saying, "Shut up, no one asked you."

"Just calling it like I see it. Face it, dude, she's just not that into you."

Annoyed, Warrick opened his mouth with a stinging retort, but swallowed it when he felt a delicate hand on his forearm. He cast a glance over his shoulder, and found his date staring up at him. The former debutante wasn't the brightest crayon in the box, but she'd been the Jet Beauty of the Week twice and dazzled in her mermaid costume.

Turning toward his date, he greeted her warmly. "Hi, Alexis. Is everything all right?"

"I see a…an old friend out on the patio. Do you mind if go over and say hello?" she trilled, adjusting her outfit to reveal more flesh. When she popped open a gold compact and cleaned the corners of her mouth with her tongue, he knew her "friend" was a member of the opposite sex. "I won't be long."

"Take your time," he muttered, watching her sail through the French doors. Popular in her own right, Alexis Nyguard exchanged business cards with the men and shared beauty tips with the women. *I sure know how to pick them,* he thought, when he saw Alexis throw her arms around a swarthy man dressed in a hot-dog costume.

Glad she was gone, he turned back to his friend. "Know anything about Tangela's date?"

"Name's Leonard Butkiss. He's a plumber."

Warrick chuckled. "You're yanking my chain."

"I couldn't have come up with something that funny if I tried."

Both men laughed.

"What does this Butkiss guy look like?"

"What does he look like?" Quinten mimicked, shaking his head. Scowling, he reached over and plucked the *S* embellished on the front of his friend's costume. "A superhero, my ass. You should have gone with something more feminine like Snow White. You're too soft to be a superhero." His harsh, grating chuckle got louder. "Why are you so hell-bent on seeing her, anyway? It's about the car, isn't it?"

"No, I'm over that. Besides, Tangela must have been really hard up for money to sell it. She loved her little Sunbeam." Four months after their breakup, he'd spotted the classic automobile in the classified section of the newspaper. When he'd seen it weeks later on a used-car Web site, he'd actually considered buying it. At five thousand dollars below value, it was a steal. But whenever he looked at the car, he remembered all the times they'd made love in the backseat, and it was hard enough *not* thinking about her as it was.

"Pull yourself together, man." Folding his thick lumberjack-like arms across his middle, Quinten scanned the partying crowd. "This desperate, R. Kelly–type vibe you're giving off ain't cool. It's scaring off the honies."

"There's nothing wrong with me wanting to see her," he argued, prepared to defend himself. "We dated for seven years, remember?"

"How can I forget when you keep reminding me?" Quinten snapped. After a beat, he said, "Did you know that fifty-three percent of marriages end in divorce within the first five years? You guys never would have made it that long. You're both too jealous and hardheaded."

Warrick blew out a breath of frustration. Why was everyone so dead-set against him seeing Tangela? First his sister and now Quinten. Was he that bad? How come everyone forgot that *she'd* walked out on him? While he was in New York negotiating the biggest deal of his career, Tangela had packed her stuff, rented a truck and moved out. He'd lost sleep over it, not her. So why was everyone rallying around poor ol' Tangela?

"Leave the woman alone. She's moved on and you should, too."

Anger flared in Warrick's belly. Running his tongue over his teeth, he lifted his glass of soda to his mouth to keep from decking his friend in the face. Quinten didn't know jack about women. His longest relationship had lasted as long as a Super Bowl commercial and there were parts of the city he couldn't drive through for fear of bodily harm. The management consultant had broken hearts in every county from Tule Springs to Charleston and showed no signs of stopping. "Like I'm going to take advice from someone who gets dating tips from *Playboy* magazine."

"It's over. She's not coming back." Quinten's eyes roved appreciatively over a shapely woman in a cocktail bunny costume. "Rejoice, man. Now she's somebody else's problem." Clapping a hand on Warrick's shoulder, Quinten swiped a champagne flute from a passing waiter's tray and raised it high in the air. "Congratulations! All your problems are gone!"

Warrick didn't join in the celebration.

"Stay away from Tangela," Quinten warned, striding off.

Warrick scanned the darkened room, peering around the tombstones hanging from the ceiling. Avoiding Tangela wasn't the answer. In fact, he was secretly hoping to run into her. Closure. That's what he needed. Wandering around, he searched for something to do. Alexis was dancing with an Austin Powers look-alike, Quinten was flirting with a sexy gypsy and couples everywhere held hands, kissed and shared private jokes. The way he and Tangela used to.

Warrick took the elevator to the second floor of the palatial home and knew instinctively that his ex was there. Her Oriental fragrance sweetened the air. Seconds later, he heard her rich, effervescent laugh. Heart pounding, mouth wet with anticipation, he resisted the urge to run full-speed down the hall. Careful not to spill his drink on the carpet, he shouldered his way through the crowd of partygoers. Warrick brushed fake cobwebs away from his face as he ducked into the game room. Standing nonchalantly in the doorway, he surveyed the scene. And there, beside the pool table, was his first love, Tangela Marie Howard.

Coughing, he rubbed his eyes with the back of his hand. His nervous system went berserk and it took several seconds before his heart rate slowed. Tangela had always had that effect on him, but tonight it was a hundred times worse. It wasn't the stylish haircut, or even her shrunken waistline that stunned him. It was her costume. He hadn't expected to see her dressed in a leather cat-woman bodysuit that accentuated every luscious slope. Her dark dramatic eyes, visible through the slits in her face mask, and her lush red lips enhanced her staggering sex appeal.

At a statuesque five feet ten inches, Tangela towered over all of the women in the room and more than half of the men. Her costume left nothing to the imagination and made the Pussycat

Dolls look like a bunch of Catholic school girls. Once, to spice up things in the bedroom, he'd suggested she dress up in one of those skimpy maid's uniforms. Not only had Tangela flat-out refused, she'd given him the cold shoulder that night in bed, but now she was boldly flaunting her salacious curves. His ex obviously had a wild streak he knew nothing about, and that made him wonder what else she'd kept hidden from him all those years.

Jealousy reared its ugly head as he watched Tangela cheer on her date. She used to look at *him* that way. Eyes twinkling, face aglow, lips holding a smile reserved just for him. Seeing Tangela with another man, even a fluffy, out-of-shape plumber, made Warrick burn inside. How had it been so easy for her to start over?

Nine years ago, when he'd met Tangela Howard at Tower Records, it had been love at first sight. A scrawny teenager had crashed into a life-size cutout of Aerosmith and sent hundreds of CDs crashing to the floor. Warrick glanced up, wondering how the kid could have missed the gigantic display. Then he noticed the crooked grins on the faces of the male customers and trailed their covetous gazes. Shoulders bouncing, hips twirling, the tall, voluptuous girl at the back of the store in the skintight jeans grooved as if she was at a hip-hop concert.

Warrick made his move and after a few minutes of polite conversation asked her out. By the end of their first date, the twenty-year-old business administration student had captured his heart. Friends labeled them polar opposites and discouraged them from dating. They had mismatched tastes in music, movies and food, but Tangela understood him better than anyone and supported him wholeheartedly.

In the beginning, she'd praised him for climbing swiftly up the corporate ladder. But soon she was complaining about his crazy schedule. Warrick wanted to spend time with her, but he wasn't cutting back his hours or delegating more tasks to his team. It was hard enough proving himself. Founded in

1978, Maxim Designs and Architects was one of the leading architectural companies in the world and was widely known for its international landmark structures and commercial projects. The other architects thought he'd been hired because his father owned the company and they didn't try to hide their contempt. They didn't care that he worked weekends or stayed at the office until midnight. He was the boss's son and they resented his success.

Then, Tangela's mother died and she became short-tempered, clingy and possessive. Calling him on the hour, dropping by his office unannounced, bombarding him with wedding checklists and seating plans. Things got so bad, Warrick moved into the spare bedroom to escape her constant nagging and resorted to picking fights with her just to get out of the house.

As he reflected on their past, Quinten's words came back to him. *She doesn't want you…she's moved on and you should, too.* As that conversation replayed in his head, he shifted his attention to her date. Leonard Butkiss had a face only a mother could love. Wide eyes, large ears and a slightly crooked nose. Warrick didn't know anything about the guy, but Tangela deserved to be with someone strong and athletic and rich. Like him.

Giving his head a shake, he turned away from the thought. Then, like a scene out of a romantic movie, their eyes connected from across the room. Seconds passed. Then minutes. Their connection was so intense, so commanding, the fine hairs on the back of his neck shot up. Time stopped and everything he'd ever felt for her came rushing back. Love, desire, passion. His heart burned for her, and he wanted to draw her into his arms. When Tangela abruptly turned away, Warrick realized that Quinten was right. A man of his stature shouldn't be pining over anyone, not even his first love.

Warrick channeled his gaze. No more ogling Tangela. Or thinking about how utterly captivating she was. There were plenty of good-looking women at the party. Women who'd love to be with someone wealthy. Wasn't that what every sister wanted? A successful, affluent man who'd shower them with the finer things in life? Determined to have a good time, he chugged the rest of his drink and searched for his date.

Spotting Alexis, who must have come upstairs after he did, at the bar, he grabbed her around the waist. He didn't have fancy footwork like Chris Brown, but he didn't let that stop him from moving to the music. They rocked in perfect rhythm and when Warrick saw the curious expression on Tangela's face, he broke into a knowing grin.

"Is the plumber good in bed?"

Tangela laughed out loud. Being outside on the deck provided privacy, fresh air and a panoramic view of the city. Stars gathered beside the moon and the warm breeze shook the palm trees shielding the expansive estate. "What kind of question is that?"

"The guy's no hunk, so there must be another reason why you're dating him," Rachael continued, adjusting her golden-blond Tina Turner wig. "Well?"

"We're not sleeping together."

"It's the nose hair, isn't it?"

"I'm taking my time, Rachael. This is only our second date, and like I told you before, I'm keeping my options open." Staring through the kitchen window, she searched the room for her date. Her gaze fell on Warrick and she sucked in a breath. Her ex was as straitlaced as a brother could be. He had no earrings, no tattoos and the only time he cursed was when his beloved baseball team was losing. Tangela had always been attracted to smart guys and Warrick Carver was a brain. Though he was studious-looking and serious, there was no denying it: the architect pulsed with sexual energy. His biceps filled out the superhero costume nicely and the cape flowing freely around his shoulders drew her attention to his chest.

The man made her mouth water. And despite herself, she

felt a rush of excitement when he glanced her way. Images of their last vacation scrolled through her mind. Swimming with the dolphins. Making love in the Jacuzzi. Frolicking on the beach. Tangela shuddered and pushed away the memories. She wouldn't go there. Not today. Not ever. This wasn't an episode of *The Young and the Restless*. This was real life. Her life. And she'd never allow her attraction to Warrick to cloud her judgment again.

Unable to pull her eyes away, she watched him for several moments, all the blood in her head rushing to her core, leaving her nursing an unquenchable longing. Feeling weak, she swayed slightly to the right. Tangela reached out and gripped the table beside her. She had to stop doing that. Yeah, he had a strong, hard body, but that didn't mean she should faint. Her goal was to find Mr. Right, get married by her thirtieth birthday and relocate to New Orleans. Lusting over her ex-boyfriend wasn't going to change the facts, and she'd wasted enough time pondering what could have been.

"Are you still seeing the dentist?"

Tangela nodded. "Uh-huh, we're going rock-climbing this weekend."

"You weren't kidding when you said you were on a mission," Rachael said, winking.

Laughing, she revisited the conversation they'd had months earlier. One afternoon while shopping at Boulevard Mall, Tangela had confessed that she was on a mission to find a husband. To improve her chances of making a love connection, she'd joined a dating agency and posted an online ad, but after six months, she was no closer to finding Mr. Right than a single woman at a gay pride parade.

"You're dating so many different guys. Isn't it hard to keep them all straight?"

"Not really." Tangela enjoyed meeting new people, but every time she went out with a guy, she couldn't help comparing him to Warrick. It felt wrong, tainted, cruel, but the more she tried to censor her thoughts, the stronger they were. Her last date had been drinks at a smoky jazz café. Warrick had taken her on a hot-air-balloon ride for their first date. A personal trainer took her hiking May long weekend. Three years earlier, Warrick had whisked her away on a Mediterranean cruise. Most of the guys she'd met through the agency were beer-and-corn-chips type of guys, while Warrick was caviar and Dom Pérignon, and there was just no getting around it. "So," Tangela began, keeping her tone light. "Warrick's seeing someone, too."

"Not that I know of."

She gestured to the window. "Who's the girl in the mermaid costume?"

"Your guess is as good as mine. I've never seen her before."

Tangela didn't know why, but she felt a perverse satisfaction knowing Warrick was still single. But any joy she felt dissolved when Warrick caught her staring. And just when Tangela thought things couldn't get any worse, he ended the conversation he was having with a man in a skeleton costume and made his way toward her.

Glancing around for an escape route, or at the very least, something to hide under, she stepped back and bumped into a potted plant. His cologne floated on the evening breeze, inciting her sexual hunger. Without his designer suit, he could pass for a college student, and his infectious white grin made him irresistible.

Tangela heard her pulse throb in her ears. She'd grieved the loss of their relationship for months and now that she could finally see the light at the end of the tunnel, he was back. Literally. Before Tangela could get hold of herself, he was there. Wearing his characteristic smile, smelling delicious, acting as though they didn't have a long tempestuous past behind them.

"Ladies." The tension was suffocating, but instead of breaking eye contact with Tangela, he closed the distance between them.

It should be a felony to look that good. That hot. That sexy. That erotic. "You guys are definitely going to win the award for best costume."

"We know!" Rachael quipped, giggling. "Are you having a good time?"

"Of course. Great company. Good food." He stared at Tangela. "Nice view."

Then to her surprise, he leaned over and planted a kiss on her cheek. Under her mask, sweat pooled on her forehead like minuscule worry beads. It felt as if the temperature had soared to a thousand degrees. Expelling a breath, she rubbed a hand across her forehead. She didn't know if it was the humidity or Warrick's kiss, but her head was spinning like clothes in a dryer.

"Welcome home." His voice, clear and steady, was filled with surprising warmth. "Mexico's obviously been good to you."

"Yeah, it was great." Feeling dry-mouthed and sick, Tangela gulped down a mouthful of soda. Anticipating his next question, she cut him off. "I learned Spanish, toured most of the country and made some great friends."

"Who's she?" Rachael asked, motioning to Alexis. "Someone you met at work?"

Warrick wanted Rachael to leave and tried to communicate his wishes with his eyes. When his sister didn't get the hint, he put a hand on her back and guided her to the open patio door. "Davis has been looking all over for you."

"Really? Is he all right?" Rachael downed the contents of her cocktail glass. "Hubby's been fighting a migraine all day. I'll go check on him, then come right back."

Tangela watched Rachael hustle inside.

"That spread in *People* magazine was really something. Every man in America will be dreaming about you tonight." Staring at Tangela, Warrick reflected on their seven-year relationship. Their intense, emotional bond had seen them through the most difficult times and he missed having Tangela to talk to. It still bothered him how things had ended, but he didn't share his thoughts with her. More than ready to put the past between them, he suggested they sit down on the wicker love seat. "We should catch up. It's been a while and I'm curious about what you've been up to." He added, "Besides appearing on magazine covers, of course."

"I should go before my date starts looking for me."

"What are you doing with him, Tangela? He's not your type."

"Exactly." Defensive, she glared openly at him. "I finally abandoned that silly Hollywood notion of true love and decided to find someone nice."

"What about love?" Warrick couldn't believe those words had actually come out of his mouth. Before he could correct himself, Tangela tossed her head back and laughed in his face.

"I forgot how funny you were." Her tone was sarcastic and her smile was ice-cold. "Like you know anything about love."

"You sound a little bitter."

Her hand shook when she lifted her glass to her mouth. "No, I'm just cautious."

"But don't you want to be with someone you're in sync with?"

For a long time she didn't speak. There'd been a time when they were two minds with a single thought. Scintillating conversation and scorching sexual chemistry had kept their relationship strong for almost a decade, but in the end, that hadn't been enough to keep them together. "Chemistry's overrated. I want somebody who's going to be there when I need him. Someone committed to me *and* our relationship."

Warrick winced. Why didn't she just come right out and call him a jerk? Smirk in place, he recovered quickly, saying, "I guess I'm looking at the next Mrs. Butkiss, then. Congratulations! I wish you nothing but the best."

Tangela regarded him coldly. She heard the humor in his voice, but resisted playing the role of the bitter ex-girlfriend.

He'd love it if she embarrassed herself in front of their friends. It wasn't going to happen. Doing everything in her power to keep her composure, she made a point of peering over his shoulder in search of a more suitable companion. Her eyes landed on their lively host. "Mr. Hawthorne promised me a dance and I'm going to go cash in."

"See you around."

"Not if I see you first," she mumbled, stepping past him.

Chapter Three

Tangela avoided Warrick like the bubonic plague. To ensure their paths didn't cross again, she stuck to her girlfriends like glue. But when she spotted Warrick's date perusing the dessert table, her curiosity got the best of her and she went over. "Everything looks so good," Tangela gushed, peering at the pumpkin-shaped chocolate cake. "I don't know where to begin."

Alexis glanced around, then leaned over and whispered, "Don't tell anyone, but I'm on my fourth goblin truffle. If I'm not careful, I'm going to split the zipper on this costume!"

The women laughed.

"Are you a friend of the Hawthornes'?" Tangela asked, picking up a plate.

"No, I came with Warrick Carver. Do you know him?"

Squinting, as if trying to place him in her mental Rolodex, she shook her head. "I can't say that I do. Is he your boyfriend?"

"I wish. If he wasn't so obsessed with his work, I'd be all over him." Alexis bit into a pecan spider cookie and chewed. "And I think he's still hung up on his ex. I can't be anybody's rebound. Not even for a hottie like Warrick."

Convinced she'd misheard, Tangela inched closer and blocked out the other voices in the room. "What kind of things does he say?"

"Not much really. He said she kept the house clean and had dinner and a cold beer ready for him when he got home from work." Laughing, Alexis raked her fingernails through her hair. "She sounds like a fifties housewife if you ask me! *Pa-th-e-tic*," she sang, rolling her eyes.

Tangela had always questioned her unwavering devotion to Warrick and hearing Alexis, a perfect stranger, belittle her, made her feel like a fool. Instead of ironing his dress shirts and scrubbing the kitchen floors to a shine, she should have been working her way up the corporate ladder. "So, there's no chance you and this Warrick guy might hook up?"

"Not as far as I can see. He has this Tangela chick on a pedestal and I'm not about to compete with Ms. Doubtfire."

Tangela winced. She remembered when she was Alexis's age and she'd never, ever been that together. Young, insecure and desperate for love, she'd put all her hopes and dreams on hold to plan her future with Warrick. Married at twenty-six. First baby at twenty-eight. Dream home by thirty. It was too bad he'd turned out to be a toad instead of her Prince Charming.

"Well, it was nice talking to you." Alexis wiggled her fingers. "Tootles!"

As she watched the woman saunter off, feelings of regret settled in. Tangela wished she'd made better decisions, but refused to beat herself up over the past. Thrilled to be working at American Airlines but wanting more, she knew it was just a matter of time before she got a management position. And once she found Mr. Right, she'd have the loving, caring family she had always longed for. The one she'd never had but knew existed.

A lump formed in her throat. Three years ago her mother had died of heart failure and as she'd watched her mother's casket being lowered into the ground at the funeral, she'd decided she, too, wanted, needed someone to care for her in her last days. Two days after the funeral, she'd sat Warrick down and told him to pick a wedding date. He'd refused. His dad was in the hospital, he was swamped at work and his family needed him. Excuses, excuses, excuses. Knowing she'd never be strong enough to move out if Warrick was around, Tangela rented a trailer the day he left for New York, loaded her things and left town.

Even now, after all this time, she remembered their last conversation. The anguish in his voice was unbearable, but she'd been strong. No, she wasn't coming back. Yes, she was sure this was what she wanted. Her eyes burned at the memory, and to loosen the tightness of her throat she downed the rest of her drink. Ready to go, she tapped her date on the shoulder. When she caught Warrick eyeing her, she grabbed her purse and made a beeline for the coat room.

Forty minutes later, Leonard turned his battered sedan into Tangela's apartment complex. "Can I come in for a while?"

"Sorry, but I have an early-morning flight," she said, discreetly scratching her arm. Tangela had fallen in love with the cat-woman suit on sight, but after five hours in it, she wanted to set the stupid thing on fire. Sweat, leather and shea butter made for terribly itchy skin, and although she'd won the prize for best costume, she'd decided that the hundred-dollar Nordstrom gift card wasn't worth all the trouble.

"Tangela, I really like you," Leonard confessed, stretching his meaty arm across the back of her seat. "I know we agreed to see other people, but I don't want anybody else. I want you."

Right words, wrong guy, she thought, unlocking the passenger door. Warrick's face popped into her head, but Tangela cleared the image from her mind. Thinking about him would lead to fantasizing and she didn't want to go down that road again. Marriage was on the horizon, not hooking up with a man with whom she'd once shared an incredible passion. They didn't have a future, and that was reason enough for her to stay far away from him.

"Come here." Eyes closed, lips puckered, he moved in for

a kiss. Minuscule pieces of spinach were trapped between his front teeth and he smelled like onion dip.

Looks like I found another winner! Convincing herself it was his bad breath and not seeing Warrick again that was turning her off, she twisted her body toward the window. His lips grazed her cheek. His mustache felt like hard, brittle whiskers and made her think of her foster mother's cat, Rufus.

"I'm attracted to you and I know you feel the same way, so what are we waiting for?" Shifting in his seat, he licked his thin lips. "A man has needs, you know."

Tangela almost choked on her tongue. Leonard had said a lot of funny things since they'd met last month, but that took the cake. "Good night, Leonard. Take care."

At the door of her apartment condo, she waved, then turned the lock and went inside. "Whoever said dating was easy ought to be shot!" she complained, slipping her aching feet out of her black stilettos. Tangela considered calling Sage to vent. Before meeting her husband, Marshall, her best friend had dated a long list of losers, and if anyone would understand how she was feeling, it was Sage. Tangela reached for the phone, but remembered that Sage was in Los Angeles watching her stepson, Khari, play in the regional basketball championships.

Fifteen minutes later, Tangela stretched out on the bed and allowed India.Arie's voice to shower her with self-love and tranquility. *Warrick looked good tonight. Good enough to take home and make love to.* Startled by the thought, she rolled onto her side, searching the room for a suitable distraction. Something. Anything that would take her mind off her ex.

Sitting up, she reached for the stack of magazines on her night table, and plopped them down on her lap. For the third time in days, she scrutinized the *People* magazine cover. When she'd opened her mailbox and seen it lying among her bills, she'd actually danced around the kitchen. But when she read the interview, her excitement had waned.

"Food addiction, my ass," she grumbled, tossing the magazine onto the floor. She was fit and fabulous whether she was a size eighteen or a size ten. Just because the editorial staff didn't believe her didn't mean it wasn't true. She'd lost the weight without even trying. Having been to Guadalajara numerous times, she'd felt comfortable walking from her host family's house to the institute where she taught English classes and studied Spanish.

Her host mother, Ima, was weight-conscious and took great pride in preparing tasty, low-calorie meals for the family. Three weeks after arriving in Mexico, Tangela had lost twelve pounds. Six months later, she was down to a size fourteen and by the end of the year, she was at the lowest weight she'd ever been.

Tangela wished she could curl up in bed and watch TV, but she had to get ready for work tomorrow and her clothes weren't going to pack themselves. After trading in India.Arie for the Black Eyed Peas, she grabbed one of the suitcases from the back of her closet.

As she heaved the suitcase onto the bed, it fell open, sending photo albums, stray pictures and DVDs crashing to the bedroom floor. For a moment, Tangela stood there motionless, unsure of what to do. She'd been meaning to get rid of these old mementos, but hadn't gotten around to it yet. Warrick wasn't her boyfriend anymore, but it just didn't seem right tossing perfectly good pictures into the trash.

Tangela had always considered herself a fairly with-it person. In spite of having been raised by a woman who had a laundry list of psychological problems, Tangela had graduated high school with a near-perfect GPA and worked full-time to put herself through college. But when Tangela had met Warrick, she'd fallen hopelessly in love. Moving in with him had cemented their commitment, and he became everything to her, the only real family she'd ever had.

Against her better judgment, she picked up the tape marked Spring in New Orleans. Tangela still remembered the time they'd spent in the Big Easy. They'd shared passionate kisses, made love on the beach and eaten at the best Creole restaurant in the city. It was there, while they celebrated their fifth anniversary, that Warrick had proposed. Tangela had been too mesmerized by the sight of the pink canary diamond to notice his tense body language, but months later, when she'd watched the video he'd secretly had taped by a hotel concierge staff person, she'd seen the uncertainty in his eyes.

Enough memories, she decided. To purge her thoughts, she turned up the music and forced all images of Warrick from her mind. It was time to cut her ties with her ex once and for all. As much as she hated destroying the video and other mementos, she couldn't hold on to them any longer. If she was serious about getting married by her next birthday, she had to quit thinking about Warrick and make room in her heart for the right man to come along.

Scooping up the albums and videos, she marched into the kitchen, dumped everything into the trash bin and slammed the lid. "There," she said, smacking her hands together. "Goodbye and good riddance!"

"Attention, passengers. The pilot has switched on the seat-belt light and we ask that you remain seated for the remainder of the flight." Stepping out from behind the curtain that separated the two cabins, Tangela delivered a smile to the sleepy-eyed passengers occupying business class. "On behalf of the pilot and the entire American Airlines crew, we'd like to thank you for choosing American Airlines and we look forward to serving you in the future."

For the remainder of the flight, Tangela handed out cups of water, retrieved headphones and collected garbage. When the plane touched down promptly at six forty-five, passengers broke out in applause, drawing chuckles from the flight attendants.

"Thanks for flying with American Airlines," Tangela said cheerfully when the final passenger disembarked. "Have a great day!" Her mouth ached from smiling, and she could feel a migraine coming on, but she kept her smile in place until the last businessperson was out of sight. After catering to a hundred and thirty people on a flight from Chicago, then bidding them all goodbye, Tangela needed an ice pack, two aspirin and an apple martini.

"You're one heck of an actress," Mr. Connelly teased, patting her on the back like a proud father. "I thought you were going to lose it when that snot-nosed kid started banging on the cockpit door, but you held it together. Good job, Tangela."

He returned to the cockpit, and Tangela glanced around the first-class cabin. This morning, the Boeing 737 had been clean enough to eat off the floor, and now it looked as if a twister had ripped through it. Scraps of papers, wads of tissue and food crumbs now littered the carpet and she could see pink bubble gum wedged between two of the second-row seats.

Mumbling Spanish expletives, she grabbed a pair of latex gloves from the overhead bin and yanked them on. After two grueling back-to-back flights, Tangela was anxious to go home, but she couldn't even think about leaving until the aircraft was spic-and-span.

"At the rate you're going, we'll never get out of here!" Poking her head into the first-class cabin was her friend and the lead flight attendant, Carmen Sanchez. "Get a move on it, *chiquita*."

"Entonces matame ahora mismo."

"Put *you* out of your misery? At least you didn't get stuck in the back thwarting the plans of kinky couples anxious to join the mile-high club!"

Tangela laughed.

"I can't say I blame them," Carmen confessed. "I know what it feels like to be in heat. I haven't seen Hugo for ten days and mama needs some sugar!"

"Please, no more stories about how magnificent Hugo is in bed." Tangela fought to keep a straight face. "I'll run out of here screaming if you do!"

Carmen stuck out her tongue. "You're just jealous."

"You're right, I am."

"It's been that long, huh?"

"Girl, you have no idea." Tangela dumped an empty water bottle into the plastic bag. "I'm going to have to watch a how-to video the next time it happens!"

"What's going on with you and that Demetrius guy?"

"He's really sweet, but I can't be with someone who smokes weed, even if it's only 'recreational,'" she said, making quotation marks with her fingers.

"Oh, no, not another one!" Carmen laughed. "My ex used to smoke pot, too. After three months of him eating me out of house and home, I kicked his sorry butt to the curb."

"Sometimes I think I should just give up on this stupid quest to find a husband," Tangela admitted. Since Halloween, Tangela had been on one bad date after another. The singles' potluck dinner at her apartment complex had given her something to do last Sunday, and although she'd met several attractive men, she hadn't made a love connection. Tangela worked hard, took care of herself and had her own money, but she couldn't find a man to save her life. "I don't know why I'm kidding myself. Mr. Right probably doesn't even exist."

Picking up on the sadness in her voice, Carmen took the garbage bag and motioned for her to sit down. "You're going to be fine, Tangela. And one day you'll find the perfect guy."

"I'm so tired of going home to an empty house. In Guadalajara, I got used to having someone to talk to and do stuff with. Now, I'm back here and there's no one. Most of my friends are either married, engaged or in a committed relationship."

"Cheer up," Carmen admonished, patting her hand. "You're seeing Oliver later and he always takes you somewhere nice."

"He sent me a text message about an hour ago. He can't make it. Something came up."

"That sucks."

"Tell me about it. Another Friday night with nothing to do and nowhere to go."

"What are you going to do instead?"

Tangela shrugged. "Oh, I don't know. Wash my hair, rearrange my furniture. You know, the usual single-girl crap."

"Wanna stop by SushiSamba tonight? It's been a while since I was there."

"What about Hugo?"

"He'll be fine. He has the Playboy channel to keep him company until I get home." Snickering, she pulled Tangela to her feet. "Let's finish up so we can go eat. Mama's starving!"

Chapter Four

Socializing with clients after hours was one aspect of his job that Warrick hated. Away from their wives and esteemed country club members, sane, upstanding businessmen propositioned women half their age, guzzled champagne like it was water and partied more vigorously than a championship-winning football team.

Known for its carnival-inspired decor and twenty-one-seat sushi bar, SushiSamba appealed to professionals and partiers alike. It was the place to be seen at, and international real estate mogul Hakeem Kewasi had requested they have dinner at the upscale restaurant lounge. Proud of his movie-star looks, he'd hit on waitresses and girls barely out of their teens, but seemed particularly taken by full-figured women.

Warrick was nursing his second beer, wondering how much longer he'd have to babysit the businessman, when he felt his cell phone vibrating in his pocket. Convinced it was his father calling to check up on him, he said, "I'm going to the men's room."

"You're not sick are you?"

"No. I feel great."

"Good because the night's still young, and I can't wait to check out Vixen."

"The topless bar?"

His eyes were bright. "My brother was here last year and he said the dancers at the club look like that Beyoncé girl."

Warrick smothered a laugh. A week after Tangela had moved out, Quinten and the guys had dragged him to the gentlemen's club on Paradise Road. He'd had a lot to drink, but he didn't remember seeing any beautiful dancers there. Most of them looked like teenagers playing dress-up, not like the Grammy-winning superstar. "Vixen's not all it's cracked up to be. It's just a lot of Las Vegas hype."

"Andre said a hundred bucks can get me anything I want."

There was no disputing that. Warrick wasn't a saint and he loved clubbing as much as the next guy, but he'd rather go home and hang out in his living room than watch some bony chicks dance. He didn't want to go to Vixen, but his dad had ordered him to show Mr. Kewasi a good time and that's what he was going to do.

Strolling through the bar, he noted the coltish smiles the female patrons were shooting his way. Most were wearing designer outfits but had colorful tattoos on their shoulders and arms. Attractive in their own right, but not his type. Classy, sophisticated women who carried themselves with grace piqued his interest every time. Tangela would never dream of getting a tattoo. Or would she? If she could show up at the Hawthorne party in a skin-tight cat-woman costume, there was no telling what else she'd do.

The brunette sitting at the bar waved. Warrick returned her smile. He thought of approaching her, but when he saw her see-through outfit he changed his mind. It looked as if she'd stuffed two hot-air balloons under her dress. It was a wonder she didn't topple over. Fake breasts didn't appeal to him, and neither did silver tongue rings.

After using the washroom, he wandered into the lounge and sat down. The inviting decor, padded leather booths and lively music created a relaxing atmosphere. Pressing his BlackBerry handheld to his ear, he listened to his messages. Making a mental note to return the calls later, Warrick slid the phone into his pocket and stared up at one of the flat-screen TVs.

He checked the score of the Mariners game, relieved to see his team was beating the Yankees. An American Airlines commercial came on and he thought of Tangela. He wondered if she was out with her friends. On the weekends, she liked to go with her coworkers to the Karaoke Hut for cocktails. Singing off-key and encouraging others to do the same was something he couldn't get behind, but Tangela always seemed to enjoy herself.

Warrick glanced over at the bar. Mr. Kewasi was gone. He combed the lounge for his prospective client. Ten minutes after his search began, he spotted the businessman in the dining area standing with a tall, slender women. The waiter was obscuring his view of her face, but he'd recognize those legs anywhere. Tangela!

Wanting to confirm his hunch, he stepped into the lounge. Tangela's look was a slam-dunk. The white belted shirtdress was tight in all the right places and unlike all the other sisters in the restaurant she didn't look as though she'd spent hours getting dressed.

Relieved to see a petite woman join them, Warrick felt the tension flowing through his body recede. He was in the middle of the room obstructing the flow of traffic and other patrons were eyeing him curiously, but Warrick didn't move. Dazzled by Tangela's stylish ensemble, he watched as she sat down at one of the round tables and crossed her long brown legs. Warrick swallowed the lump in his throat. At the Hawthorne party Tangela had been a seductive temptress, but tonight she looked more like her old self. The golden tones in her auburn hair made her eyes sparkle and a smile sat beautifully on her rosy lips.

Warrick didn't know how he got across the room, but he pulled up to their table and stood there, studying her. He waited impatiently for Tangela to acknowledge him, but when she didn't, he said, "Twice in one month. This has got to be some sort of record."

Tangela spun around, her smile frozen in place. "What are you doing here, Warrick?"

"Entertaining a client."

Surprise splashed across Mr. Kewasi's face. "You know these two beauties?"

"Yes. Tangela and I used to date."

"A long, long time ago," she added, shifting in her chair.

The businessman gestured to the chair beside him. "Sit down, Warrick. I'm buying these lovely ladies dinner. Carmen was just telling me how stressful her job is."

"Stressful?" Warrick started to make a joke, but thought better of it. The last thing he wanted to do was antagonize his ex-girlfriend and her friend. They were being nice to his client and that was a very good thing. "The pay's not the greatest, but I bet you've been to some amazing places," he said instead.

"I have, but being a flight attendant isn't a walk in the park. There are days when I'm so tired I fall asleep in the shower!"

Mr. Kewasi wasn't convinced. "But you can travel anywhere in the world and your friends and family can accompany you for just a fraction of the cost."

"Every job has its drawbacks and being a flight attendant is no different."

"Drawbacks? Really? Like what?" Mr. Kewasi asked, studying the brunette thoughtfully.

"For starters, there's a common misconception that we're waitresses. We're not. We're highly skilled flight specialists, equipped to deal with everything from ill passengers to operating cabin equipment and handling unexpected safety matters."

Mr. Kewasi grinned. "No offense, ladies, but you *do* serve drinks."

"Imagine this," Tangela began, facing him. "You're on an eight-hour flight to Paris and a few minutes after takeoff, you start to have trouble breathing. Sweat's dripping down your face, your hands are clammy and it feels like your heart is about to explode out of your chest."

The businessman adjusted his collar.

"You don't want a waitress coming to your aid, do you? No, you want a trained, proficient flight attendant to keep you from dying in your first-class seat, right, Mr. Kewasi?"

Warrick hid a crooked grin behind his menu. Tangela was as sharp as ever. She'd lost some weight, but she hadn't lost her sense of humor. It didn't matter that they hadn't seen each other for two years; she was still the same saucy woman he'd fallen hard for nine years ago.

"Well put, Tangela. I'll never disrespect flight attendants again!"

The waiter arrived, and addressed Tangela first. "What can I get you to drink?"

"An apple martini with a dash of calvados and three maraschino cherries."

Warrick didn't realize he'd spoken out loud until Carmen bumped his elbow with her arm. "You still remember how she likes her cocktail? Wow, I'm impressed!"

"It just slipped out," he mumbled, hating the way the Latina woman was eyeballing him.

"So, you guys dated, huh?" Carmen began. "What happened? Did you have a roving eye? Or a little problem with recreational drugs?"

"No, of course not."

"Well?"

Warrick tripped over his tongue. "I…she…we…"

"We fell out of love," Tangela offered, wearing a thin smile. "We were barely out of our teens when we met and over time we changed."

Warrick felt as though someone was pelting him in the back with golf balls. Was that what she thought? That he'd stopped loving her? He'd never heard anything more ludicrous. Just because he didn't walk around quoting Nikki Giovanni or buy Tangela flowers every day didn't mean he didn't love her. He'd let his actions speak for him. Wasn't that what women wanted? Money, gifts and jewelry? He'd kept her in designer clothes, took care of the bills and gave her money on a weekly basis. Tangela was a hopeless romantic and wanted his attention all day every day, but Warrick wasn't going to sacrifice his career so they could stay home and cuddle.

"He was finishing his IDP training and working crazy hours." Tangela folded and unfolded her napkin. "We stopped making time for each other, and after seven years of dating we both got a little bored."

Her voice was light, carefree, free of spite, but he felt the sting of her words. Tangela had a great capacity for love and affection, and after a few dates he'd known she was the one. They'd grown up together and she'd been there through every trial and every success. He kept his eyes on her as she spoke, amazed that she could discuss the demise of their relationship with such detachment. Warrick was the first to admit he hadn't been the perfect boyfriend, but he'd never imagined those words coming out of Tangela's mouth.

"It's hard to maintain a relationship when one person wants out."

As if sucker punched in the gut, Warrick slumped back in his chair, shoulders bent in defeat. Clearing the cobwebs from his mind, he swallowed a curse. He considered giving his side of the story, but didn't want to lose his temper. Tangela didn't look at him and carried on as though he wasn't even there. Was she putting on an act or did she really believe he'd stopped loving her? Warrick didn't know what to think. Women were confusing and even now, at thirty-one, he didn't understand them any better than he had at thirteen.

"Our breakup was the best thing to ever happen to me," she admitted, laughing at nothing in particular. "I learned to stand on my own two feet and stopped looking to someone else to make me happy."

The waiter arrived with the appetizers, putting an end to all conversation. Over king crab and wine, the group discussed movies, music and Las Vegas's thrilling nightlife. Mr. Kewasi asked Tangela about her stint in Mexico and she talked about her host family, the vibrancy of the culture and the sweltering heat. Warrick pretended to be watching the Mariners game, but he was listening to every word. He wanted to ask Tangela if she was planning to go back to Gaudalajara, but didn't. She was being cordial, and he didn't want to push his luck. Stealing a glance at her, he watched as she opened her purse and took out her pink, diamond-studded cell phone. The one he'd bought her years earlier in Japan.

When it rang, her eyes lit up. He strained to hear what she was saying, and listened intently as she greeted the caller. *"Buenas noches, Marcello. ¿Cómo es usted?"*

Warrick broke into a sweat. Who the hell was Marcello and why was she speaking in a sultry Spanish whisper? Back in the day, they'd lain in bed long after midnight, laughing about the crazy things that happened on her flight or planning their next vacation. Now, she was on the phone with some guy, asking questions about his day and listening intently to his answers.

Infected with lust, his wanton eyes roamed over her tight, toned physique. The sound of her laughter drew his gaze back up to her face. He couldn't believe his ex—the woman he'd planned to marry—was on the phone with another man, flaunting her single-and-available status in his face.

Thanks to his sister, he knew Tangela had shown up at the Chrisette Michele concert with some blue-eyed geek, who was so smitten with her he'd escorted her to and from the ladies' room. He'd pressed Rachael for more details, but she'd abruptly ended their conversation.

Staring down at his hands, he used his fingers to tick off the number of guys Tangela was dating. There was Leonard

Butkiss, the concert guy and now some dude named Marcello. How many more were there? For all he knew, she could be dating someone from Mexico. Or an oil tycoon from Saudi Arabia. What was Tangela up to? Personally doing her part to bridge the racial divide?

Throwing down his napkin, Warrick searched the room for their waiter. He'd had enough. Enough of her giving him the cold shoulder, enough of her speaking in hushed tones to the mystery man on the phone and enough of her superior attitude. He had a hole in his heart the size of a basketball and she was dating more guys than the Bachelorette.

Tangela said something to Carmen, then got up from the table. Warrick watched her leave. She moved with a rhythm all her own. A confident, magnetic grace that made all the blood rush to his groin. Despite their acrimonious breakup, one thing was clear: he still desired her.

"You're right, Mr. Kewasi, the American legal system has become a joke, but there are legitimate cases where people *should* sue their employer. Look at what happened to Tangela." Carmen appealed to Warrick. "Don't you think she should have sued Flight Express for discrimination? Or at least told her story to the news media?"

Her words didn't register. "I don't know what you're talking about," he said, frowning at her. "Tangela quit her job to study in Mexico."

"That was after they cut her hours."

Warrick felt his blood go cold. What the hell? Tangela told him she'd scaled back on her hours so she could devote more time to planning the wedding. Angry at her for dropping by his office unannounced every day, he'd suggested she return to work. In the weeks leading to their breakup, they'd argued about the ever-increasing guest list and soaring wedding costs. And when he stumbled across a five-thousand-dollar florist bill, he'd told her to quit wasting *his* money. "Carmen, I want to know exactly what happened."

"Her boss said some mumbo jumbo about her not reaching her full potential. Apparently, she wasn't reflecting the right image and the airline wasn't satisfied with her work."

"What does that mean?"

"Translation? She'd gained too much weight and they wanted her out."

"Her supervisor actually said that?"

Carmen grunted. "They're not *that* stupid. The airline didn't want a lawsuit on their hands, so they cut her hours in half."

"Can they do that?"

"It's their company. They can do whatever they want." Carmen continued, "Tangela quit and moved to Mexico. It was good for her to get away for a while. She needed it."

He filled in the rest of the story. "But she missed flying, so she returned home and applied at American Airlines." Warrick looked up just in time to see Tangela exit the ladies' washroom. A slim, lanky guy in a white fedora stopped her as she entered the lounge. The woman was like a magnet. Everywhere she went, men followed.

Minutes later, Tangela returned to the table, clutching a thin stack of business cards. *His ex, the social butterfly.* While they were dating, he'd encouraged her to get out and make friends, but Warrick had never imagined his words would come back to haunt him.

As he watched Tangela sipping her second apple martini, he considered asking her about what had happened at Flight Express. She'd never admit it, but her appearance, or rather, other people's opinion of her, had always been a sore spot for her. He'd loved her curvy figure, and the male attrention she garnered whenever they were together. Or at least he used to.

A cell phone shrilled and Tangela reached for her purse. When she greeted the caller and rose from her seat for a second time, giggling as she strode off, Warrick stabbed a shrimp ball with his fork and plunged it into his mouth. He wasn't going to confront Tangela about what Carmen had shared with him tonight, but this wasn't over.

Chapter Five

Warrick doused his face with water. The ice-cold liquid coursed down his cheeks like rain, cooling his overheated body. Returning it to the cup holder, he increased the speed on the treadmill and jogged to the beat of the song playing. At 6:00 a.m. on a Friday morning, the gym was practically empty. Four junior draftsmen lifted weights, three female clerks did sit-ups and Payton was on an exercise bike, reading a women's magazine.

He ran with grace, fluidity, like a long-distance runner on a wide-open track. He was in a zone, a sphere, a place free of stress, deadlines and difficult clients. A row of exercise machines stood in front of the window providing runners a clear view of the pink-orange horizon. The clouds were piled onto each other like a stack of buttermilk pancakes. Warrick licked his lips. After he finished his workout, he'd stop in at Guido's for breakfast. He had a long day ahead of him and needed to eat while he still had the chance.

A plane glided across the sky. An American Airlines plane. Even from miles away, he recognized the distinctive logo on its wings. Before he could guard against it, an image of Tangela surfaced. It was the first time since running into her at SushiSamba that he'd allowed himself to think about her.

Every time she'd interrupted his thoughts or sneaked into his dreams, he'd resisted her. But he couldn't run forever.

Sweat dripped from his chin. He felt good. Strong, powerful, resilient. Then Tangela's words came back to him, blaring in his head. *We fell out of love...we...we...we...* Warrick gripped the sides of the machine. He still couldn't believe Tangela had said that. She'd been polite at the Hawthorne party and had even chatted with Alexis. Warrick had been stunned to learn that Tangela hadn't revealed her true identity. Was that what things had come to? Avoiding each other and lying about their past? He was even more confused by her behavior at SushiSamba, but more than anything, he wanted to know when she'd stopped loving him.

Running full-tilt, he thought about his plans for the weekend. He'd planned to catch up on sleep, but when Marshall had called and requested his help moving into his new Lake Las Vegas home, he'd said yes. And thanks to his buddy, he knew that Tangela would be there, too.

The timer beeped, cuing Warrick that his hour was up. In thirty minutes, he was showered, changed and dressed to impress in a three-piece charcoal suit. On his way up to his office, he went to Guido's and ordered pastries for his staff. As he was leaving, he spotted Dr. Marc Solomon sauntering toward him.

"Carver, it's been a while. How are you doing, man?"

Warrick didn't answer. The pediatrician was full of himself, but according to his female employees, Dr. Marc Solomon was the best thing since fat-free ice cream. Warrick didn't see what the appeal was, but some women liked pretty-boy types and Marc Solomon looked like the Latin version of Brad Pitt.

"Did you get your car fixed yet?" Marc asked, wearing an innocent smile.

Warrick's jaw tightened. Last month, Marc had scratched his Aston Martin DBS, but when the repair bill arrived, had refused to pay. The damage was minuscule, but a dent on a luxury sports car was a very serious matter—at least to him. "I took care of it."

"Next time, don't park so close to my truck," Marc advised.

"I'm late for a meeting. See you around," Warrick said, stepping past Marc, almost knocking him down as he strolled through the restaurant doors.

"I ran into Tangela at the mall a few weeks back." Marc sneered.

Warrick stopped. Marc had whetted his curiosity and despite himself, he wanted to hear more. "And? So what?"

"Back when the two of you were dating, I thought she was all right for a chubby girl, but now she's a babe." Pushing a hand through his dark wavy hair, Marc licked his lips lasciviously. "We exchanged numbers. We're going out tomorrow night."

Cautioning himself to remain cool, Warrick turned around and faced the arrogant physician. The idea of Tangela with the slick-talking creep was sickening, but he didn't let his disgust show. "We're not together anymore. I don't care what she does."

"Good. I just wanted to make sure I wasn't stepping on your toes." Marc flipped open his cell phone and when he realized Warrick was still there, smirked. "Don't worry, Carter," he chided. "I'm not trying to steal your girl."

Warrick sighed inwardly.

"I just want to bang her."

He reached out to snatch Marc up by the collar, but reason seeped in. Now wasn't the time and the Truman Enterprises building was certainly not the place. Later, when there were less witnesses and no one to intervene for the good doctor, he'd teach the jerk a lesson. "Hurt Tangela and you'll have me to deal with." His voice rose slightly, drawing the attention of the customers in the waiting area. "And this time, I won't let you off the hook, pretty boy."

Marc held up his palms. "Relax, tough guy. I'm a lover, not a fighter."

A woman wearing heavy eye makeup approached. "Hi, Marcello," she purred, sticking out her chest. "Have you eaten already?"

"No, *mi amore,* I was waiting for you."

Warrick frowned. "Marcello?"

"The ladies find it sexy, and I like to give the ladies what they want." Grinning from ear to ear, he slipped an arm around his date's shoulder and disappeared into the restaurant.

Scratching his head, Warrick tried to remember where he'd heard that name before. Inside the elevator, it came to him. The other night at SushiSamba, Tangela had spent twenty minutes on the phone with some guy named Marcello. Marc was posing as a gentleman and by the looks of things it was working.

Flying down the hall toward his office, Warrick decided he couldn't wait until tomorrow to speak to Tangela. He'd call her, order her to stop seeing Marcello and if that didn't work, he'd have to take matters into his own hands.

"That concludes the agenda for today." Arms folded, Warrick sat down on the edge of the square glass table. "Does anyone have anything else they wish to add?"

His gaze circled the room, and when no one answered, he ended the meeting. "All right, everyone. That's it. Have a good day." He turned to one of the junior draftsmen. "Can you have the preliminary designs for the Mega Mall Tokyo site on my desk by noon?"

The man nodded. "Sure thing, boss."

As his employees packed up and filed out of the room, he caught sight of his dad in the reception area, chatting with the Human Resources manager. Warrick's shoulders sagged. Normally, he loved seeing his dad, especially when he had a problem and needed his ear, but this wasn't one of those times. He had a deadline to meet, a business lunch with a prospective client and a stubborn ex-girlfriend to deal with. Tangela hadn't returned his call. There was a good chance she was out of town, but he knew she checked her voice mail regularly. He was trying to save her from Marcello-the-Latin-playboy, but she obviously didn't want to hear what he had to say. Fine, he decided, shrugging on his suit jacket. If she wanted to be another notch on the good doctor's belt, then he wouldn't intervene.

Why was he sweating her, anyway? She might be a beauty, but she wasn't the right woman for him. At least not anymore. It wasn't until their breakup that he'd realized how heartless Tangela could be. She didn't even have the decency to leave him a Dear John note or send him a crummy text message to break up with him, she just up and left like a thief in the night. Never to be seen or heard from again. She'd left the country without giving him a second thought, and he'd never forgive her for that.

Warrick pushed himself to his feet. Remembering he needed Payton to make copies of the Mega Mall Tokyo design, he popped open his briefcase and retrieved the file. At the bottom of his attaché case, underneath his sketch pad, was the November issue of *People* magazine. Taking it up, he noted Tangela's blinding smile and her firm, mile-long legs.

Full of longing and regret, he thought back to the night they'd made love for the very first time. Caught up in a sexual trance, Warrick didn't hear the phone buzz or the whirl of voices outside the conference-room door. His eyelids grew heavy and his eyes closed, taking him back to that sweltering August night. Inside his master bedroom, they'd kissed and groped each other, more desperate than they'd ever been before. Resplendent in a white lace gown, Tangela had stretched out on the bed, waiting for him, hungry for him, begging him to join her. At ease with herself and her body, she'd pulled the flimsy material over her head and giggled when it sailed to the floor. When he'd stretched out on top of her, her perfume had surrounded him, subduing him with its enticing sent. Rolling her hips as though she was spinning a hoola hoop, she'd clamped her legs around his waist and ridden him so hard he'd seen the sun, the moon *and* the stars.

"Not reading one of those girlie magazines are you, son?"

Warrick swallowed hard. "Hey, Pops."

"What you got there?" Jacob Carver asked, motioning with his head to the open briefcase. "*Playboy,* maybe?"

"Dad, this is a place of business. I'd never bring something like that here."

"Too bad." Chuckling, Jacob walked inside the office. "I'm all out of my little blue pills and my new girlfriend is on my ass *literally.* I need something to get the black stallion up—quick."

Warrick rubbed a hand over his stomach. The picture his dad has just painted made him queasy. Ever since his old man had gotten a prescription for Viagra pills, he'd been acting like a sex-crazed fiend. Warrick was happy his dad was dating someone, but he didn't want to hear what they did in bed. "What are you doing here so early? I wasn't expecting you until this afternoon."

"Our meeting with Mr. Uchiyama and his associates has been bumped up to ten o'clock, so I thought we'd run through the presentation one more time before they arrive."

Jacob Carver took a seat, and Warrick poured two cups of coffee. Initially, he'd thought his dad was coming by the office to check up on him, but after talking to Rachael, he realized how much his father missed going to work every day. Eight months ago, his doctors had given him a clean bill of health, but he still didn't have the energy to return to work full-time.

"You're going to nail this presentation. Just like all the others."

"It's been a team effort, Dad. You should see what one of the structural engineers added to the 3-D model. It's a hundred times better than the last time you saw it."

"My son the humble leader."

"The quality of the people you hire determines how successful the business is. Isn't that what you used to tell me?" He took the chair across from his dad. "Everyone's been working their butts off around here and it shows."

Mr. Carver tasted his coffee. Gesturing to one of the plaques displayed on the far wall, he said, "Win three more of those Architect of the Year awards and we'll be tied."

Warrick grinned. "Is that a challenge, old man?"

"I'm proud of you, son. You've stepped into the CEO position so smoothly it feels like you were born to chair the company."

"Thanks, Dad. I'm enjoying it, but it's a ton of work."

"Now you understand what it takes to be number one."

Warrick worked seventy hours a week, but he liked the prestige and respect that came with spearheading the most successful architecture firm in the country. His father was the heart and soul of the company, but in just six years he'd built a reputation of being an innovative designer. Initially, he'd balked at the idea of taking over for his dad. He didn't have enough experience to run the company, but when the board of directors had backed his father's decision, he'd proudly accepted the interim-president position.

It had been an uphill battle earning his employees' respect, but he'd refused to crumble under the pressure. New to the game and eager to learn, he'd asked questions, worked late and read everything he could get his hands on about architecture and design. Being president definitely had its perks, but Warrick missed sketching on Sunday afternoons and taking his nephews to Game Zone. These days, free time was a luxury he just didn't have.

Mr. Carver snapped his fingers. "I almost forgot. I talked to Bernard this morning and he suggested we come to New Orleans this year to help out, instead of just writing another check."

"I thought he'd be thrilled to get another donation."

"Bernard's no fool. He's taking the money!" Mr. Carver chuckled heartedly. "He just needs some extra manpower. We have to show the community that we're behind them. The rest of the world may have forgotten what happened in New Orleans, but we haven't."

"You're right," Warrick agreed with a nod. "We should *both* go."

"I want to, but I have a physical that week."

"Everything okay?"

"I'm as fit as a fiddle. It's just a case of bad timing." His face was alive with nostalgia. "I was really looking forward to seeing Bernard again. It's been years since I saw him."

"Bernard's the guy you roomed with at the University of Louisiana, right?"

Mr. Carver cracked a sly smile. "We were the hottest cats on campus."

"Must have been a small school," Warrick joked.

"You could learn a thing or two from us. As you young people like to say, we were the bomb!" Pride flickered in his eyes. "We had more girls than Little Richard has curls!"

Warrick chuckled. "Well, what happened, Mack Daddy?"

"Your mother. Cupid shot me in the ass and I was never the same again."

Father and son laughed.

"How'd you know Mom was the one if you were dating all those other women?"

"It's not something you can explain or even put into words. But if I had to, it's like the rush of adrenaline you feel when you're going two hundred miles an hour on the autobahn."

Warrick knew the feeling. Every time he saw Tangela, he felt as though he couldn't breathe. Their relationship had ended disastrously, but that didn't mean he didn't want her. He did. And who could blame him? Her smile was electric, her walk hypnotic and her girlish laugh brought memories of happier days. And even after all this time apart, the sexual energy between them was still devastating.

"Your mother was an incredible woman, and if she was alive today she'd be bragging to her friends about how smart and successful her son is." Clearing his throat, he reached for his coffee cup and took a swig. "Back to the matter at hand. Can I count on you to make it to New Orleans at the end of next month?"

"I'll check my schedule. If I can't reschedule my appointments, I'll send some of the draftsmen. I know they'd love to help out."

"Great, I'll let Bernard know."

"Anything else on your mind?"

"Nope, that's it." Staring down at his watch, Jacob tapped the glass with his forefinger. "But we'd better get started. I promised Daphne I'd be home in time for an afternoon quickie and—" He must have seen Warrick grimace, because he swallowed the rest of the sentence. "Show me the blueprints, son. We don't have much time."

Warrick sighed. What was the world coming to? The last time he'd had sex George Bush was President, but his dad was getting all the loving he could stand. So were his boys. Last night, at their favorite pub, Quinten had bragged about his marathon sack session with a perky dance choreographer and now his father had his own raunchy tale to share.

Turning away from his sad, depressing thoughts, he uncoiled the blueprint, spread it out on the conference-room table and said, "Let's get down to work, old man."

Chapter Six

"Be careful with my coffee table!" Sage bellowed from the steps of her new Lake Las Vegas home. "It cost more than your raggedy-ass car!" Following her husband's friends back through the vestibule, she barked orders like a military commander in chief.

Focusing her acidic gaze on the shortest of the four men, hands propped on her hips, she stomped her right foot. "Dammit, DeAndre! You almost knocked over my lamp. If I see any scratches on it, you're going to replace it. You hear me?"

"I told you it wasn't my fault. The sidewalk was slippery and I tripped. Maybe you shouldn't have watered the lawn this morning."

Before Sage could tear a strip off the part-time carpenter and full-time loser, her husband grabbed her around the waist. "Baby, bring it down a notch. If you keep this up, the neighbors' association will kick us out before we even unpack."

"Did you see the crack on my vanity mirror?"

"I'll replace it," he promised.

"It was eighty-five hundred dollars."

"What?" Marshall pulled back so he could see his wife's face. "You paid almost ten grand for that thing?"

"It's from Saks Fifth Avenue!"

"We'll discuss it later, okay?" Closing his arms around her, he told her to take it easy on the guys. "Be nice, Sage. They're not professional movers. They're our friends, remember?"

"Not all of them," she mumbled, peering around him into the living room.

"Why don't you go finish up in the kitchen while I supervise out here."

"Are you sure? Because those guys need a firm hand, and, baby, you're kind of soft."

Marshall kissed the side of her neck. "That's not what you said last night."

Sage giggled. "You're so nasty!"

"Quit playing, girl. You know you love it when I talk smack."

Resting her head on his chest, she played with the buttons on his plaid shirt. "Baby, can you just make sure that idiot DeAndre doesn't destroy anything else? And watch Jonas, too. He had three beers at lunch." Snapping her fingers, she nodded emphatically. "Oh yeah, have the guys carry the hutch into…"

Putting his hands on her hips, he steered her in the direction of the kitchen and swatted her playfully on the behind. "Sage, go. I got this."

"Mmm…" she purred, shooting him a coy look over her shoulder. "I like when you take charge, baby. It *really* turns me on!"

"There's a lot more where that came from, *Mrs. Grant*."

"Bring it on, big daddy. I'm up for a little—"

"Would you two knock it off already!" Quinten strolled through the foyer, his face the picture of disgust. "It's bad enough you forced us to watch your wedding video at lunch, but do we have to listen to you talk dirty to each other, too?"

Marshall gave his bride another quick kiss, then followed his friend into the living room. "You don't know what you're missing, Q. Marrying Sage was the best decision I ever made."

"Sure," he said skeptically. "You have to say that or she'll whup your ass!"

Everyone in the room chuckled.

"A woman who has worked on her spirit more than her body is truly beautiful and I have that and more in Sage. With her by my side, there's nothing I can't do." Marshall's smile was brighter than the morning sun. "It's like they say—behind every great man is an even better woman. Look at Barrack and Michelle Obama."

Jonas groaned. "Please don't subject us to another one of your marriage-is-the-best-thing-that's-ever-happened-to-me speeches." He heaved an encyclopedia onto the wooden bookshelf. "I hated it the first time you gave it and I'll hate it even more the second time around."

"All right. I won't say any more on the subject." Marshall picked up the cable box and set it on top of the big-screen TV. "But don't say I didn't warn you when you're a shriveled-up old prune playing spades in the nursing home with all the other geezers."

"What the hell does marriage have to do with getting old?" Theo scratched his head. "I know I'm a numbers guy, but I don't see the correlation."

"Married men live longer."

"Bullshit!" Quinten lobbed a velvet sofa cushion across the room, smacking Marshall upside the head. "That's what you get for lying."

Jonas laughed the loudest. "Take it from someone who's been divorced twice. Marriage sucks. And anyone who says differently has been brainwashed. Or tortured!"

Marshall stood his ground. "There was a segment about it on the evening news. Researchers have been studying the correlation between marriage and life span for decades," he explained. "I'm going to live a longer, fuller life and you guys are going to be old, miserable and lonely. It's a proven fact."

"I'm surprised Sage lets you watch TV," Quinten joked.

Warrick entered the living room, carrying a toaster oven in one hand and a plastic bag in the other. "You guys on another break?" he asked, glancing at DeAndre and Theo. "You better get your sneakers off the coffee table before Sage goes postal."

"Ask Warrick," Marshall challenged, gesturing to his friend with his chin. "He'll tell you. We'll see who's right and who's wrong."

"Ask me what? I hope it's not about that chip on the hardwood floor. Sage just finished questioning me. I passed the lie-detector test, y'all!"

The group laughed.

"I'm not asking Warrick jack." Quinten sneered. "He's still hung up on Tangela, so he'll likely side with you. Your women are friends. You guys always back each other up."

Ignoring the dig, Marshall turned to Warrick. "Isn't it true that married men live longer? The topic was featured on the *CBS Evening News,* right?"

Warrick had seen the segment and remembered his female employees discussing it at lunch the following day. But if he'd learned anything from his father, it was how to defuse conflict. "This needs to go in the kitchen." He stepped out of the room. "I'll be back in a minute." *Or never,* he thought, relieved to have dodged that bullet.

After spending the entire day together, everyone was on edge. Warrick didn't want to butt heads with Sage again, but he didn't feel like playing peacemaker, either. He'd hang out in the kitchen with the women, have a beer and, if he was lucky, catch another glimpse of Tangela in her cute denim overalls.

As Warrick passed the foyer, he admired the winding, gold-rimmed staircase. The French Provincial–style house had been built on three acres of land and had taken ten months to complete. During the consultation phase, he'd advised Marshall and Sage on which upgrades to choose and when he peeked inside the main-floor bathroom and saw the limestone sinks and skylight, he knew his suggestions had been put to good use.

Warrick was en route to the kitchen, thinking about his Monday-morning conference call with a prominent British developer, when he heard Tangela say, "Men just don't get it. It's not about how much money they make or how nice their car is. I like flowers and candy as much as the next girl, but that's not what I wanted from Warrick. I wanted to spend quality time with my man, without his stupid cell phone going off every two seconds."

He stopped short. *Is that all she wanted? Time and affection?* Warrick heard the genuine longing in her voice and considered her words. When he'd gone away on business, he'd always brought a gift home for her, but he'd overlooked how important it was to do things as a couple.

He'd fallen in love with her caring nature and high-energy personality, but in the end, it was her exuberance that drove him away. Tangela felt the need to tell him everything, no matter how trivial it was, and after a grueling ten-hour day, he often didn't have the energy to keep up.

Interest piqued, he decided to wait until there was a break in the conversation before interrupting. Back flat against the wall, Warrick listened as Tangela shared the most personal and intimate parts of their relationship with her girlfriends. He felt as though there was a target on his back and the more Tangela spoke, the angrier he got. Calling off the wedding and walking out on him obviously wasn't humiliating enough. Now, she was back to finish the job.

"Warrick made time for his friends, but not for me. He was too tired to go look at reception venues, but not too tired to shoot pool with the guys. In the end, that's what it came down to. He put everyone before me and when we stopped making love I knew it was—"

Someone gasped. Warrick couldn't see inside the kitchen,

but he could imagine the stunned expressions on the women's faces.

"You never told me you guys weren't having sex! Why didn't you say anything?"

"Because I was embarrassed."

"Well, just how long was it?" someone questioned.

Warrick held his breath. Yeah, how long *was* it? Surely it couldn't have been longer than a week or two. As his responsibilities increased at the office, he'd spent less time at home, but his furious schedule hadn't diminished his appetite for Tangela. When they'd first started dating, they couldn't get enough of each other. They'd had a hot, passionate sex life and although the flames had cooled over the years, she'd never failed to excite him.

"I can't believe I'm telling you guys this." A pause, then, "Three months."

The box slipped out of Warrick's hand, but he caught it before it hit the ground. *What the hell?* It couldn't have been that long. Could it? He tried to remember the last time they'd made love, but the weeks leading up to the breakup were a blur. His dad was in the hospital, and he'd been named as interim president. For weeks, he'd split his time between the office and the hospital and even though Tangela had been very supportive, he knew she resented him for not helping her plan the wedding.

"Damn, girl! I know we punish the brothers sometimes by withholding the booty, but that's torture! It's a wonder he didn't come down with scarlet fever or something!"

Laughter flowed out into the hall.

"I wasn't the one holding out."

The giggles skidded to a stop. "You mean he turned *you* down?"

"All the time," he heard Tangela say. "Back in the day, we used to make love three or four times a week. Over time, it dwindled to once a month. I finally got tired of initiating things and quit trying. He obviously didn't want me, so why would I waste my time?"

Warrick hung his head. He'd never known she felt that way. Every relationship went through rough times, but in spite of their problems, she'd always been his rock. Her smile, her warmth, her love made everything right in this messed-up world. Tangela was the only person outside of his grandmother who could keep him in line, and when she left, he felt like he'd lost the best part of himself. Work was the perfect distraction, but when he was home alone in the house they'd loved and laughed in for years, he thought he'd go insane with boredom. Vodka numbed the pain, but when the alcohol wore off, melancholy returned.

"Men always complain that women hold out. According to my male colleagues, we put the booty under lock and key and brothers have to pull a Houdini to get some!" The women shrieked with laughter. "But men rebuff us, too."

"I heard that," a high-pitched voice agreed. A cupboard slammed, plates clanked and the microwave hummed to life. "The only time a man turns down sex is when he's—"

"Cheating," Tangela finished. For a moment, she fell silent. "He probably was. He wasn't sleeping with me, so he had to have been getting his needs met somewhere."

Warrick's face stiffened. This had gone on long enough. He couldn't have Tangela trashing his family name. Carver men didn't cheat, they didn't abandon their families and they always lived up to their responsibilities. She'd walked out on *him*. Why was everyone overlooking that vital piece of information?

"Why didn't you hook up with that Javier guy you met in Mexico?" someone asked.

"I wasn't feeling him."

"You weren't feeling him or you were still carrying a torch for Warrick?"

"No one's thinking about Warrick." Tangela laughed. "I'm *so* over him."

For the first time all afternoon, Warrick smiled. If he didn't know Tangela as well as he did, he might have believed her. But the high-pitched giggle was a dead giveaway. She wasn't over him, and the news pleased him.

"I know what you should do." Sage's voice was so low, Warrick had to press his ear to the wall to hear what she was saying. "When Marcello comes over tonight, put some of that old-school whip-appeal action on him!"

The women cheered.

"Forget Warrick. Give that sexy doctor a chance," Sage advised.

"You think so?"

"Hell, yeah!" encouraged another. "You have an itch and that suave Latin hunk is the perfect guy to scratch it! Meow!"

Warrick's heart galloped like a thoroughbred. *This issue with Marc is worse than I thought!* Shifting the toaster oven in his hands, he blew out a deep breath. His fingers were numb and his arms ached, but that didn't compare to the pain he was feeling inside. And if he didn't do something soon, Tangela would become Marc's flavor of the week. Determined to thwart her plans, he stepped into the sunny kitchen. "Sage, where do you want me to put this?"

The fork in Tangela's hand slipped and fell to the ground. *Sweet mother of Joseph!* she thought, taking in the view. Her gaze swept over Warrick's solid physique. His biceps were hard, enticing mounds of muscle and although she couldn't see under his polo shirt, she still remembered the remarkable definition of his broad chest. Tangela often drooled over the young, the black and the famous, but Shemar Moore had nothing on Warrick James Carver. The man was a force of nature. Wholly and deliciously fine with a hard butt. She didn't want to be attracted to him, didn't want to desire him, but she didn't have a say in the matter. He'd stepped into the room and now every nerve in her body was on high alert.

Needing a diversion, she retrieved the fork and resumed organizing the cutlery drawer, but seconds later, she was staring again. His back was wide, his legs strong and when he hoisted the toaster oven onto the countertop, Tangela caught sight of a dark nipple. Warrick's entire body was glistening with sweat and memories of making love in a cramped Maui cabana showered her mind.

Her mouth wet with desire, Tangela put a hand to her chest in the futile hope of grabbing hold of her emotions. Heart failure wasn't common in healthy twenty-nine-year-old women but there was no mistaking the burning sensation in her chest. Lust coursed through her body, leaving her feeling hot, bothered and more aroused than ever before.

From across the room, their eyes aligned. His lips flared into a smile and she momentarily lost her bearings. Her mouth was drier than dust and she could feel a baseball-size lump in her throat. What was the matter with her? Pouring herself a drink, she fought their intense, mind-numbing attraction. Warrick would always be tied to her past, but he'd never be part of her future. It didn't matter how good he looked or how lonely she got, she wasn't going to take him back. They had no business being together and she'd sooner join the three-ring circus than date Warrick James Carver again.

"Girls, look who decided to stop in for a visit," Sage announced, opening the microwave and taking out the plate of mixed vegetables. "It's Warrick, y'all."

Warrick flashed that dreamy, lopsided smile and the women's faces softened like butter. Overcome with longing, fully and completely lost in his provocative scent, Tangela tried not to stare at his muscles. Slack-jawed, eyes wide, Tangela stared in disbelief as Nadine surged to her feet and poured Warrick a tall glass of orange juice. "That should quench your thirst," she cooed, touching his forearm. "Is there anything else I can get you?"

Tangela's eyes were flaming red coals. Five minutes earlier, Nadine had called Warrick a selfish jerk and now she was standing so close to him her D cups were grazing his chest. *So much for sisterly solidarity,* she thought, deciding she'd better keep a close eye on the attractive Chicago native. She'd met Nadine at a dinner party months earlier, and remembered how she'd impressed the men in attendance with her knowledge of politics, sports and real estate. All of the things Warrick loved. Tangela didn't want him back, but she wasn't going to stand by and let Nadine have him, either.

"Warrick, can you go get the guys?" Sage asked, carrying the roasted chicken into the dining room. "Dinner's ready."

"Sure, no problem."

"I'll come with," Nadine offered.

Tangela looked on helplessly as the single mom sauntered off with Warrick. Nadine hung on his arm like a Christmas wreath and as they exited the room she heard the backstabber say, "I hear you have a vacation home in the Hamptons. I'd *love* to see it sometime."

Chapter Seven

Wild, boisterous laughter drowned out the painfully tender voice of John Legend.

"You slashed his tires, keyed his car *and* put sugar in his gas tank?" Quinten asked.

"I had to," Cashmere replied matter-of-factly. "I'm sure I'm not the only one here who's gotten revenge on an ex. It's normal to want to get even when you've been hurt."

Tangela agreed, but she wasn't about to voice her opinion. She placed herself back to the day she'd moved out. Tangela would keep the secret until her grave, but as she'd heaved clothes and shoes and toiletries into her suitcases, she'd actually considered destroying Warrick's prized model-airplane collection. Intent on getting even, she'd stormed into his office, but stopped short when her gaze fell across the picture on his desk. The one they'd taken with his grandparents during Christmas. Misty-eyed and overcome with guilt, she'd bolted from the room and didn't stop running until she was inside the garage.

"Cash, you're like a sister to me, but I can't help you out on this one," Sage admitted, snuggling closer to her husband. "I've done a lot of crazy things in my life, but I always drew the line at messing with a man's stuff. You saw *A Thin Line Between Love and Hate,* didn't you?"

The group broke out in laughter.

"Y'all don't know some of the assholes I've dated. I've met brothers who didn't know how to do right by a woman, so I have to teach them a thing or two about honesty. It's like my grandmother used to say, 'All's fair in love and war!'"

Theo, Cashmere's boyfriend of two months, coughed so loudly it sounded as though he'd come down with a serious case of whooping cough. He tried to act normal, tried to project calm, but his voice was swathed in fear. "You'd never do something like that to me, right, baby?"

Shrugging innocently, Cashmere donned a mischievous smile. "Well, that depends. If you're the honest, hardworking studio engineer you told me you were, then we'll be cool. But if it turns out you're a polyester-wearing, walkie-talkie-carrying security guard with two baby mamas, we're *definitely* going to have a problem."

Her response incited the Third World War.

"What's wrong with blue-collar men? Everyone can't go to the Harvard Business School you know." Jonas slouched in his seat. "All you women care about is what kind of car a man drives and how big his bank account is. What's up with that?"

Nadine joined the discussion. "I busted my butt to finish law school and saved for years to buy my own house. It's only natural that I'd want to be with a man who has worked just as hard. So Roscoe, who flips burgers at a fast-food joint, just isn't going to cut it!"

The women laughed, and the climate quickly changed from friendly to hostile. "Cashmere, you should've given the guy a break. Maybe he really was separated." DeAndre pointed a thumb at his chest. "Take it from a guy who knows. Before you get married, you get all the sex you want. After you say 'I do,' you're on some kind of strict military diet."

Sage smirked. "It sounds like *you* don't know how to please your wife."

"Tell him, girl!" Nadine cheered, nodding vigorously. "Sex is like pizza to you brothers. You can enjoy it even when it's so-so. It's not like that for sisters. It has to be damn good for us to want it. I'm talking deep-dish with a cheese crust and everything on it." She licked her lips. "And I do mean *everything*."

Laughter rang out.

"I don't mind taking care of a woman, as long as her body's bangin'," Quentin said.

"A bangin' body isn't what makes a woman beautiful or valuable, Q."

Tangela glanced up from her peach cobbler. Warrick reclined on the brown armchair, a pensive look on his square face. He'd been so quiet, she'd almost forgotten he was there. His gentle voice stilled the clamor and captured everyone's attention. A man of great intellect, he preferred to listen than to talk, but when he spoke, it was profound. He was a calm, introspective type, and although he'd been educated at one of the best architectural schools in the world he didn't flaunt his credentials or boast about his numerous awards.

"Beauty is someone who takes care of others, someone who exhibits compassion, empathy and love." He turned to her and Tangela felt her face flush. "Ever see a woman walk into a room and command the floor? It's not her hair or her dress that grabs them. It's her spirit, her soul, her aura. She has an inherent grace that can't be defined or duplicated."

"Have you been reading Maya Angelou again?" Quinten bumped elbows with Jonas. "Quick! Someone call Pimp Don Juan. Warrick's starting to sound like a punk!"

The men burst into laughter, and Tangela rolled her eyes. One thing she'd always loved about Warrick was the depth of his mind. The other guys might be superficial jerks, but he'd been raised well and didn't get tricked into believing beauty came in a size-two package.

Maybe badmouthing him to her friends had been a little harsh, she thought, stealing a glance at him. After all, he had done some nice things for her during their relationship. He'd massage her feet at the end of a rough flight, run out to buy her aspirin whenever she had cramps and surprised her with romantic, spur-of-the-moment trips a couple of times a year.

"Are we going to Bar 890 or what?" Quinten asked, standing. "My friend's working the door tonight, and if we get there before nine he'll let us in for free."

Tangela stood. Walking down the hall toward the main-floor bathroom, she thought about her late-night rendezvous with Marcello. After using the bathroom, she washed and dried her hands. Inspecting her hair in the antique mirror, Tangela wondered if she could really go through with it. Sleeping with Marcello was risky. What if he was a player? Or worse, only interested in her because she'd been on the cover of *People* magazine?

Deciding she needed to talk things over with Sage, she shut off the lights and exited the bathroom. But her girlfriend wasn't in the living room and neither was anyone else. As she picked up her plate, she caught sight of someone on the recliner. Warrick. Eyes closed, he tapped his fingers to the beat of the song playing. He looked relaxed, dreamy and oh-so-fine. Tall, dark and hot, she decided, smiling indulgently to herself. Worried she might get carried away, she turned toward the kitchen.

"Tangela?"

She stopped. "How did you know it was me?"

"Your perfume," he explained, his eyes open and burning into her with a firelike intensity. "I'd recognize that scent anywhere."

"Where is everyone?"

"The guys left." He motioned with his head to the ceiling. "Marshall's on the phone and the girls are upstairs trying to find something to wear in Sage's closet."

"And you're…"

"Waiting for you."

Genuinely surprised, she frowned. "Why would you be waiting for me?"

"You're going to the club with us, right?" he asked, standing and crossing the room toward her. "It'll be like old times. You have to come."

"I have other plans."

"At eight-thirty? You're usually asleep by now or in bed watching *Grey's Anatomy*."

"That was then and this is now," she snapped, annoyed that he remembered her routine. "And if you must know, a friend of mine is stopping by. A *male* friend."

"Anyone I know?"

Hoping to put more distance between them, she picked up the dessert plates from the coffee table and went into the kitchen. Instead of staying put, he followed.

"Have your friend meet us at Bar 890."

"I can't. I have to get…" She stumbled for the appropriate word. *Sexy?* No. *Bootylicious?*

Wrong again. "Why do you care whether or not I come? It never mattered to you when we were dating." Unrepentant about her strong remarks, she folded her arms across her chest. "You preferred when I stayed home. According to you, I was too clingy and you didn't want me hanging on you all night."

"Tangela, before we became lovers we were friends. Good friends." He reached for her hand. His touch ignited sparks and his cologne was refreshing, as though he'd just stepped out of the shower. Unwanted memories surfaced. Clad in boxer shorts, a rose between his teeth, one night he'd slipped into bed and made love to her with such tenderness she'd had to fight back the tears. Tangela erased the image. She refused to think about that night, no matter how passionate and exhilarating it was.

Slamming the door on her memories, she listened to Warrick talk about seeing her on the magazine cover for the first time. "I feel like I've been left out in the cold. Everyone knows what's going on with you except me. I want to hear what's new and exciting in your life.

"Tangela, our relationship wasn't all bad and I'd like to think after dating for seven years, we could be friends. Things weren't perfect, but you must have been happy at some point, or we wouldn't have lasted as long as we did."

Warrick gave her a long once-over, then slowly returned his eyes to her face. The truth was he had more than friendly feelings for her. There, he'd admitted it. He still desired her, but he wasn't going to be stupid enough to cross the line. "You've always been a part of the gang and I think it would be cool if we hung out tonight. You know, for old times' sake."

"Well, I don't."

He'd need a blowtorch to melt her heart, but he wasn't giving up. One thing he'd always loved about Tangela was how much she valued her friendships. And tonight, her sense of loyalty would work in his favor. "Look at you. You're working up the ranks at American Airlines, you bought your first place and you're on the cover of *People* magazine. That's worth celebrating."

Tangela felt her face warm. Blowing the air out of her mouth, she pushed a hand through her hair. Someone with a sick sense of humor must have jacked up the heat because the temperature had suddenly gone from a cool seventy degrees to a sweltering inferno.

"I just want to get to know this new side of you. This side of you that you kept hidden from me all of those years."

Swept up in the moment, she lost her ability to speak. And when his scent enveloped her, she felt as though her feet were glued to the hardwood floor. *Move! Run! Call for backup!* a voice screamed inside her head. *You're not going to stand there and let him put the moves on you again, are you?*

"I have no ulterior motives, Tangela. I just want my best friend back."

He gave her something to consider. Staring up at him, her eyes probing his face, she judged the sincerity of his words. Her ex might be a lot of things, but he wasn't a liar. Warrick gave it to you straight, a cold, hard dose of the truth served with a smile. Tangela caught herself eyeing his lips and channeled her gaze. For the first time ever, she liked who she was and what she was doing. She had her own thing going on and she didn't need Warrick complicating her simple, stress-free life. The man might look harmless in his polo shirt and khaki shorts, but his touch was lethal and his lips honey. It was time to make a run for it. If she wanted to keep her sanity *and* her heart intact, she had to get far away from him. "I'm going to say goodbye to the girls. I'll see you later."

Warrick blocked her way. "There's one more thing I have to say."

There was no way out. He'd expertly pinned her against the wall between the microwave stand and the potted fern. *How in God's name did I end up here?* Unnerved, she licked her lips and forced herself to remain calm. No matter what happened, she wouldn't lose her cool. "Warrick, what are you doing?"

Her breathing came in quick, short spurts. Over time, they'd lost interest in each other and ultimately stopped having sex, but her desire for him was still there. One kiss was all it took and she'd be a bumbling, love-struck fool. "I have to go. It's—"

"I know you think the worst of me, Tangela, but the truth is I never meant to hurt you."

Taken by surprise, her hands dropped to her sides. *You never meant to hurt me?* her mind repeated dubiously. *Then why did you string me along for seven years?* Narrowing her eyes, she studied him for several long seconds. Warrick was a hard man to read, but he looked dead serious. He honestly and truly believed he'd done nothing wrong. Deciding she wouldn't interrupt or argue, she listened to his impromptu speech. It sounded rehearsed, but she found herself being sucked in by the smoothness of his voice.

"If I could do things differently, I would. I'm not proud of the way I acted or the way I treated you, but we had a lot of problems in our relationship and instead of fixing things, we ignored them. The night you left was…" He paused, organized his thoughts and continued. "We both said a lot of things that we didn't mean."

"Speak for yourself, Warrick. I meant what I said."

A long, awkward silence followed.

"Okay," he conceded with a curt nod. "*I* shouldn't have yelled at you and I'm sorry."

Tangela blinked rapidly. She must have misheard him. Warrick never apologized. At least not to her. Obstinate and proud, Warrick thought he was above asking anyone else for forgiveness. "I'll apologize when hell freezes over," he liked to say. They'd dated for seven years, but he'd only said sorry twice. And both times, his grandmother had ordered him to.

"You were good to me, Tangela, and I'll never forget all the thoughtful things you did for me and my family. You're a very special woman and all I want is for you to be happy."

Tangela's jaw dropped. The implausible had happened. Hell had officially frozen over.

Chapter Eight

All Tangela could hear was the clock on the wall ticking. Warrick's confession set her mind to rest and she was glad they'd finally put the past behind them. He used to be the single most important person in her life, and a big part of her still missed him. But that didn't mean they were going to be buddies again. They weren't.

His grin was contagious and no matter how hard she tried she couldn't wipe the smile from her face. Warrick had apologized for hurting her, and finally after two long years, all was right with the world. She could finally stop lamenting over what could have been and focus on her future. "Warrick, I appreciate you saying that."

Overcome by the intensity of his gaze, she stared down at her hands. Tangela often played the role of the blameless ex, but it was time she owned up to her part in their breakup. "I'm sorry, too. I should have been more understanding about the pressures you were under at work."

"Speaking of work," he began, his face showing disapproval, "why didn't you tell me about the problems you were having at Flight Express? Did you think I wouldn't understand?"

"Your dad had just had a heart attack, and I didn't want to burden you with my troubles," she explained. Her heart ached when she remembered the day she'd turned in her badge and uniform, but she said, "There are far more opportunities for personal and professional growth at American Airlines. I love working there, so let's just drop it."

Warrick stayed the course. "If I'd known what was going on, I would have been there for you. If you'd given me the chance, I would have supported you the way you'd supported me all those years. Losing your mom and your job at the same time must have been devastating."

He didn't ask the question outright, but Tangela knew what he was getting at. "It was an incredibly difficult time in my life, but that's not what drove me to move out. Warrick, in loving you I lost a piece of myself, and over time I became a woman I never thought I'd be. You didn't want to get married, and our arguments about the wedding became vicious and mean. I knew if I didn't leave soon, things would escalate."

"I don't want you ever to think, not even for a second, that I'd ever put my hands on you, Tangela." He wore a sad, joyless smile. They stood face-to-face without a word, then he broke the silence. "I want to be clear about one other thing. Tangela, I never, *ever* cheated on you."

Her eyes popped. *Had he been talking to Sage?* Tangela didn't have time to consider the idea, because the next thing she knew, his hands were traveling down her arm. Leaning over, he bent down and kissed her gently on the forehead. *Who knew a chaste kiss could evoke such pleasure?* And when his mouth moved over her cheeks, then slowly swept over her lips, the nerve endings between her legs shot up.

Tangela didn't have the strength to turn away from his touch. The truth was she craved him. Like wine. Chocolate. And sensuous lovemaking. Caressing her cheeks with the back of his fingers, he weakened her resolve. Then the unthinkable happened. Their lips came together in a passion-filled reunion. His kiss—his sweet, gentle kiss was like balm on her wounded heart and soothed away her deepest pain. Since running into Warrick at the Hawthorne party, Tangela had imagined what she'd do if he ever tried to kiss her again. Screaming seemed childish and she was too weak to fight him off, so Tangela did what any woman who hadn't had sex in eight months did: she kissed him back!

Desire gripped her, filled her, swallowed her whole. He brought her to him; every part of their bodies connected now. His lips moved beautifully, expertly over her mouth. Tangela didn't feel that any of this was real. They were enemies. Bitter, angry exes who couldn't stand each other. They'd had a volatile breakup and before last month, hadn't laid eyes on each other in two years. But when she felt his tongue inside her mouth, seeking her own, Tangela slanted her head to the right, hungry for more.

His mouth was sweet. Trapped in a web of hunger, need and lust, she ignored the conflicting thoughts spinning in her brain and took everything Warrick offered. She'd wanted him the moment he strolled into the Hawthorne party, looking buff, fit and as handsome as ever. He'd filled out the costume better than Dean Cain and she'd had a hell of a time keeping her eyes *off* him and *on* her date. Her desire for Warrick would be there until she died and when he ran his hands up the slope of her hips, she moaned. Tangela felt confident, empowered, sexy. They weren't a couple anymore, and weren't ever getting back together, but he still wanted her and that was an incredible feeling.

Warrick gave Tangela what she was craving. He nipped her earlobe, stroked her shoulders and told her she was beautiful. Kissing her, he buried his fingers into her hair, inhaling a lungful of her scented shampoo. A combination of light and urgent caresses, his deep, passionate kiss electrified her. She felt his erection, strong and thick, against her throbbing core. *No!* screamed in her head, but "Yes" spilled from her lips. The heat of his body aroused her. Every touch, every sound and every smell was magnified. He took his time kissing her, exploring her mouth with his tongue, then pausing to stare deeply into her eyes.

"I never even looked at other women," he murmured, his warm mouth flitting over her ears. "Why would I mess around with someone else when I had perfection at home?"

Tangela came to her senses when she felt his fingers under her T-shirt. Stepping back, she covered his hands with her own, stopping him. Never again would she lose control like that. She was playing with fire and one thing she'd learned as a single woman in the twenty-first century was that she had to be honest, no matter the cost. "We shouldn't have done that."

"I just wanted you to know the truth."

"And the only way to do that was by kissing me?"

His eyes twinkled. "I got a little carried away," he confessed, with a wry shrug. "But can you blame me? You're stunning."

Tangela lacked the words. A little carried away? They'd been only one French kiss away from having sex on the granite countertop. In spite of the gravity of the situation, a smile broke through. Damn Warrick and his silver tongue. He had sex on the brain, and thanks to *that* kiss, so did she. Warrick Carver was the only man she'd ever met who could talk her into almost anything, and it had been that way from day one. Why else would she have put her dreams of marriage and motherhood on hold and moved in with him after only dating for three months? "I'm glad we finally got everything out in the open."

"Me, too," he said in a low, disarming voice. "I'm glad we finally talked things through." Sage's high-pitched laugh and Marshall's deep chuckles floated into the kitchen.

Careful not to touch him, she stepped out from beside the microwave stand and exited the kitchen. The living room was dark but the glow from the TV prevented Tangela from tripping over the piles of unopened boxes. "What are you guys watching?"

"Tangela?" Marshall lowered the volume of the TV and turned on the side lamp. "Warrick, you're here, too? I thought you left."

"We were in the kitchen talking."

Sage snorted. "Is that why Tangela's clothes are crooked?"

"Shut up, Sage." Staring down, Tangela inspected her wrinkled outfit. Her face flushed when she looked at the sagging neckline of her T-shirt and noticed her push-up bra was exposed. When had that happened? Combing the end of her hair with her fingers, she avoided her friend's menacing gaze. "Are the girls still trying on clothes?"

"No, they left about fifteen minutes ago."

"But Cashmere was my ride!"

"That's what you get for making out in the kitchen with Warrick," Sage grumbled. "Will the two of you be breaking in our guest room, as well?"

Ignoring the dig, she went over to the sectional sofa, picked up her purse from the floor and flipped open her cell phone. She had two messages. One was from Carmen and the other was from Marcello. Her heart sank when she heard his voice.

"What's wrong?" Warrick asked. "Everything all right?"

His gentle smile coaxed the truth out of her. "My date canceled."

"I can give you a lift home if you'd like."

"That's the least you can do after—" Sage began.

Marshall pinched Sage's arm and she yelped.

"Warrick offered to give Tangela a ride home. Isn't that nice, honey?"

"He's as charitable as they come," Sage agreed, grinding the words out between her teeth. Rubbing the sore spot on her forearm, she cut her eyes at Warrick, as if issuing a silent warning. "No funny business, you got it? Just drop her off and be on your way."

Biting back a laugh, Tangela shook her head. Sage was acting like her mother, and if Marshall hadn't been sitting there, she probably would have cursed Warrick out. "Aren't you going to the club?" she asked, addressing him. "Isn't dropping me off out of your way?"

"You're right, it is." His frown had a tinge of humor to it.

"This is what we'll do. Go by the club, have a drink with the gang and then go home."

In the ensuing silence, Tangela considered his offer. Why not? Marcello was working, Carmen was at a family function and she had nothing else to do. If they were going to be alone, she wouldn't chance it, but they'd be with their friends and there was no way Nadine would ever let them out of her sight.

Tangela stared at Sage and Marshall. Hugged up on the couch, they spoke quietly to each other, their hands clasped fiercely together. Envy formed a thick knot in Tangela's chest. Seeing happily married couples got to her every time. This— this idyllic scene of marital bliss—was what she wanted, what she'd dreamed of her entire life. And Tangela was determined to have it all. A fantastic career, a loving husband and kids cute enough to model.

Taking Warrick up on his offer was a good idea, she decided, eyeing the starry-eyed newlyweds. It was the couple's first night in their new home and she didn't feel right asking Sage to drive her across town. "Warrick, look at me," she said, glancing down at her dirty clothes. "I'm not exactly dressed for the club."

"It's impossible for you to look anything but beautiful."

Head inclined to the right, she concealed a smile. "Been watching *The Bachelor,* huh?"

He chuckled. "I'm sure Sage can lend you something to wear."

Throwing her hands up in the air, a crazed, wild-eyed expression on her face, Sage surged to her feet. "Oh, sure, why not? Everyone else is helping themselves. Just take a number!" Grumbling to herself, she marched across the room and stomped up the winding staircase. "At this rate I'll have nothing to unpack into my new Louis Vuitton dresser!"

Decked out in framed mirrors, crimson walls and mood lighting, Bar 890 exuded a fresh, hip vibe that appealed to the over-thirty crowd. The bar was heavy on style, and the wrap-around terrace offered a stunning, 180-degree view of the Las Vegas Strip. Home of the Hollywood elite, the sophisticated nightspot was the place to be on a Saturday night.

Champagne flowed, women danced in clusters and business deals were made over pan-fried sirloin steak and fifty-year-old bottles of wine. Worried he might lose Tangela in the crowd, Warrick slipped an arm around her waist. When she glanced over her shoulder and favored him with one of her wide smiles, he closed the gap between them. He quickly scanned the terrace for their friends, but didn't see them. "Let's just grab one of those empty tables," he suggested, steering her toward the far wall. "We'll catch up with the group later."

"There's DeAndre!" Tangela said, pointing at the DJ booth. "The others have to be around here somewhere. Let's keep looking."

"Yeah, let's," he grumbled. Warrick didn't want to share Tangela tonight. He'd hoped they could spend some more time together—alone. Not because he wanted to kiss her again, but because he…he… Who was he fooling? Of course he wanted to kiss her again! Tangela had put it on him and like a single man at the Playboy mansion, he was hungry for more.

On the drive over, he'd had a hell of a time keeping his eyes off Tangela and on the road. When she'd returned to the living room in a flirty, head-turning number, he'd been too surprised to speak. The printed halter dress highlighted her feminine curves and the bright amethyst necklace and bracelets completed her sultry look.

They'd chatted about music and business, but it was the stories about her most lively passengers that cracked him up. There was the young record producer who mutilated the English language every time he spoke, the mother who insisted on breast-feeding her second-grader at her first-class seat and the seniors who got busted having sex in the lavatory. But amid all the laughter and joking, he'd felt an ache in his heart for the woman he'd stupidly let get away. He'd dated some over the years, but he enjoyed how easy it was to being with her. With Tangela, he didn't have to fake interest or break his back trying to impress her.

"There's Nadine, Quinten and Jonas!" Waving, Tangela hustled through the mass of partygoers and greeted their friends with hugs. "We've been searching all over for you guys!"

"Hey, bro." Quinten pushed a beer bottle into Warrick's hand. "I called your cell. When you didn't answer, I thought maybe you'd changed your mind about coming."

"Tangela couldn't decide what to wear," he explained. "You know how long it takes her to get dressed."

"Yeah, about that, why's she here?" Jonas stared at the women, who were admiring each other's shoes and shrieking every two seconds. "I didn't expect you guys to show up together."

Warrick frowned. "I gave her a ride. What's the big deal?"

"You're not going to be able to cut loose with her around," Quinten explained.

"Don't worry about me. I'll be fine."

Jonas wasn't convinced. "Do I have to remind you what happened the last time we were here? Tangela flipped out when you started dancing with that MTV vee-jay."

"That's nothing," Quinten said, his face pinched tight. "Remember when she stormed into Leon's bachelor party looking for you?"

Warrick chuckled. "Just my luck. Tangela walks in just as the dancers are starting their routine." A grin on his face, he shook his head ruefully. "I never did get that lap dance!"

Chuckling, he cast his eyes slowly around the crowded terrace. Drawn by the sound of her laugh, he turned around in time to see Tangela on the dance floor, waving her hands in the air and rocking her hips in time with the music. He remembered how good it had felt to hold her in Sage and Marshall's kitchen.

"There's plenty of hot chicks here," Quinten told him,

gesturing toward the dance floor with his hands. "Check out the honey at the bar in the fishnet stockings. She's hot!"

Peeling his eyes away from Tangela, he redirected his gaze to the circular bar. His eyes skipped over the brunette and landed on the greasy-haired man pawing her. Marc. In a flashy red suit and collarless off-white shirt, he was hard to miss. Warrick didn't know who Tangela's late-night rendezvous was with, but after overhearing her conversation with her girlfriends that afternoon, he'd bet the mystery man was Marc. Warrick didn't want to see Tangela with the slick-talking pediatrician, but he didn't want her to get hurt, either. Or worse, going berserk like Cashmere. The woman Marc was groping looked like a *Flavor of Love* contestant, but if Tangela saw them, she'd lose it, Terminator-style.

Without thinking, he shouldered his way through the crowd, and reached Tangela in five seconds flat. Obscuring her view of the bar, he rested a hand on her back. "Guess who's eating in the VIP lounge?" he announced. "It's one of your favorite actors."

Her eyes shone. "Rick Fox?"

Warrick nodded and she squealed. Tangela didn't know anything about basketball, but once the three-time NBA champion had joined *The Game,* she'd become his biggest fan.

"You have to show me where he is! Oh my God! Wait until I tell Nadine and Cashmere!"

She did, and seconds later, Warrick was ushering Tangela and her girlfriends into one of the wide glass elevators.

Chapter Nine

"Enough about my messed-up love life," Tangela said, once Warrick slid into the driver's seat of his sleek black sports car and clicked on his seat belt. On the walk from Bar 890 to the parking garage, he'd asked about the guys she was dating, and now she was flipping the tables on him. "Are you still dating that Alexis girl?"

"No, she just accompanied me to the Hawthorne party."

"Oh." Turning toward the window so he wouldn't see the smile stuck to her lips, she watched people spill out onto the strip from clubs, restaurants and casinos. "I wish dating wasn't so stressful. Hollywood makes it look so easy!"

"Maybe you just haven't met the right guy." His voice was low, charged with feeling and emotion. "You'll know when you do. You'll share an intense, immediate connection, stronger than anything you've ever experienced before."

His lascivious gaze fell across her face. Tangela cleared her throat. Pulse soaring, hands trembling, she tried not to let her anxiety show. His lips looked so damn good. He had a soft mouth, strong hands and every time he kissed her, her legs wobbled. Desperate to refocus her thoughts, she stared out the windshield. It was so hot in the car, the windows had fogged up. "We'd better get going. Someone might think we're fooling around in here and call the police."

"That wouldn't be so bad," he joked, starting the engine. "My stocks would go way up! You know what they say, no press is bad press."

"You'd like that, wouldn't you? Sisters from all across the country would be flocking to Las Vegas to meet the single, illustrious son of Jacob Carver."

"I don't need a troop of women," he confessed. "Just one."

Shivering, she inched toward the passenger door. Warrick had given her his sports coat as they left the club, and as she pulled it tighter around her shoulders, he slipped an arm along her seat. Tangela raised an eyebrow. Her ex-boyfriend boggled her mind. Inquisitive and incredibly discerning, he could read her thoughts without her ever saying a word. They'd been sexually, emotionally and spiritually connected, but he'd refused to marry her. So, why was he making eyes at her now? He was trouble, and if she wasn't careful, she'd get sucked in by his hearty laugh, that boyish smirk and his rich, invigorating scent. Caution had to be the order of the day when he was around. "Have you dated a lot?"

"I don't have much free time." The truth was, he'd tasted the singles' scene and hated everything about it. He was a relationship type of guy and had quickly grown bored taking out a different woman every night. When Tangela left, there'd been an enormous gap in his life and it didn't matter how many attractive females he met, the hole in his heart remained.

"What's the quickest way to get to your place?" he asked.

"Head west on the I-15, then merge onto Frontage Road and hang a left on…"

Warrick glanced over at Tangela and wish he hadn't. She ran a hand through her thick, silky hair, and his thoughts ran wild. To refocus, he flipped on the stereo and hit Play on disc one. The smooth, languid voice of Jon B flowed into the convertible as they cruised down the narrow downtown streets. Tapping his fingers in beat to the catchy, midtempo song, he made a sharp turn at the next intersection.

"I can't believe you still listen to this CD," Tangela said, staring over at him. "This song takes me *way* back. God, I haven't listened to Jon B in ages."

"You know what this song reminds me of?"

Tangela's hand shot up. "Don't *even* think about bringing up that god-awful camping trip to Meadow Valley." Her voice was stern, but he saw laughter in her eyes. "I'm warning you," she threatened. "I have Mace in my purse!"

Chuckling good-naturedly, he effortlessly shifted gears. "To this day, every time I unfold that tent, I smell that hideous stench. I think *you* should pay to replace it."

"It's not my fault that skunk sprayed you." Wearing a cheeky smile, she quipped, "I told you to put the chicken in the cooler, but you wouldn't listen. Serves you right."

"Hey, you're the one who left the door to the cabin wide open. Not me!"

Their laughter mingled with the music sweetening the air.

"We had some great times, didn't we?"

"Yeah, we did." With a pounding heart and a dry throat, she pointed out the windshield. "That's me on the corner. Number fifty-one."

"Here we are, safe and sound," he said, turning off the car. Warrick wasn't touching her, but the power of his gaze and the soulful music fueled her lustful thoughts, thoughts she had no business having about him. "Do you have plans next Sunday?"

"You don't want to go camping again, do you?"

His deep, guttural chuckle coaxed a smile from her lips. It had been years since they'd laughed together. Stress brought out the worst in people, and at the end of their relationship they'd argued so fiercely, Tangela had thought she hated him. But tonight, she burned with passion, a fire so hot, it could flatten the whole apartment complex.

"It's my grandparents' anniversary."

Tangela nodded. "You guys are throwing them a surprise party, right?"

"How did you know?"

"Rachael mentioned it."

"Does that mean you're coming?"

"I don't know. It's a family thing and I'm not—"

"Tangela, don't," he warned, cutting her off. "You know my grandparents would love to see you. You're like another daughter to them."

"Are you bringing Alexis?"

"Why would I?"

"I'm just checking." Her laugh was dry. It would be great to see Mr. and Mrs. Carver again. The couple had opened their home to her and she would forever be grateful for their love. Why not join the family and celebrate such a joyful occasion? Now that she and Warrick had cleared the air, it was puerile to fret over being around him. She was still very much attracted to him, but nothing was going to happen. "I'll think about it."

His eyes had a friendly twinkle and the smile on his lips made her warm all over. *Get out of the car!* the voice in her head screamed. *What are you waiting for? For him to pounce on you like he did in Sage and Marshall's kitchen?*

"I don't know if I should walk you to the door or not," he confessed, leaning over the center console. His mouth was at her ear and the dulcet sound made her drowsy. "I want to, but you remember what happened at the end of our first date, don't you, Tangela?"

After a pricey dinner, outrageous flirting and a steamy grind on the dance floor of a hot new club, he'd escorted her back to the apartment she shared with her roommate. Pressing her flat against the wall, he'd tilted her chin to receive his kiss. It was heaven, and one kiss hadn't been enough. One kiss had led to another and soon she was down to her bra and panties. They'd stood in the open doorway kissing for what felt like hours. If her roommate hadn't interrupted them, they probably would have gone inside and made love in her cramped closet-size bedroom. They didn't make love for another month, and when it finally happened, Tangela was sorry she had made Warrick wait so long.

"Should I or shouldn't I?"

Heat rose up her neck. Why was he doing this to her? Why was he playing racquetball with her heart? Tangela gripped the door handle so hard, she feared it would come off in her hands. Yes, they'd been broken up for years, but they still shared a deep, undeniable attraction and the sensible thing to do was to keep her distance.

"I'm thirsty," he announced, his mouth against her ear.

Tangela reclaimed her voice. "W-Warrick, don't."

He put a hand on her leg.

"I'm serious, *stop.*" She didn't want him to stop—ever, but she wasn't prepared for where they might end up. It was 2:00 a.m., and the only time a single woman invited a man inside her house at this time of night was when he was staying for breakfast. "Thanks for the lift."

"It's a long drive to the penthouse." Running his fingers across her forearm, he asked if he could come inside for a cup of coffee. "I always loved how you made it. Not too sweet, with a dash of cinnamon and rum. Mmm…"

"I'm all out," she lied. "How about a bottle of water instead?"

"You're inviting me inside?"

Was she? Allowing Warrick into her apartment was begging for trouble. In designer eyeglasses and a crisp oxford shirt he might look harmless, but she knew another side of him. A daring, sexier side that she couldn't resist. He could outwit a magician and make it look easy and Tangela didn't want to be his next victim. "You wait here. I'll bring it out."

His smile slid away, but his eyes still sparkled. He was teasing her and having a good time at her expense. Deep in concentration, he studied her like a painter with his muse. "You don't trust yourself to be alone with me," he announced, his eyes creeping down her figure. "That can only mean one thing. You still have feelings for me."

"It's not that," she argued. "We have a long history and I don't want to end up—"

"In my bed?" His hand traveled up her thigh.

Tangela swallowed. What was wrong with her? She'd never had a problem telling her dates to back off, so why was she letting Warrick feel her up? If anyone else had tried to get fresh, she would've smacked them upside the head, but for some reason she didn't rebuke him.

"This is nice." His smile stretched the length of his mouth. "It kind of reminds me of old times. Back in the day, we used to go to Lover's Peak and sit in the car talking until sunrise." When she nodded in acquiescence, her eyes blazing with desire, his imagination ran further. "We never did more than kiss, but I wanted you so bad, Tangela. I had it all planned out in my mind, too. I'd undress you on the banks of the river and…"

"We've been out here for a long time," she said, interrupting his erotic daydream. "I'd better get inside before one of my nosy neighbors calls security."

"Just a few more minutes." The urgency in his voice bordered on desperation and she'd never heard him sound sexier. "We're having a good time, aren't we?"

"It's been a really long day and an even longer night. I'm exhausted."

Grabbing her purse, she pushed open the passenger door and stepped out of the car. When Warrick appeared at her side and offered his hand, she hesitated for a moment, then took it. A long, meaningful look passed between them. Her stomach lurched when Warrick stepped forward. The man gave her butterflies and heart palpitations. "I guess I'll see you around."

Warrick closed the gap between them. Her lips looked appetizing. At war with himself, he took a moment to consider what he was about to do. He felt as if he was being pulled in two directions. Being with Tangela reminded him of all the good times they'd had. There was a gravity about her, an energy, and he wasn't strong enough to turn away.

Abandoning himself to his need, he allowed his gaze to crawl over the contours of her hips. Taking her hands in his, he gave her a gentle kiss. He tasted wine on her lips and though the kiss was brief, it was deadly. He'd never felt more connected to her or wanted her more than he did now. "I've thought about you every day for the last two years," he confessed, whispering in her ear. "Every minute of every single day."

"I don't believe you, Warrick. It's just the beer talking."

"Ask Rachael. Ask the guys. You're all I talk about." His hands slid down her hips. Self-restraint had never been one of his strong points, especially when it came to Tangela. She wasn't just his first love, she was his *only* love. "I know we shouldn't be having this conversation now, but I want everything to be out in the open."

Respectable, well-bred guys didn't make out with girls in public, but he didn't know when this opportunity to be alone with Tangela would come again. "I should have married you when I had the chance. I thought we were too young."

"You were right. We don't belong together."

"You're wrong. We do." After a moment of silence, he tilted her chin upward, studying her for several seconds. "We dated for seven years. Don't you think we owe it to ourselves to see if we could work?" Desperate to get through to her, he spoke openly, truthfully, from the heart. "I'm a changed man. I'm not the person I used to be."

"It's only been two years since we split up. How much could you have changed?"

"I don't know, you tell me," he said, concealing a grin. "I'm not the one who moved to Mexico, lost eighty pounds and landed on the cover of *People* magazine. Next thing I know, you'll be starring in your own hit reality show!"

Warrick saw a smile form on the corners of her lips, and knew he was making progress. "Mistakes were made on both sides and I'm the first to admit that I should have treated you better, especially after your mom died. All I want is another chance to prove that I'm—"

"We did that already, remember?"

"All I remember is coming home and you not being there. You left without giving me a chance to fight for you, Tangela. To fight for us."

"Nothing's changed, Warrick. You still have an insatiable drive to achieve professionally and I want to raise a family. I'm open to us being friends and hanging out every now and then, but that's about it."

"I can accept that." He wouldn't, but he didn't want to argue with her, especially when he was dying to taste her mouth again. Tangela possessed an incredible warmth, but she was no pushover. No one could force her hand. "Did you know that forty percent of people end up marrying their first love?"

Her cheeks grew warm and the heat spread south. *Way* south. "You shouldn't believe everything you read." She paused then sighed. "I'm not interested in getting back together."

Eyebrows raised, he waited expectantly.

Never one to beat around the bush, she gave it to him straight. "I'm in the market for a husband, not another long-term relationship."

"What if I told you I wanted the same thing?"

Her heart stopped. Blocking out the sounds spilling onto the street from open windows, she studied the expression on his face. The cocktails she'd ingested earlier were giving her a nice buzz, but Warrick looked as serious as a Supreme Court judge.

"It took me a long time to get over you, but I did." Scared her lies would crumble if their eyes met again, she stared up at the light post. "You really, *really* hurt me. I'm finally in a good place and I don't want to go there with you again."

"I need you in my life, Tangela. Nothing's been the same since you left."

"You don't miss me. You just hate to see me with somebody else."

"And why wouldn't I?" Warrick would never admit it, but it was the image of Tangela on Leonard's arm that had spurred him to action. A woman as vivacious as Tangela had no business dating a balding plumber. Truth was, competition fueled him. In his mind, nothing was out of reach. Not even the woman he'd once lost. Drawing her to his chest, his arms coiling around her waist, he planted light kisses on her nose and cheeks.

His hands stroked the back of her neck, and Tangela did the unthinkable. She whimpered. Over and over again, until he finally put her out of her misery and kissed her hard on the lips. "Angie, you've always been my world, my better half, the best of me. Everything I've achieved means nothing without you to share it with."

More soft, melodic words streamed from Warrick's mouth. "Do you have any idea how much I've missed you…." Trailing off, he leaned into her, burying his face into her lustrous hair. Taking her murmurs as consent, he used his tongue to part her lips and gently probe her mouth. Pressing her flat against the passenger door, he slid a hand under her thin halter dress. "I don't want anyone else. Only you."

Convinced it was the alcohol talking, she dismissed his impassioned declaration. Tomorrow, he'd have no recollection of this conversation and probably wouldn't even remember what had happened back in Sage and Marshall's kitchen.

A shiver tore down her spine when his fingers grazed her panties. This was wrong. They shouldn't be kissing or caressing or rubbing their private parts against each other. He roughly palmed her breasts, squeezing and tweaking her erect nipples. Sensations of pleasure flowed. If she wanted to find her soul mate, her one true love, she had to resist Warrick. Things were spinning out of control and it was up to her to take charge of the situation. It was hard to think with his tongue gliding around her mouth, but it was time she got off this sexually charged ride.

Battling a killer blend of passion, need and longing, Tangela chided herself to get a grip. No more Warrick, she decided resolutely. No more daydreaming or fantasizing about all the delicious things he could do with his tongue, either. And no matter how badly she wanted him, she wouldn't, under any circumstances, sleep with him. She was in control of her body, not the other way around.

Stepping back, she broke off the kiss. With a speed that could earn her a place on the U.S. Olympic track team, Tangela raced up the stairs to her second-floor apartment, pretending she didn't hear Warrick calling her name. Only when she was inside, and the dead bolt was securely locked, did she realize that she was still wearing his sports coat.

Chapter Ten

Tangela smiled at the hostess greeting patrons inside the door of the House of Blues restaurant. The gospel brunch was the hottest ticket in town, and when Tangela saw the packed waiting area, she was glad she'd had the foresight to make reservations. "I'm meeting a friend for brunch. Do you know if Rachael Carver's arrived yet?"

After searching the thick black book displayed on the podium, the hostess said, "Just give me one moment to locate your party."

Tucking her clutch purse under her arm, Tangela took in the eccentric decor. Candles hung from low-hanging trees, the walls were painted red and servers were dressed in Western-style garb. Famous for its lively atmosphere and its international cuisine, the House of Blues restaurant was one of the oldest and most renowned establishments in all of Las Vegas. And when the scent of fried catfish filled the air, Tangela felt like she'd pass out if she didn't eat in the next ten seconds.

"Good morning."

Startled at the sound of the husky male voice, Tangela glanced to her right. *What is Warrick doing here? Has Rachael invited him to join us?* Looking smooth and debonair in a dark suit, leather shoes and personalized cuff links, he slipped off his rimless aviator sunglasses. *The man sure knows how to wear a suit!* she thought, closing her gaping mouth. He was a great dresser and an even better kisser. Tangela frowned. *Where did that come from?*

"How did you sleep last night?" he asked, invading her personal space.

Was this a trick question? She was anxious to discuss what had happened last night in the parking lot, but suddenly lacked the courage to bring it up. She wasn't ballsy like Sage or Cashmere. She was a simple, small-town girl who had dreams of settling down and having a family of her own. Confronting Warrick was out of the question. If he wanted to play dumb, so could she. "Fine, thanks. Where's Rachael?"

"She couldn't make it. The twins have the stomach flu, and since Davis is out of town on business, she's stuck at home," he explained. "Rachael tried to call you, but when you didn't answer your phone, I volunteered to come by and give you the message."

Tangela nodded. "I didn't have time to charge my cell and it died on the drive here."

"I didn't mind coming. Besides, you have something that belongs to me."

"Your jacket!" Wearing an apologetic smile, she slowly shook her head. "Shoot, I knew I was forgetting something when I left this morning."

"No problem. I'll come pick it up."

"I'll just give it to Rachael the next time I see her."

"That won't work," he answered with a firm shake of his head. "I need it ASAP."

Annoyed, she frowned up at him, a hand planted on her hip. "You have dozens of other sports coats, Warrick. I'm sure you can live without it for a few more days."

"You're right, I could—if my iPhone handheld wasn't in the breast pocket."

"Is that what that beeping sound was?" Giggling, she

shrugged her shoulders as if to dismiss her rudeness. "Good thing I didn't run it through the washing machine, huh?"

"Thank God for small miracles."

They both smiled. He was hungry for another taste of her lips, but Warrick fought his desire. Baring his heart to her last night had been a mistake. Tangela Howard was synonymous with heartache and he wasn't going to be burned twice. Next time, he'd drink less, leave Jon B in the CD case and keep his hands in his pockets.

"You look stunning as usual." Her makeup was light and she smelled like tulips. Everyone inside the restaurant was dressed in their Sunday best, but Tangela had glammed it up as though she was going to a movie premiere. The yellow pantsuit matched her bright disposition and she was wearing her hair the way he liked, up off her shoulders, gathered in an elegant French roll with slim curls grazing her ears. The sexy flight attendant lived life beautifully and looked damn good doing it.

Watching Tangela fiddle with her necklace, he realized he'd never really appreciated what she'd meant to him. She'd always been a prize, but now she had the three Bs—beauty, brains and brilliance. Generous by nature and incredibly loyal, she'd drop everything at a moment's notice to help him out. "We should get out of here," he said, taking her by the arm. "I'll follow you back to your place and grab my jacket."

Stopping abruptly, her lips holding a pert smile, she released herself from his grasp. "I came to hear gospel music and eat brunch, and *you're* paying, Warrick."

"You want to stay?" he asked, his mouth breaking into a half grin. "Well, praise the Lord and pass the corn bread!"

Seated in the balcony at a small table at the rear of the restaurant, Tangela and Warrick shared a seafood appetizer and discussed their plans for Christmas holidays.

"I'll be in New Orleans," Tangela announced, wiping plum sauce from her fingers. "American Airlines is really committed to the urban-development project and they gave me the two weeks off I requested starting the day after Christmas. They've been involved since the beginning, and donated more money than any other airline carrier."

"It's too bad more corporations won't get behind the city." Warrick stuck a cherry tomato into his mouth and chewed slowly. "Thousands of families still live in those cramped FEMA trailers and rebuilding has been a slow undertaking."

"It's tragic. Many of the residents I've talked to feel like they've been forgotten. If everyone did their part, we could get the city cleaned up a whole lot faster."

"That's what my dad keeps saying. He wants me to head down there, but I don't know if I can find time in my schedule."

"Make time," she told him. "The camera crews are gone and all of the volunteers have returned home. Those families need help now more than ever."

"Maxim Designs and Architects will be well-represented. When I told my staff about the event, everyone volunteered to go. Payton will be there and she'll be thrilled to see you. In fact, she was the one who showed me your *People* magazine cover."

Tangela forked salmon into her mouth. She didn't want to talk about the interview and had hoped he wouldn't mention it. Steering the conversation to a safer topic, she asked if he was still coaching his nephew's soccer team. "The season's about to start up again, right?"

"Yeah, and I'm still trying to whip the little rug rats into shape."

She laughed. "Warrick, they're in preschool!"

"Never too young to be the best," he quipped, smiling easily. "I love coaching Brandon and every time he scores a goal, he breaks out into the widest grin. As much as I enjoy it, I might not be able to coach the entire season. I have too much going on at the office."

"Are you still working six days a week?"

Warrick nodded.

"That's got to be tough."

"It is, but it's nothing I can't handle. You know me, I thrive under pressure."

"That you do," she agreed, studying him quietly. "That's one thing I loved about living in Mexico. The people are just as busy as we are here, but they make time to kick back and unwind. They go to the beach, play cards or pile into a family member's house for dinner."

"Did you go to the Mayan ruins while you were in Mexico?"

He sat quietly, listening, thinking, contemplating. Tangela knew how to tell a story and shared all the ups and downs of living in one of his favorite countries. Turned on by the sudden vibrancy of her voice, he found it a challenge to remain in his seat.

Itching to touch her, but aware of his surroundings, he circled his hands around his glass, but wished he was palming her full, curvy waist instead. The animated expression on Tangela's face brought back warm memories. Memories of sunbathing in St. Croix, roasting marshmallows by the fireplace and curling up in bed watching their favorite movies.

As Warrick listened to Tangela talk about her new four-bedroom condo, he realized it wasn't her body or her incredible cooking that he missed, it was her companionship. No one was at home to greet him at the end of a long day or listen to him vent about his employees and clients. His friends were cool, but no one understood him or supported him the way Tangela did. Not even Quinten, and they'd been boys since high school.

"You must be so bored. I've been talking about myself nonstop."

"Well, nothing's changed," he joked, winking at her. "You still talk a lot!"

Laughing, she picked up her napkin and threw it at him.

"Ha, ha, you're a regular Chris Rock. They should give *you* a star on the Hollywood Walk of Fame!"

When their waiter returned to collect their plates, Tangela sneaked a look at her watch. She couldn't believe they'd been chatting for the last two hours. Warrick was a student of the world, unlike anyone she'd ever met, and as committed to his family as he was to his career. He was every inch a businessman, but a kindhearted soul, too. Too bad he hadn't wanted to marry her.

"Maybe after lunch we could—" Warrick broke off when his cell phone rang. Smiling sheepishly, he pressed Talk and greeted his friend. "Hey, DeAndre, what's up?"

"Nothing. I'm just crawling out of bed. Took a fine-ass honey home last night."

"Lucky you."

"You want to roll? She has a twin sister."

Warrick didn't even consider the offer. "No thanks."

"Are we still going to Henderson?"

"Yes, but it has to be later on in the day," he explained. "I have to go into the office for a few hours this afternoon."

"Well, shoot, let's go now. I can be ready in—"

"I can't. Tangela and I are having brunch."

"What? Don't tell me you took her home last night.…"

Warrick turned away, but Tangela could hear DeAndre through the phone, as clear as a whistle. She thought of going to the ladies' room to give Warrick some privacy, but when the lights dimmed and a hush fell over the crowd, she decided against it. The concert was about to start and she didn't want to miss a second of the show.

"DeAndre, we'll talk later." Eyes glued on Tangela, he watched her rock back and forth in her seat, a wide smile on her face. She was clapping to the foot-stomping beat and when the emcee asked the audience to stand, she shot up out of her chair. "Call me back in an hour."

"Don't take her back to your place," his friend warned,

his voice colder than steel. "You're headed for disaster if you do."

"Later, man." Warrick ended the call, switched his phone to Vibrate and pocketed it. Clapping to the beat of the loud, thumping bass guitar, he listened as the choir belted out a toe-tapping rendition of "Oh Happy Day."

Wanting to be closer to Tangela, Warrick stood up and went over to where she was standing. He was enjoying the show, but he couldn't keep his eyes off Tangela. She didn't shop in high-end boutiques or buy five-hundred-dollar jeans, but she was always well put together. Perfect hair. Classy outfit. Inviting smile. A rush of feeling came over him, and he stepped behind her, circling his hands around her hips.

Tangela exhaled. The guitar was thumping, the drums were loud and the singing high-pitched, but she could still hear the staggered beating of her heart. His touch warmed her and fueled thoughts of what had happened yesterday in Sage and Marshall's kitchen. She stole a look over her shoulder. He loosened his hold around her waist, but didn't release her. When he leaned in close and whispered in her ear, her smile came back. He was right. She *was* beautiful and nothing made her feel sexier than being in his arms.

At the end of the show, the audience was invited to join the band onstage for the final song. The jazzy, upbeat rendition of "Amazing Grace" drew men, women and children out of their seats and into the aisles.

"Tangela, you should go down there and join the group."

"Quit teasing me. You know what a horrible singer I am."

"You're not *that* bad," he teased. "But you should sing backup. There are little kids here and we don't want them to cry."

Laughing dryly, she bumped him with her hips. "Thanks for the vote of confidence."

"Can I see you sometime this week?" Worried his voice

didn't carry over the music, he leaned and spoke directly into her ear. "Are you free on Thursday night?"

"No, I have my Spanish-language class."

"What about the day after?"

She shook her head. "I'm going bowling some with friends, and the following night I have a date. The next morning I fly out to New Orleans."

"When did you get so busy? You used to enjoy staying in with a good book." *Or with me* went unsaid. These days, Tangela was always out—mingling, socializing, dating. So unlike the woman he'd fallen in love with. "Every time I went out with the guys you'd give me a hard time, and now you're partying like it's 1999!"

"When I got back to town, I joined every club I could think of," she said. Chin up, shoulders squared, Tangela oozed self-confidence. "If not for our breakup, I probably never would have moved to Mexico, or discovered how much I love playing certain sports. Now I surf, jog and even do a little yoga."

"I'm really proud of you."

His touch was deliberate, but she pretended not to notice. Better not to encourage him. A man of extraordinary wealth and power, Warrick James Carver looked the part, dressed the part and didn't ever let his competitors forget it. If she was ever foolish enough to let her guard down, she'd be toast. "I'm glad you finally feel good about yourself, Angie, but you didn't need to lose a single pound." Lowering his head, he moved his hands up and down her shoulders. "You know I love thick, curvy types, and, baby, you were stacked."

Her stomach coiled in knots. Tangela couldn't concentrate when Warrick was standing this close, and she felt a dull ache between her legs. Praying the feeling would pass quickly, she fingered the ends of her hair. "I've never heard such a unique arrangement to this song. This choir is really amazing."

"And so are you," he confessed. "I still can't get over how much you've changed. You're more confident, more outgoing and there's nothing sexier than an independent woman who knows what she wants and works hard to get it."

A strange sensation came over her. Amid the music, the dim lighting and the appetizing aromas in the air, she felt a sudden, irrepressible need to kiss Warrick. Not just kiss him, but to wrap herself up in his arms and have her fill. Conscious of what had happened last night and not wanting to humiliate herself in public, she returned to her seat, silently vowing never to be alone with Warrick Carver again.

Chapter Eleven

"Happy Holidays!" Tangela said, glancing down at the man's electronic boarding pass. "Good evening, Mr. Heinrich. Your seat is on the right, two rows down."

Watching the elderly man march off, she noted the plane was more than half-full. Fifteen minutes from now they'd be airborne, en route to New Orleans. When she turned around to greet the remaining passengers, Warrick was standing there, smiling down at her.

He smelled delicious and his musky cologne suited him. Well-dressed in an exquisite cream suit, accessorized with a gold Concord watch, he reminded her of a young black business tycoon she'd once seen on the cover of *Newsweek*. With Warrick's drive and tenacity, it was only a matter of time before he was bestowed with the same honor.

"Do you mind showing me to my seat, Ms.? I'm a business-class passenger in 3B."

Tangela concealed a smile. "Not a problem, sir. Please follow me."

When his suitcase was safely stowed and he was seated comfortably, she flipped through the stack of magazines in the overhead bin and pulled out his favorite publications. "We have *Time, Business Today* and the *Wall Street Journal* if you're interested."

He held out his hand. "Oh, I'm very interested."

"Are we going to keep pretending we don't know each other, or are you going to tell me what you're doing on this flight?"

"Urban Development is an organization that's near and dear to my heart and you're right, I should be there," he answered, loving the way she looked in her cute American Airlines uniform. None of the other flight attendants filled out the polyester sweater and skirt like she did.

"So, you'll be there for the weekend?"

"No. I'll be there for two weeks. Dad's holding the fort while I'm away."

They fumbled through small talk, and when a teenager asked for help with her carry-on bag, Tangela made a quick getaway. Seeing Warrick left her rattled, and she couldn't seem to get anything right. She accidentally slammed the lavatory door on Carmen's finger and knocked over a kid playing in the aisle. Tangela could recite the safety announcement in her sleep, but when she caught Warrick watching her, she stumbled over her words like a felon on the witness stand.

Once the pilot switched off the seat-belt light and dinner was served, Tangela joined her coworkers in the galley. "Thank God this is a direct flight," she said, breaking the tab on her diet soda. "I don't know how much more of 12C I can take."

"You had a run-in with her, too?" Carmen asked, shoving potato chips into her mouth. "Could she be any more obnoxious? 'Get me a blanket. Reheat my coffee. I want mineral water.' What does she think this is, Club Med?"

"Forget Ms. Collagen Injections," Marilyn said, smoothing down the hair on top of her head. "Did you guys see the hottie in first class?"

"Oh, yeah," Carmen sang, winking at Tangela. "He's a fine one, all right."

"He'd be even sexier if he ditched the glasses. They make him look nerdy."

Tangela choked on her soda. *Nerdy* wasn't a word she'd ever use to describe Warrick. *Intellectual,* yes, *staid* even, but *nerdy?* Never. He had a voracious thirst for knowledge and his dreams and imagination were far beyond what most people could fathom. Then, there were all the naughty things he enjoyed doing in bed.

"Who's the filet mignon for?" Tangela asked, eyeing Marilyn. "Everyone in first class has been served."

She winked. "I know, but I thought Mr. Carver might want seconds."

"Good idea," Carmen agreed, prying the tray from her coworker's hands. "Back off, Pocahontas. He's taken."

Tangela laughed, but stopped when Carmen shoved the tray at her. "Get going."

"No way. He'll think I'm making a play for him or something."

"You are!" Carmen pushed her back into the aisle. "Tangela, this isn't the Victorian age. You don't have to sit around and wait for the man to choose you. If you want him, go get him."

"Or *I* will." Marilyn winked. "I could use a man like that."

"All right, I'm going. I'll drop this off and come right back."

"No, you won't," Carmen told her. "Take your time. Sit, talk, catch up." Shielding her mouth with the back of her hand, she whispered words of encouragement. "You can do it, *chiquita.* Hell, kiss him if you feel the urge. We won't tell!"

As Tangela stepped away, she overheard Carmen issue a warning to Marilyn. "Back off of 3B. He belongs to Tangela.…"

Did he? It was a dizzying, exciting prospect. Her emotions were conflicted, but one thing was for sure. Warrick was in a class all by himself. She looked forward to seeing him, and felt giddy whenever he was around. Until the Gospel Brunch, she'd never imagined them getting back together, but now it was a real and frightening possibility.

Tangela stopped beside Warrick's first-class seat. His head

was lowered, his fingers were intertwined and he was breathing deeply. She'd finally worked up the nerve to come talk to him and he was sleeping. Disappointment set in as she turned away.

"Where are you running off to?" Yawning, he stretched his hands out in front of him. "I was just resting my eyes. Once we land, I'll be off and running, so I figured I'd better sneak in a power nap now."

Releasing the latch on the tray, she put down his plate. "Enjoy."

"I always loved that about you. It didn't matter how long my meeting ran or how late I came home, you always had a hot meal waiting for me." Warrick took her hand and gestured for her to sit down. "And you served it with a smile, too. In this day and age, it's hard to find a woman who still believes in spoiling her man."

Unsure of what to say, Tangela stared out the small, streaky window. Dark amorphous clouds floated across the afternoon sky, and the awkward silence stretched on for several minutes. "How does everything taste?"

"Your steak is *way* better than this," he announced, after tasting his food.

"You think so?"

"I wouldn't say it if it wasn't true."

After a long second, he turned so they were facing each other. What he had to say couldn't wait until they arrived in New Orleans. "It's been years since we broke up, but I still feel guilty for the way things ended. You deserved much more than I was willing to give."

Swallowing the lump in her throat, she glanced nervously around the first-class cabin. Tangela wanted to hear him out, but she wasn't going to put her career on the line. Fraternizing with passengers was frowned upon and there was no telling who was watching. Aside from breaking company rules, Tangela was terrified of losing her heart to the man she'd once loved more than life itself. "Not here, Warrick. Not now."

"Just hear me out. I promise to be brief." His eyes tried to reach her. Thankful the seats across from them were empty but mindful of the couple behind them, he lowered his voice.

"I'm sorry for all the times I yelled at you, for all the times you ate dinner alone or had to attend an event without me. The truth is, life isn't nearly as good as it was when we were together. Angie, do you think there's hope for us? I'd like to give our relationship one last…"

His fingers played on her thigh, and Tangela felt hot down below. She wanted to believe Warrick when he said he wouldn't hurt her, but she still had the scars from the last time she'd been burned. Two years ago, blind devotion had left her penniless and sleeping on Sage's living-room couch. But she wasn't a needy, self-conscious girl anymore. Like every woman, she struggled with the occasional bout of insecurity, but she no longer succumbed to the issues that had plagued her in her early twenties. She was confident, secure and for the first time in her life, playing by her own rules.

"Think about all the great times we had, traveling across the country, dining at the best restaurants, going to concerts." Warrick hated to play the sympathy card, but he wanted to have some plans firmly in place before they arrived in New Orleans. How could they be in the same city for two weeks and not go on a date? "The times we spent together were some of the best moments of my life, Angie. I still care deeply for you and I can't shake the feeling that we made a mistake breaking up."

"When I moved to Mexico, I made a pact with myself not to get involved with anyone for at least a year. Once I was ready to date again, I decided I'd only date men I could see myself marrying and—" she forced the words out of her mouth "—you no longer fit in that category."

"You can see a future with someone like Leonard Butkiss, but not with me?" He looked sad, confused. "We dated for seven years and even lived together. Didn't the time we spent together mean anything to you?"

"Of course it did! How can you even ask me something like that?"

"Because from the day you packed up your stuff and skipped town, I've been doubting everything you ever said."

Tears stung her eyes, and her ears were ringing. His words hurt, pierced, cut with the accuracy of a double-edged knife. From the second they'd met, they'd clicked and even after all these years she still cared about him. There was no magic pill to make her doubts go away, so this time around she had to be smart. God, what was the matter with her? Why was she even considering dating him again? Hadn't he hurt her enough? Although she was open to them seeing each other, Tangela wasn't going to end her search for Mr. Right. "I paid Love Match a thousand dollars and I intend to get my money's worth. So, let's just keep things casual."

"I can accept that." He wouldn't, of course, but until Tangela was his woman again, he had no choice but to go along with it. Taking her hand, he lowered his mouth and kissed her palm. As he listened to Tangela discuss her plans for the next two weeks, Warrick decided it was time to implement the next phase of his plan, and not a moment too soon.

An hour after arriving in New Orleans, Warrick met Bernard Robinson at the Urban Development office. On the drive over to the construction site, the project manager brought him up to speed on the six housing properties. As they drove through downtown, Warrick found his thoughts straying to Tangela and the conversation they'd had on the flight.

Was he finally ready for marriage? The question circled his mind, deepening his fears and anxiety. Warrick took marriage very seriously, and, as much as he loved Tangela, he didn't want to rush into anything. His parents had divorced when he was nine and in the subsequent years his father had married twice and lived with a fleet of younger women. As a child, he'd decided he was only going to get married once. He'd thought Tangela was the one, but when they got engaged everything changed. Suffocated by her constant attention, he'd looked for excuses not to come home and stayed out late on the weekends. But now Tangela was back, sporting a new look and a sexy, confident vibe. One that turned him on big-time.

"The community has come a long way since the last time you were here."

Surfacing from his thoughts, he nodded his head in agreement. "You're right, Bernard, it has. I hardly recognize this place." The Lower Ninth Ward had once been a wasteland of abandoned homes, graffiti and small-time hoods, but with the financial support of several major corporations, the community was being transformed.

On the corner of the littered block, a band of teenage boys sporting jeans, boots and braids smoked cigarettes and whistled at girls. "Your ride's tight," a teen in a baseball cap said as Warrick emerged from the truck. "Are you a music producer?"

Warrick chuckled. "No, I'm an architect."

"How much you makin' at your job?"

"I do okay. You know, boys, we could use some more volunteers to help paint."

"I'll paint if you let me take your whip for a spin around the block."

"Do you have a license?" The kid nodded and produced his permit. "All right, you paint and I'll take you out to lunch," Warrick proposed. "I might even let you drive on the way back."

The teen stuck out his hand. "Dude, you've got yourself a deal!"

The joviality Warrick felt chatting with the teens eroded the minute he stepped into the house on Lamanche Street. To the naked eye, the twelve-hundred-square-foot home was a sleek, contemporary bungalow furnished with leather couches, lively paint and sunlight. But as he inspected the main floor, he spotted scratches on the hardwood floor, crumbling concrete in a corner of the bathroom and mold behind the bookshelves.

Inside the kitchen, he found evidence of shoddy framing. Smoothing his hand over the wall, he found dozens of cracks originating from the baseboard and spreading up toward the ceiling. "This place won't be ready by Friday. We're looking at another week of work."

Shaking his head, Bernard smoothed a hand over his mustache. "Warrick, you're just like your old man. A hard-nosed perfectionist who's rarely satisfied."

"Thanks. I'll take that as a compliment." Annoyed that Bernard was taking the matter lightly, but remaining calm, he said, "What is worth doing is worth doing well."

"After Katrina, more than half of the workforce relocated and never came back. Prices skyrocketed, businesses closed and it's been hard to find skilled, competent workers anywhere. The construction industry is under pressure to keep costs down and Lyndon's feeling the heat."

Lyndon Siegel was the owner of the construction agency Bernard had insisted on using, and although the New Orleans native was popular and well-connected, he had a terrible work ethic. "I wish you would have listened to me from the beginning and hired Elite Construction," Warrick said. "I've worked with them on other projects and not only do they use the highest-quality materials, they're meticulous to a fault."

"What's done is done. We can't start second-guessing ourselves now." Scratching the top of his head, a concerned expression on his face, Bernard released a deep, troubled sigh. "Do you want to tell Lyndon or should I?"

"I'll handle it. You have enough on your plate without having to worry about confronting Lyndon. Now, show me what's wrong with the wiring."

Warrick and Bernard were inspecting the fireplace when

the front door swung open and Lyndon Siegel stepped over the threshold. "How are y'all doing?"

"Lyndon, I'm glad you could make it. I was just showing Warrick around," Bernard said, walking over and clapping the construction foreman on the shoulder. "I have to stop in at the community center, but I'll be back in fifteen minutes. I have my cell with me, so call if you boys need anything."

Bernard left, and Lyndon closed the door behind him.

"Isn't this place incredible? You had reservations about hiring us, but we stayed within the budget, finished on time and did the landscaping, too," Lyndon boasted, his eyes filled with pride. "I don't want to blow my own horn, but my boys did a damn good job."

"The deck looks good, and I think Mrs. Porter will appreciate the extra cupboard space, but—" Warrick didn't want to clip anyone's heels, but he couldn't stand back and say nothing, either. The work was poor, mediocre at best, but instead of rattling off a list of complaints, he asked Lyndon to follow him through the house. He showed him what needed to be done and told him what materials he wanted used. "How soon can you get some men over here?" Warrick asked. "Bernard's pretty adamant about staying on schedule. The mayor will be here for the dedication ceremony next Friday and—"

"My men and I have jobs lined up through to the summer."

Warrick curbed his anger. Butting heads with Lyndon would make for an acrimonious relationship, and he didn't want to make trouble for Bernard. Worried the other houses were in the same shape, he asked when the building inspector would be out to assess the property.

"The city sent someone two weeks ago."

"This place passed inspection?"

The construction foreman chuckled, revealing a mouth full of cavities. "Don't look so surprised. I have a lady friend who works downtown. I take her out for nice dinners and she overlooks a few minor details when she writes her reports."

"Do you have the paperwork? I'd like to see it for myself."

Lyndon looked at Warrick as if he'd taken leave of his senses. "Don't go stirring up trouble, Carver. Faye Smith and I have a sweet thing going on and I don't need you poking your nose around *our* arrangement."

"I'm not satisfied with the work your men did, and I want it redone."

"There's nothing wrong with this house and I won't have you running my reputation into the ground, either." Spit shot out of his mouth and his dark eyes were filled with hate. As he cracked his knuckles, he issued a warning. "Leave it be, Warrick. Just leave it be."

Arms crossed, Lyndon mumbled feverishly under his breath. His behavior was almost laughable, but Warrick didn't find anything funny about the condition of the house. Realizing Lyndon couldn't be reasoned with, he pointed with his chin, hoping to draw his attention to the cracks. "Would you move into a house with uneven floors, crumbling walls and mold?"

"These families are from low-income neighborhoods," Lyndon explained. "They'd never dreamed of owning a house as nice as this, and they won't care if there are a few kinks. It's taken six months and hundreds of hours of overtime to bring everything together. I ain't fixin' shit. If you don't like it, that's your problem."

The two men stared each other down.

"We wouldn't be having this conversation if *you'd* done your job right." It felt good knocking the construction foreman down a few pegs. Warrick knew careless work when he saw it. "Are you going to do what I paid you to do, or do I need to find someone else?"

His eyes filled with disdain, and Lyndon Siegel's lips stretched into a sneerlike grin. "While you were in Las Vegas, sipping merlot in your plush, air-conditioned office, I was here, with my men, working my ass off in harsh ninety-five-degree temperatures."

"This wasn't a labor of love," Warrick said, keeping his tone even. Talking to Lyndon tested his nerves to the fullest, but he wasn't going to lose his cool. "You were paid *very* well to build four homes and restore the community center, but you dropped the ball. You're lucky I'm not suing you. Or reporting you to the Construction Workers' Association."

Lyndon coughed out a harsh, raspy laugh. "Are you forgetting who I am? I'm warning you, Carver. Back off or you'll regret the day you were born."

"You don't scare me, Lyndon, and if you don't want to lose your business, I suggest you get a team of men over here, *now*."

The front door swung open. "What's going on here?" Bernard asked, confused.

"This is *my* city," Lyndon spat. "I run things here, not you. I practically built this neighborhood with my bare hands. The house passed inspection and there's nothing you can do about it. I'm not calling my men back over here because you're on one of your power trips, so get that stupid notion out of your head."

"Then our contract is null and void."

"Let's not act in haste, fellas. This house is for a single mother and her three kids, remember?" Bernard waited expectantly. When nothing happened, he appealed to the younger of the two men. Eyes filled with trepidation, he turned to Warrick. "The dedication ceremony will go on as planned, but we won't let the Porter family move in until all of the changes are done to our satisfaction. Agreed?"

Chapter Twelve

New Orleans wasn't the romantic getaway Warrick had hoped it would be. He left his Bay Shore home every morning at sunrise, put in a full day at the Urban Development site and, much to his disappointment, only saw Tangela in passing. With all the work that needed to be done at the recreation center, they didn't have time to talk or even have a quick lunch together.

On Thursday afternoon, Warrick told Bernard he had a meeting downtown and left the construction site at four o'clock. It was a lie, but he wanted to take Tangela out for dinner and he couldn't risk her leaving the center before he got there.

Warrick turned onto Franklin Avenue, parked his rental car in front of the Urban Development center and strode up the driveway. "Hey, boss, how's it going?" Payton greeted when he approached. "You ready for the big day?"

"Yeah. Everything's finally coming together."

"Was there ever any doubt? You're far too controlling to let anything go wrong."

Warrick chuckled. He peered into the backyard and when he didn't find Tangela, asked where she was. "Let me guess, she did another ice-cream run with the kids, right?"

"You didn't hear what happened?" Payton asked, her eyes wide. "I thought she would've called you from the hospital."

"Hospital?" His voice carried around the yard. "What happened?"

"She tripped on one of the workers' tool belts."

Like a pit bull on the verge of attack, Warrick's hands clenched and his lips curled. "How serious are her injuries?"

"Tangela has a small gash on her forehead, but she'll be all right. I think she was just shaken up. One minute she was painting, and the next she was flat on her face."

"Where is she now?"

"Lyndon took her to the hospital to get checked out."

"Which one?"

Payton answered with a shrug. "I don't know. I went inside to get her some ice and when I came out, they were gone. Do you want me to—" She broke off when Warrick threw open the iron gate and disappeared around the corner.

An hour later, Warrick plopped down on an armchair at the Drury Inn and Suites Hotel. Dropping his head in his hands, his mind racing, he blew the air out of his cheeks. Where was she? After leaving several messages on Tangela's cell phone, he'd driven to three area hospitals and even phoned Payton to see if she'd heard from her. He'd been at the hotel for the last ten minutes and there was still no sign of her.

His thoughts tormented him. What if she was badly injured? He considered calling Payton again to find out more about the accident, but changed his mind. Tangela was fine. She *had* to be. His feelings for her were stronger than ever before and these days she was all he could think of. Tangela was the kindest, most selfless woman he knew and he didn't know how he'd lived without her for two years. He could date a hundred women and he'd never find someone with her class, charm or inherent grace.

Warrick leaned back in his chair as his eyes wandered aimlessly around the room. Perched on one of the French Quarter's busiest quarters, the Drury Inn and Suites was one of the largest and flashiest hotels in all of Louisiana. Accentuated by dark wood, contemporary art and showy lights, the elegantly decorated hotel captured the essence of old New Orleans.

Wild, frenzied laughter drew his attention to the entrance. A dashing European couple strolled through the sliding-glass doors, and a cool breeze swept inside. The air was still and the sky was a deep, soothing blue. As he turned away, he spotted a black truck idling at the curb. Eyes tapered, he scrutinized the vehicle. The female passenger lifted her head, affording him a quick glance at her face.

Tangela! Warrick bolted upright. Gripping the sides of the chair, he stared at her striking side profile. Jealousy was a useless emotion. It was foreign to his nature and he'd never envied anyone in his life, but every time he saw Tangela with another man, resentment flared in his belly. How long had she been sitting in Lyndon's truck? And what were they talking about?

Warrick was outside, knocking on the passenger window, before either of them saw him coming. "Tangela, open up, it's me."

Not wanting to argue or cause a scene, she reluctantly obliged. Resting her weight on his shoulders, she allowed him to help her out of the truck. "Warrick, what are you doing here?"

"I heard what happened," he said, angling his body toward her. How could he tell Tangela he was worried about her without sounding sappy? Taking a few seconds to sort out his thoughts, he pretended not to notice Lyndon hovering nearby, glowering. "I came by to make sure you were okay."

"I'm fine, really. It was nothing."

"What did the doctors say?"

Tilting her head sideways, she gingerly touched the bandage on her forehead. "They stitched up the gash, gave me a prescription and sent me on my way."

"But you're favoring your ankle."

Lyndon spoke up. "She tweaked it. A couple of painkillers and she'll be as good as new."

Acknowledging Lyndon's presence with a flick of the head, Warrick said, "I hope you've given your men a stern talking-to about leaving their equipment lying around."

"You heard the little lady. It was an accident." A smug, self-satisfied expression was on his face. "None of my men are careless or—"

"Then why was there a tool belt lying in the middle of the yard?"

"It was my fault," Tangela explained. Dividing her gaze between both men, she prayed they wouldn't come to blows. Glowering at each other, they stood with their legs apart and their hands propped on their hips. They reminded her of Old West gunslingers, but without the cowboy hats and pistols. "Warrick, you of all people should know how clumsy I am."

He wasn't buying it. "It shouldn't have been on the ground in the first place. Anyone could have tripped over it. A kid or a volunteer. We'd be looking at a lawsuit if—"

"Are you sure you don't want me to come up?" Lyndon asked, facing Tangela. "We can sit in the lounge and finish our conversation—"

Warrick stuck his fists into his pocket. Was Lyndon making a pass at Tangela right in front of him? Was he out of his mind or spoiling for a fight? Nostrils flaring, he stepped forward, shielding Tangela with his body. "She'll be fine. *I'm* here now."

Their eyes lined up. After several seconds, Lyndon's face broke into a sly smirk. "Tangela, I'll see you tomorrow. Maybe we can do lunch or something."

"Thanks for the lift, Lyndon. I really appreciate it."

"It was my pleasure." He shot her a wink. "Sleep well, gorgeous."

Warrick wished Lyndon would drop dead. Where did he get

off flirting with Tangela? Taking her gently by the elbow, he hustled her through the luxury hotel.

"What was that all about?" Tangela asked, motioning with her head toward the entrance. "Why were you such a jerk to him? I told you what happened."

"I should be asking you the same thing. Is there something going on between you two that I need to know about?" There was something wrong with this picture and Warrick couldn't shake the feeling that there was a lot more going on. "Did he ask you out?"

"Lyndon suggested we grab a bite to eat." Slowly parting her lips, Tangela slid a hand up to her mouth to conceal a yawn. "But my head is killing me. I'm going to take a couple of aspirin and go to sleep."

Warrick's face felt harder than clay. He was right. Lyndon *was* interested in her. Why was everyone after his woman? If it wasn't one of her male friends blowing up her phone, or a construction worker showing off his chiseled pecs, it was one of the volunteers hitting on her. Tangela's natural charm had always drawn men to her, but now that she'd been on the cover of *People* magazine, she garnered more attention than ever.

"Lyndon told me you came by the site today and picked a fight with him in front of his employees," she reported, her pretty features contorted into a glare. "I'd seen the house on Pritchard while out driving one day and I think it looks good."

"Well, there's good and then there's better." Warrick raked a hand over his head. "Each family committed to putting in three hundred volunteer hours toward building their home but Ms. Drummond did twice as much. I'm not going to let Lyndon or anyone else ruin it for her and those kids. After all they've been through, they deserve some happiness."

"I'm not questioning your views, just your methods. Threatening people doesn't produce results. Everyone here is working hard, but you're so focused on what's wrong you don't see all the things that are right. Cut Lyndon and his men some slack." After a moment of silence, she asked, "How are things coming along for the wrap party?"

Warrick cursed under his breath. "Damn! I was supposed to order more cases of wine this afternoon, but it slipped my mind."

"You'd better get to planning, then. Everyone's really looking forward to it." Touching the bandage on her forehead, she wore a sad smile. "I'm going up to bed. I'm exhausted."

Something came over Warrick. Something he'd never experienced before. He didn't know if it was seeing her with Lyndon or the helpless look on her face, but he wanted to protect her. Starved for her touch, he drew her to his chest. His willpower eroded when her body touched his. Subtle but enticing, her perfume induced visions of that rainy afternoon they'd spent making love in his cottage in the woods.

Minutes passed. Warrick couldn't get enough of her, but tonight, holding her was enough. Running his hands along her back, he thought about all they'd been through over the last nine years. Tangela had always been a calming presence in his life. His love for her hadn't diminished and as he caressed her cheek with his thumb, the truth became painfully clear. Tangela Howard was still the only woman he loved and wanted to be with.

Hands wet with perspiration, he stared down at her, wondering what was going through her mind. Warrick held the back of her head in his palms and her silky hair slipped through his fingers. Even without makeup, she was a looker. Straight-up sexy without even trying. He was aroused by the feel of her warm flesh, and his eyes traced the outline of her lips. Their hug was as sensual as any kiss and he heard the catch in her voice when she said good-night. "I'll walk you up."

"No. Go on, I'll be okay. I'm only on the second floor."

In the vain hopes of persuading her, he smoothed his hands

over her shoulders and said, "Tangela, there's nothing I'd love more than tucking you in."

Her eyes were three times their usual size.

"See what you've done to me?" He wore a sly smile. "You have me saying and doing things I wouldn't normally do."

"Thanks for checking up on me. That was very thoughtful of you."

Warrick watched Tangela leave, his heart sinking in his chest. He knew what the problem was, but he didn't know how to fix it. There were a million things to do and no one to shoulder the load. And now on top of everything else, he had a party to plan. How could he romance Tangela with fifty other people in the room? He had to get her alone, far, *far* away from the crowd, but how?

Deep in thought, he stalked through the lobby of the bright, luxurious hotel. Warrick didn't have a plan, but he wasn't going to just sit back and let Lyndon steal Tangela right from under him. He'd always been laid-back in matters of the heart, but it was time to pull out the big guns. If he wanted Tangela to take him seriously, he had to kick things up a notch. *No more Mr. Nice Guy,* he decided, handing the valet his keys. *I deserve to be happy, and that will start with having Tangela back in my life.*

Chapter Thirteen

There's nothing sexier than an intelligent, articulate man, Tangela decided, her eyes crawling down Warrick's slim physique. And as she listened to his speech at the ribbon-cutting ceremony on Friday morning, she had to ward off sinful thoughts. Passion ruled her body and her legs tingled every time they kissed. Humble, down-to-earth guys were damn sexy, but it was his dedication to the community that she admired most about him. Tangela had never known someone who cared so selflessly about the poor and when the audience broke into feverish applause, her heart overflowed with pride.

"We're all bonded by our desire to see New Orleans become the vibrant, captivating city it once was. For real, effective change to begin, we have to remember that we're a unit, a family, a strong, unified brotherhood. In union there is strength and this community has some of the most courageous men and women I know!"

From her place behind the refreshment table, Tangela saw one of the female volunteers hand Warrick a pair of oversize scissors. Seconds later, he concluded his speech and invited the mayor to join him onstage.

Rubbing her chilled hands up and down her shoulders, she stared up at the sky. The air smelled like rain, but the cool weather didn't dampen the crowd's enthusiasm. They applauded when the mayor cut the ribbon and cheered when Bernard gave each home owner a gold key.

Tangela felt as if she had a minor stroke every time a beautiful woman approached Warrick, but she didn't let her anxiety show. Her days of chasing him were over. If he wanted to talk, he knew where to find her. Helping herself to a cup of juice, she allowed her eyes to comb over his firm, lean body. Tastefully dressed in a dark suit and designer shades, he moved among the crowd, shaking hands and talking to prominent members of the community. No one dressed better than Warrick and he paid close attention to every aspect of his appearance, from the color of his handkerchief to the design of his cuff links. He walked with self-assurance and had a soft glint in his eyes.

The ribbon-cutting ceremony was the culmination of two long, tiring weeks, but thanks to Warrick, Tangela felt calm and relaxed. Since her fall, they'd seen the sights, hit up a cool club and bar and even taken in a show. Staying in the moment was a concentrated effort, but she'd stopped thinking about all the things that could go wrong and just enjoyed his company. It was easy to be around him, easy to like him, to love him. Warrick celebrated her intelligence, wasn't intimidated by her strength and, unlike most men, didn't want to change her.

"I'm glad this week is finally over," Payton confessed, pouring sparkling cider into disposable cups. "Warrick's been a bear to work for the last six months and it'll be nice to have my evenings back again. I hardly see my husband these days."

Tangela sympathized with the personal assistant. "He's always been a bit of a control freak and I doubt he'll ever change. Take this project for example. It was Bernard's brainchild, but Warrick practically stole it right from under him."

Frowning, Payton tilted her head up, as if deep in thought. "Tangela, I think you have your facts mixed up. After Hurricane Katrina, Warrick's dad contacted Bernard and told him about his desire to rebuild his old childhood neighborhood. When Mr.

Carver fell ill, he turned the project over to Warrick and here we are."

"Maxim Designs and Architects is funding this project?"

She nodded. "And that's not all. Warrick designed all six homes, selected the furniture and accessories, right down to the shower curtains and bed linens and paid for the renovations at the recreation center out of his own pocket. It's no surprise this community loves him. Warrick puts his money where his mouth is, and does what needs to be done."

Lips parted wordlessly, Tangela considered what Payton had just told her. She knew that Warrick was generous, but this blew her mind. He'd downplayed his involvement with the Urban Development project and insisted that Bernard was the one running the show. Raising her eyebrows, she thought over the last week. Warrick worked around the clock, and yesterday when they went shopping at Hamilton mall, he'd received a flurry of calls from Bernard, Lyndon and other staff members. If he wasn't in charge, than why was everyone around here so desperate for his approval?

"There's a rumor going around that Warrick's dad is the anonymous donor who gave a hundred thousand dollars to the Lower Ward Scholarship Fund. I don't know if it's true, but I wouldn't be surprised. The Carver family are some of the most giving people I know."

Shock loosened Tangela's tongue. "Warrick said all of the senior architects contributed to the designs and that more than a dozen companies offered financial support. Isn't that true?"

"Yeah, but Warrick was the one who worked nights, who came in on the weekends and who pressured those corporations to get involved," she explained. "Sometimes I'd come in on Monday mornings and find him asleep at his desk. But instead of going home, he'd shower, change and head off to the morning meeting. I don't know where he gets the energy from."

Eyes filled with admiration, Tangela stared openly at Warrick. She waited for him to notice her, then smiled. And just like that, he ended his conversation with a city councilman and met her at the refreshment table. "Someone looks happy to see me," he greeted, gently caressing her arm. "How's the patient this morning?"

"I'm good. Your speech was incredible, Warrick. It was very heartfelt and sincere."

"Thanks. I put a lot of thought into it." His gaze was intense and meaningful. "I don't expect things to change overnight, but I hope the healing process can finally begin."

Tangela coughed. Was he talking about the community or their relationship? "Why didn't you tell me this project was your doing?"

"Because it wasn't. Everyone played a part in the development, construction and completion of all six homes. There's no hierarchy here. We're all equal."

"So you *did* finance this venture!"

"How does your ankle feel?" he asked, gesturing to her foot. "Is there anything I can get you? Ice, aspirin, a pack of—"

"For the twentieth time, I'm fine." She wore an exasperated look, but inside, she was touched by his concern. He'd been doting on her since her accident and refused to let her out of his sight. "I'm not sick, Warrick. It's just a tweak. I'll rest later."

"You haven't changed your mind about coming to the wrap party tonight, have you?"

"Why, would you rather I stay home?" Affecting surprise, she widened her eyes and tilted her chin up. "Oh, I get it. There'll be a lot of single women there and you don't want me to throw ice on your game, is that it?"

"Don't be ridiculous. You're the reason I'm even throwing this party." He stood taller and took a step forward. "It's my way of saying thank-you."

"For what?"

"For reminding me what matters most in life." His eyes glazed over, an indication that he was about to kiss her. And he did. The sweet, tender kiss aroused her desires and ended much too soon. Cradling her chin in his hands, he said, "I had to throw this party. How else could I be guaranteed a slow dance or two with you?"

"I'm a simple girl with simple tastes," she replied, loving the sound of his smooth tone. "I shouldn't even have to tell you that. All you had to do is ask, Warrick. You know I've never been strong enough to say no to you."

His eyebrows climbed up his forehead. "I wish you'd told me that before I spent five hundred dollars on booze!" he joked, chuckling.

Tangela loved to hear his laugh and the vigorous sound made her heart go pitter-patter. "Everything ready for the party?"

"Yup, all systems are go," he said, flashing a thumbs-up sign. He turned serious and the light in his eyes grew dim. "I overheard you talking on your cell phone earlier and worried that you might have to fly out tonight. Do you?"

"No, but my supervisor asked me to work an overnight to New York tomorrow."

"But you hate that shift. The turbulence is always bad and the business passengers are more annoying than usual." He added, "Your words, not mine."

Surprised that he remembered, she held back a smile. "I slacked off a lot when I was at Flight Express and I think that's why the managers never took me seriously. If I want to show the company I'm managerial material, I have to be a team player."

"It sounds like advancing at American Airlines is really important to you."

"It is. I'm tired of being passed over for promotions. I want to be in head office and I'm going to get there, one overnight shift at a time."

Warrick gave a long, slow nod, then curled an arm around her waist. "Let's say we get out of here and go get some real food. Those mini-cheese-ball things just aren't cutting it."

"Don't you want to mingle with the mayor?" she asked, pulling back to look at him.

"No, I want to be alone with you."

Tangela smiled at the tuxedo-clad man who opened the front door of Warrick's Bay Shore home. Her mouth watered at the appetizing scents drifting from the kitchen. It had been another long, exhausting day, but seeing the radiant smiles on the faces of the new home owners at the dedication that afternoon had made all the aches and pains worth it. Now that the homes were finished and the recreation center up and running, everyone could finally kick back and unwind.

"Please follow me," the server announced, presenting his left arm in a gallant gesture.

Amused, she took the hand he offered. This wasn't what she'd expected. It was a beer-and-pizza party, wasn't it? At least that's the impression she'd got when she'd spoken with the other volunteers. Who'd ever heard of servers at a wrap party? Glancing down at her casual, loose-fitting dress, she hoped she wasn't outshone by the other guests. Warrick had made an impression on all of the female staff and she'd be lucky if they had a minute alone tonight.

Marble flooring, alabaster chandeliers and the rich blue walls gave the home a relaxed, modern feel. It was elegance and simplicity at its best and as Tangela admired the oil paintings and framed artifacts, she was reminded of what had happened the last time she was here. New Orleans held special memories for her, but nowhere was more special than this house. Specifically, the four-poster bed in the master bedroom.

When Tangela entered the dining room and saw Warrick standing next to the mahogany table, her stomach jumped up in her throat. He was handsome in a tan sweater and loose, dark slacks, and she felt her body inflame with a righteous, dizzying heat. He looked gorgeous, and everything about him, from his smooth skin to his solid frame was a turn-on. His scent had a hint of citrus and his beckoning smile encouraged all sorts of naughty thoughts to overtake her mind.

"Thanks, Ricardo. We'll start with the first course promptly at eight o'clock."

The server went into the kitchen, leaving them alone.

"Baby, you look…" The words stuck in his throat as he took in all of her. Hot-to-death in a short, seriously sexy mauve dress, her hair hanging gracefully down her back, she was easily the most beautiful woman he'd ever seen. He had a deep, emotional craving for her, but tonight, he was going to satisfy a craving of another kind. But first, he had to execute the perfect date.

"Where is everyone?" she asked, peering down the hall. It had been years since she'd been to the lavish, three-story home, but she still remembered the unique layout. There was a den to the right, a library across the hall and a living room the size of a university gymnasium off the main floor. Could the other guests be in there? Tangela listened for several seconds. When she didn't hear anything, she laughed lightly. "Please don't tell me I'm the first one here."

"You are, but I'm not expecting anyone else."

"Where's the crew, the volunteers and the Urban Development staff?"

Sliding his hands into his pockets, he shrugged nonchalantly. "At the Crowne Plaza."

In her haste to speak, she tripped on her tongue. Feeling as though her mouth was full of glue, Tangela took a deep breath, let it out slowly and tried again. "What are they doing there?"

"I got to thinking," he began, lifting a bottle out of the ice bucket. For the first time since entering the room, Tangela took a good look around. Warrick had gone all out. China, candles, red wine and chocolate. Pleased, she watched him fill two wine goblets to the brim. He was putting on a show and she was loving every minute of it. Cute and romantic would never go out of style, at least not with her. "Why spend my last night in town with the crew, when I'd rather be alone with you?"

His salacious smile coaxed her away from the window. Her legs quaked as she crossed the room, but they didn't give way. "So, you paid everyone to stay away?"

"I arranged to have the wrap party in one of the Crowne Plaza's banquet rooms." Tapping the face of his watch, he said, "Right about now they're finishing dessert and getting down and dirty to Rick James."

Warrick chuckled. The muscles around Tangela's eyes tightened and his laughter dried up. Had he gone too far? Was she angry? In his desire to please her, he'd rushed ahead with his plans without considering how she might feel. He felt guilty for deceiving her, but it was too late to second-guess himself. Self-doubt had no place in his mind, so he picked up his glass and said, "I planned for us to have a quiet evening alone. I hope that's okay with you."

Her eyes sparkled with delight, blinding him with their intensity and warmth. Raising his glass high in the air, he flashed an even bigger smile. "How about a toast?"

Placing his free hand on her waist, he pulled her close, and breathed in her sweet, decadent perfume. His stomach rumbled, and he didn't know if it was because he was hungry or because she smelled so damn good. Desire barreled through him, but he didn't act on his impulse. Given the choice, he'd skip dinner and go straight to dessert. It was a challenge keeping his hands to himself, but he admonished himself to be patient.

"What should we toast to?" he asked, his voice thick and husky.

Their eyes locked. Then, in a voice that fanned the flames, she leaned forward and said, "To new beginnings."

Chapter Fourteen

"What's the matter with us?" Warrick asked, eyeing Tangela from across the table. They'd fumbled through small talk, then sat in silence while they waited for the main course. In the hopes of re-creating their first date, he'd asked the chef to prepare all of Tangela's favorite foods. Every dish was full of flavor, rich with seasoning and layered in rosemary and garlic. "We've known each other for almost ten years, but this feels like a blind date."

"I don't mean to be quiet, but the food is so good, it's hard to eat *and* talk."

"I'm glad you're enjoying it." Her face was the picture of happiness and the flickering glow of the candles magnified the twinkle in her eyes. Tangela was the same woman he had met and fallen in love with all those years ago, but she was different, too. "I never thought about it before, but in some ways we are strangers. We're not the same people we used to be."

"I am," she argued. "I lost some weight, but I'm the same fun-loving girl inside."

Pointing at her with his fork, he swallowed the piece of chicken in his mouth and said, "You've changed the most! You were on the cover of *People and* you were on *Ellen.*"

She wore a coy, closemouthed grin. "You saw my interview?"

"Payton was watching it in the staff room and I caught the tail end of it."

"What did you think?"

"You were nervous, but—"

"Was it that obvious?"

"Not to the audience, but I can read you better than anyone. When you're uncomfortable, you shift in your seat, crossing and uncrossing your legs." He lifted her hand, intertwined their fingers and flashed a dirty little grin. "It's adorable, sexy even."

Tangela laughed. "You're very observant. I didn't even realize I did that."

"Want to know something else?" He wet his lips. "I think you're stunning."

"Flattery will get you everywhere," she quipped, downplaying his praise.

"Angie, these aren't lines. You're all those qualities and more." Tangela was the woman of his dreams, but it wasn't her shapely thighs or her long legs that excited him, it was the way she treated him. She supported him, cheered him on and spoiled him. "Do you hear that? Our song is playing." As if overtaken by emotion, he took her hand and squeezed. "I'll love you when your hair turns gray…" He continued singing.

Warrick couldn't sing worth a lick, but she giggled at his off-tune rendition of the Musiq Soulchild song playing on the stereo. Every time she heard "Don't Change," her thoughts turned to Warrick and she mentally relived all the good times they'd had.

"May I have this dance?" he asked, standing and bowing gallantly at the waist.

That got a smile out of her. She couldn't resist *that* look and he knew it. Sliding her legs from underneath the table, she said, "I'd love to."

Inside the living room, they swayed their bodies in time with the beat. The song soothed, caressed and uplifted. It was about hope, possibilities and overcoming the odds and made Warrick reflect on how far they'd come. He lost himself in every movement of Tangela's hips. Wanting more of her, all of her, he pulled her into a body-enveloping squeeze. They stood so close, he could smell red wine on her breath and feel her raging heartbeat.

Warrick ran his hand along her back. Staring down at her, he read the expression on her face and felt his stomach muscles knot. Their chemistry couldn't be denied any longer. The glint in her eyes said what she couldn't. She wanted this, needed this, desired him as much as he did her. Doubts filled his mind, but he dismissed his thoughts. It all came down to what he wanted in life and he wanted her.

Starving for her kiss, he lowered his head. When their lips touched, a thousand bolts of pleasure zipped down his spine. It was an awesome, unexpected feeling and he needed more. Much more. Her body was his wonderland and every part of her, from her neck to her breasts, was sensitive to his touch. She was his heart, his desire, his future, the single best thing that had ever happened to him. He wanted to please and be pleased and the freedom of being in the moment, kissing and touching and stroking, intensified his desire.

"My life's been empty without you," he whispered.

He drew her tongue slowly into his mouth and sucked on the tip. Warrick knew the sexiest region on his body was definitely his lips and he knew how to use them. Soft and sensual, they reached hungrily for her, crippling her resolve and pushing her to the brink of delirium. For as long as she lived, she'd never, ever get tired of his kisses. Or the feel of his fingers in her hair. Wanting to savor the moment, she cradled his head in her palms, deepening the kiss.

"Letting you go was the biggest mistake of my life."

His announcement stunned her. "It was?"

"I love you, Angie. All of you. Your scent. Your eyes. Your sexy little mouth."

Tangela held her breath. Warrick had a way of making her feel beautiful and it wasn't anything he said, it was the depth of his kiss, his loving gaze and the tenderness of his voice when he whispered her name. It didn't matter what size she was, he appreciated her full, womanly curves and called her his queen. "What if Ricardo comes back?" she asked, her voice breathless with anticipation. She felt his hands under her dress, tracing the top of her thong, then massaging her butt, warmly, expertly, reverently. Abandoning herself to the sensuousness of the music, she closed her eyes and threw her head back. "I don't...want him...to catch us."

"He was only scheduled 'til nine. He's long gone."

Rattled, breathless and desperate for more, she shoved his sweater up over his shoulders. All the kissing and dancing and grinding had whetted her erotic appetite so much that her nipples hardened and her heart rate spiked when she felt his erection against her thigh. She felt light, like air, no, lighter still, she thought, as her eyes fluttered closed.

They collapsed onto the couch. Adrenaline pumping, hormones raging, Warrick pulled her down on top of him and showered her face with hot, wet kisses. Insane with desire, he unzipped her dress, yanked it down over her hips and tossed it onto the living-room floor.

Squeezing her breasts, he ran his tongue around a nipple before plucking it into his mouth. His fingers slid inside her and a curse shot out of her mouth. Tangela liked what he was doing. His touch was sweet, his lips divine, his kiss exhilarating. Rotating her hips, she rocked with such force, the couch banged against the wall like an old wooden headboard. He teased her, tantalized her and stroked her to a superintense orgasm that stole her breath. Warrick knew her body intimately, privately, and took great pleasure exciting her. He stroked her to her desired destination and her temperature soared when he whispered in her ear.

Discarding his undershirt and boxer shorts, he rejoined her on the couch, naked.

"Warrick, you have such a gorgeous body. I could never get tired of touching you," she confessed, stroking his chest. Enraptured, she stared at this incredible male specimen standing before her. They continued kissing, but Tangela didn't want any more foreplay, she wanted the main course. She felt a fire in her belly, a raw, deep-rooted hunger that no one could fill but him.

"Do you have any condoms?"

"We never used condoms before," he pointed out, tracing his finger along the inside of her thigh. "I don't have any here. You're not going to make me run out to get some, are you?"

"Warrick, I want us to have a good time tonight, but *safely*. We've both dated other people and…well, you know."

Tilting his head down, as if in deep thought, he rubbed a hand over his head. He was obviously having a problem with his conscience, which could mean only one thing: he'd bedded more women than Mick Jagger. The thought of Warrick with someone else made her heart ache.

"I haven't been with anyone else."

The revelation was like a thunderbolt in the chest and even something as simple as breathing was a challenge. None of this made sense. Warrick loved sex. Or at least, he used to. When they stopped making love, she'd thought he'd found another woman, but now she knew it wasn't someone else, it was *something* else stealing his energy—work. Struck for words, Tangela waited until her head cleared before she said, "You've been celibate for two years?"

Warrick winced. He hated that word. Although he'd never use it to describe his sex life, it was painfully accurate. Unlike Quinten and the guys, he'd never felt compelled to put as many sexual conquests under his belt as possible. The truth was, if he couldn't have Tangela he didn't want anyone. "I haven't had time for anything but work," he lied smoothly. "And whatever you do, don't tell the guys. They'd tease me mercilessly if they knew."

He chuckled, but Tangela didn't laugh. Sitting upright, her heart began to thud and her hands shook just enough for her to rethink what she was doing. Staring down at the floor, she peered around the couch in search of her clothes. Tangela wished she had something to cover herself with. A cushion, a magazine, the remote—anything. Her dress along with her bra and panties were strewn across the floor, while she was stuck to the leather sofa freezing to death. Great, now she was cold, horny *and* humiliated. "This was a mistake. I have to go."

Gripping her shoulders, he bent down and grazed his lips across her mouth. He looked into her eyes and stared deep. What he saw bothered him. Tangela was worth the wait and Warrick didn't care if they made love in a week or a month. All that mattered was that she was finally back in his life. "I didn't invite you over here to have sex, Angie. That's not what tonight is about. I want a relationship with you."

His smile was real, but she heard something in his voice. Disappointment, definitely, but there was something else, something more….powerful. She'd never seen him this vulnerable before. It was sweet, endearing, charming even. Raking a hand through her hair, she deliberated over what to do. She didn't want to leave, but the mood had changed and the tension was stifling. "This isn't how I thought the night would end," she confessed, turning her body away from him.

"Me, neither," he joked, lifting her chin. Their eyes aligned, and for several seconds, he couldn't speak. God, she was beautiful. Naked, with nothing on but her diamond jewelry, her wet, pouty lips begging to be kissed, she made something as simple as breathing difficult. "There are lots of other things we can do besides making love, you know."

"Really? Like what?"

Grinning, he dropped to his knees and slowly parted her long, glistening brown legs. "Close your eyes and relax. You *won't* be sorry."

Swathed in a fluffy blue towel, Tangela padded over to the bathroom mirror and sprayed on perfume. Her flight wasn't for several hours but she wanted to be long gone before Warrick woke up, and he never slept past six. That gave her forty minutes to get dressed and hit the road.

Applying eyeliner required supreme concentration, but it was hard not to think about Warrick and all the delicious things they'd done last night. When he'd dropped to his knees and positioned his mouth between her legs, she'd been a reluctant participant, but once he started licking and sucking and probing, she'd given in to the delicious sensation of his mouth on the most sensitive part of her body. He'd slid his tongue around every curve, contour and slope. Pleasing, sucking, caressing.

Shamelessly arching her back, she'd gripped his head, drawing him deeper still. His tongue snaking in and out of her center had stroked her senselessly. When she came for the second time, she'd collapsed onto the bed—breathless, dizzy and spent. But good loving could do that to a girl. The stereo must have been set to repeat, because it was still playing when she'd woken up hours later and Warrick lay beside her, snoring louder than a tractor-trailer.

"You weren't going to leave without saying goodbye, were you?"

The eyeliner fell from her hand and landed in the sink. Eyeing him in the mirror, she watched him stretch, then pat back a yawn. Remembering the plastic shower cap on top of her head, she snatched if off and tossed it on top of the toilet seat. "Warrick, hi. Good morning."

"How did you sleep?"

"Fine, thanks." Hyperaware of his presence, she lifted her eyes from his bare chest to his face. His gaze held her captive for several seconds. When she came to, she apologized for being in his way. "If you give me ten minutes, I'll be dressed and out of your hair."

"You're leaving?" Coming up behind her, he watched her in the mirror, a frown stretched across his face "Your flight isn't until tonight. I thought we'd spend the day together."

Mesmerized, she scarcely heard a word he said. That long, meaningful look brought back memories. Hot, erotic memories that made her nipples throb. His erection grazed her butt and her mouth went dry. What was the matter with her? He hadn't touched her, but she got wet just thinking about them making love. When it came to Warrick, she had two minds. She loved him, but by the same token, she was afraid he'd break her heart again. Bound and determined to leave with her heart still intact, she said the only thing she could. "We had our fun, but now it's over. I think the correct protocol in this situation is for me to leave."

"The correct protocol?" His voice conveyed his surprise. "It sounds like you've done this sort of thing before."

"Hardly, but I know it would be a bad idea for me to stay."

"Says who?"

"Says *Glamour, Cosmo* and every other women's magazine."

"You shouldn't believe everything you read," he joked, wearing a crooked smile. "Don't rush off. Hang out for a while and keep me company."

Tangela stuck to her guns. "Warrick, I don't want things to get complicated between us. We both know what this was and—"

"No, enlighten me. I don't know what *this* was."

Words escaped her. But that was known to happen when he was around. "We had a great night. Let's just leave it at that." Serious, but hoping to lighten the mood, she said, "What happens in the Big Easy, stays in the Big Easy, right, Warrick?"

"With our history, it could never be just about sex." His hands careened down her shoulders. "I want more and I know you do, too."

"We've been down this road before," she said, leaning heavily on the last word. "I still want to get married and have a big family, while you want—"

"You, Tangela. I only want you."

She stood motionless, completely and thoroughly enthralled. He kissed her slowly. Full of tenderness and love, the kiss felt too good to be true. Aroused, but unwilling to concede defeat, she broke away, refusing to lose control as she had so many times before.

"You know what my favorite part of last night was?" Stepping forward, he dropped a kiss on her bare shoulder. The pleasure of her scent, her voice, her smile, excited him every time. It was hard not to picture her naked underneath the towel, but he kept telling himself, *focus, focus, focus.* "The best part of last night was holding you in my arms," he confessed, brushing his nose against hers, "I've wanted you ever since I saw that *People* magazine cover, but I didn't want us to make love until I was sure."

"Sure of what?"

"That you loved me." Warrick breathed deeply. In Tangela, he'd found more than just a lover, he'd found a confidant, a helpmate, a best friend. She was his rock, his ace, the single most important person in his life. They had love, respect and truth, all of the criteria for a successful relationship, and he wasn't losing her a second time. "After you left, life became an endless stream of board meetings, conference calls and late nights at the office. That's what I thought I wanted, but when I saw you at the Hawthorne party, I realized I was dying a slow death without you. If I've learned anything since you left, it's that…"

Her eyes grew moist as she listened to him speak. Conflicted voices whirled in Tangela's brain. No, she wasn't going to confuse a night of passion with true love. They were attracted to each other, but that didn't mean they were soul mates. Truth was, she wanted him to paw her, grab, grip and squeeze until she was insane with desire. Then, she'd get dressed and be on her merry little way.

Gripping her shoulders, he turned her around, so they were standing chest-to-chest. Face flushed, legs weak, she watched as he loosened her towel and sucked in a gasp when it fell to the floor. His hands were in her hair, then along her hips and down her thick thighs. Keeping her back straight, her body upright, she gripped the edge of the sink for support. How was she supposed to resist him when he was doing all the things she loved? Sucking her earlobes, tweaking her nipples, rubbing his penis hard against her. She opened her mouth to protest, but when he smashed her breasts together, aggressively licking each one, a moan fell from her lips. "Warrick, I don't want this."

"Yes, you do," he insisted, nudging her legs farther apart. "I ran out and got condoms while you were in the shower, so this is going to happen and it's going to happen now."

He ran his thumb along her vulva, parting and spreading her lips wide open. His touch weakened her, crippled her, making her feel delirious with need and excitement. Swallowing a whimper, she allowed her head to fall back. She was breathing hard, her eyelids were heavy and she felt sharp, intense jolts of pleasure. "If you didn't love me, you wouldn't be here. And you wouldn't have spent the night in my bed, but you did, which means…" He cupped her chin, forcing her head up, forcing her to meet his eyes. "You still love me."

It felt so good to be wanted. Not because she was thin or because she'd been on the cover of *People* magazine, but because of who she was. Warrick made her smile, encouraged her to dream big and loved her righteously. They still drove each other crazy at times, but when it came to the bedroom they were completely in sync. Almost nine years after meeting, and Warrick was still the only man she wanted. And she was hungry for him.

Snuggling against his wide, expansive chest, she put a hand inside his boxer shorts, wanting more. Kissing her deeply, passionately, Warrick stroked her to euphoria. Never in a rush or anxious for sexual release, he loved her and he loved her well. He was a patient lover with a wealth of sexual moves, but what they had was more mental than physical. She felt safe in his arms, and the tender, honest way he loved her made tears spring up in Tangela's eyes.

Tangela watched Warrick roll on a condom. Then, he lifted her onto the limestone countertop and made himself comfortable between her legs. In and out, his fingers swirled. Spreading her labia, he slowly, expertly rubbed his sheathed penis back and forth over her slick core. His only goal was to make her come and he did. Again and again and again.

A dizzying sensation poured over her. She felt lost. Completely and utterly lost in the moment. Tangela was floating, flying, out in another stratosphere. Warrick was snug, tight inside her, thrusting, pumping, filling her with his sex. Pleasure powered through her. Shot through her veins. Knocked her backward with its intensity. Moaning, shifting, squirming to get away, she sucked in a breath and pushed the strands of hair stuck to her face out of her eyes.

"Baby, I want you to speak to me in Spanish."

"But you won't understand what I'm saying," she protested, surprised at how raspy her voice sounded. "I'll feel silly doing that."

Stroking her G-spot with his thumb, he playfully nipped at her earlobe. "Please?"

"I don't know what to…" Warrick thrust himself back inside her and she faltered over her words. "Okay, baby, I'll do it. I mean, *bueno, bebé, yo lo hare.*" Tingling all over, she ran her fingertips across his shaft, crooning softly in Spanish. *"Eres tan grande y fuerte y hermoso y he extrando tu amor."*

"More, baby. I want to hear more," he whispered.

"Tu deseo es mi orden. Soy mojado, bebé. ¡Es tiempo!"

Massaging his chest to the rhythm of his thrusts, Tangela shut her eyes, sealing herself in the moment. Deep down, this was what she wanted. *He* was who she wanted. Feelings of hurt and rejection still remained, but Tangela had to decide if she was going to live in the past or embrace the future. And her future with Warrick had never looked brighter.

Staying in character, she said all of the things she'd kept hidden in her heart for the last two years. Telling him how much she loved him, and how much it meant to have him in her life. *"Te quiero, Warrick. Yo no nunca parare adorarte. Mas que nada, quiero casarte y construir una vida contigo. Yo te no parare amando nunca."*

Driving into her, Warrick watched their reflection in the mirror. Being good in bed wasn't a badge of honor, but he was glad that he could still please her. Her happiness was his ultimate quest, his joy, his reason for living. Aroused by the sight of their damp, naked bodies, he clutched her hips and increased his pace.

He excited her with soft words, promises of tomorrow and deep, meaningful kisses. Since their first date almost nine years ago, she'd always imagined them getting married and starting a family. Warrick was the prototype of what she wanted in a man, and when he came inside her, Tangela felt at peace about their relationship and their love.

Chapter Fifteen

January brought sunshine, rain showers and love into Tangela and Warrick's lives. After returning from New Orleans, they spent every available moment together and they easily slipped back into their old routines. They went shopping together, played racquetball at the YMCA and visited his grandparents on the weekend. To prove his commitment, Warrick ditched happy hour and was home every night by six. In return, Tangela cooked his favorite foods, and traded her comfy flannel pajamas for racy lingerie.

"Are we still going to that gallery opening tonight?" Warrick asked, chewing the last of his cinnamon waffle. He picked up his plate, put it into the sink and guzzled down his orange juice. "It's okay if you've changed your mind. I don't—"

"Don't even try it, buster. We're going." Grinning, she held out his jacket and slipped it on over his shoulders. His executive-chic attire and the scent of his aftershave made her feel light-headed. "Good luck at the meeting, baby. You're going to knock 'em dead!"

"I hope so. We've invested a lot of time and energy into making this deal happen."

Nodding, she adjusted his silk pinstripe tie. "Try not to worry, and don't forget to call and let me know what happens."

"I love when you boss me around," he teased, gripping her

hips and rubbing her against his erection. "Especially in the bedroom. Maybe we could re-create the night of the ribbon-cutting ceremony again."

Tangela milked the feeling of being back in his arms for all it was worth. Sheltered in his embrace and the security of his love, she lowered her head onto his chest. She closed her eyes and her mind wandered back to the night in question. While Warrick was at the grocery store, she'd taken a shower and slipped into a red teddy. He'd taken one look at her and dropped the eggs. The rest of the night had been given to tender lovemaking. Tangela didn't know what was so different about that night. She'd always held back when she came, but for some reason, she couldn't control herself. Panting, her breath coming in quick gasps, she'd hiked her legs up and squeezed down on her pelvic muscles. It made his orgasm more intense and even now, weeks later, Warrick was still raving about it.

"What are you doing today? Not going to that coed spin class, I hope."

"No, I promised Carmen we'd go for a run. I have some errands to do later, but that's about it." Craving his touch, she backed him up against the fridge and brushed her lips against the hollow of his throat. "Maybe I'll swing by your office later with a victory lunch."

"But I haven't closed the deal yet."

"You will." Tangela giggled when he whispered in her ear. His scent was her undoing, but she didn't want to encourage him. Despite his clean-cut appearance, Warrick was an animal in bed and once they got to kissing, there was just no stopping him. "Call me around eleven."

"Or, you can just come by at noon."

"I shouldn't. I've been at your office a lot lately."

"So what? I'm the president, remember?" Hugging her, he rubbed his nose against her shoulder. "Besides, I'm all for a hot, midday snack."

Giggling, she wiggled her eyebrows. "Are we still talking about food?"

It was times like this when they were laughing and joking that Tangela still couldn't believe they were back together. Even after a month of clandestine dinners and romantic dates, none of it seemed real. "Let me walk you out. I'd hate for you to be late on one of the biggest days of your career."

"Dad's chairing the meeting. I'm just there to make sure everything goes smoothly."

In the foyer, he gave her a kiss. Hugging her lower lip between his and gently sucking on it, he buried his hands in her hair. Tangela loved her new life. She went to bed laughing and woke up with a big, cheesy smile on her lips. Latching her hands around his neck, she held him close. "Go before we end up back in bed."

"Would that be so bad?"

"What's that saying about too much of a good thing?"

"Hell if I know." Winking, he cupped her bottom. "I could never get enough of you."

They kissed again, and then he was gone. Tangela was inside the kitchen filling her plate when she heard the front door jiggle. A smile crossed her lips. Warrick did this at least once a week. Sometimes he'd return to tell her she was beautiful or to give her another kiss. Taking to her heels, she rushed down the hall. But when Tangela reached the foyer, she heard female voices on the other side of the door. A feeling of dread coated the walls of her stomach.

"Tangela, open up! We know you're in there!"

Sucking in a breath, she closed one eye and stared through the peep hole. Yup, it was Sage and Cashmere. Decked out in black, her girlfriends looked like well-dressed spies, and even through the tiny hole, she saw the furious expressions on their faces. Days after returning from New Orleans, she'd received a blizzard of angry phone calls and text messages from her friends, wanting to know why she was out cavorting with

Warrick. She'd ignored them all. Now, the busybodies were banging on her door like Dog the Bounty Hunter.

"Oh, brother," she mumbled, heaving a deep, tortured sigh. Leery about seeing her friends, but faced with no other options, she slowly unlocked the door. "What are you guys doing here? Shouldn't you be at work?"

"We're staging an intervention," Sage announced, marching inside.

"A what?"

"You heard me. An intervention." Sage folded her arms. "We saw Warrick leave here a few minutes ago."

"And?"

"And you said if you ever took him back, that we should talk some sense into you. So, here we are." Cashmere pushed back her trench coat and bolstered her hands on her hips. With the outrageous blond weave and skintight leggings, she reminded Tangela of a female action hero. "He's sleeping here now, isn't he?"

"I don't have time for this, you guys. I have a flight this afternoon…to…to…Washington." Lying to her girlfriends was childish, but she wasn't in the mood for their jibber-jabber. It was her day off and she wanted to spend a quiet morning alone watching soaps and eating ice cream. "Why don't we get together when I get back?"

Sage slammed the door. "We're not leaving until you give us some answers. You've been dodging us for weeks and we're sick of it. It's time you tell us what's going on."

Tangela rolled her eyes. Hoping they'd take the hint and leave her alone, she shook her head in annoyance. Spinning around, she returned to the kitchen, Tweedledee and Tweedledumb in tow. "Are you guys hungry? I was about to eat breakfast."

"Damn, something smells good up in here!" Cashmere quipped, smacking her lips together. "Did you make cinnamon waffles?"

Pointing at the stove, Tangela said, "Help yourself, there's plenty left."

"You cooked for him?" Sage asked, eyes narrowed, lips pursed tight. The women exchanged worried glances. "It's worse than we thought."

Tangela refused to be drawn into a discussion about her love life. Wanting to distance herself, she grabbed her plate and sat down in the living room. She felt their eyes on her and pretended to be interested in the morning news.

"Tangela, why are you doing this?"

"Doing what?"

"Screwing Warrick."

After sneaking around for weeks, Tangela was relieved to finally have everything out in the open. But she didn't appreciate her friends storming into her house, disrespecting her and insulting the man she loved. Annoyed, she broke her vow of silence. "For the record, Warrick and I are in a committed, monogamous relationship." Her heart skipped a beat at the mention of his name. "Honestly, you guys, things are so good between us it hardly seems real. It's like we're dating for the first time. He's attentive and loving and…"

Cashmere snorted. "How long do you think *that'll* last?"

"I'm serious. We both really want this to work." Tangela considered the last three weeks. Being with Warrick and having his love meant more to her than anything. He was a dream—her dream and she couldn't get enough of him. There was never a shortage of laughs when they were together and the sex was so hot she needed fireproof sheets.

"Why are you so weak for a man who has done nothing but hurt you?" Sage interrogated her as though she were a hostile witness, firing one question after another. "What's the matter with you? Are you that desperate? Warrick doesn't love you and he's never going to marry you. You know that, I know that, hell, the whole state of Nevada knows that!"

Mouth contorted into a tight grimace, she glared at her

childhood friend. Sage was working her last good nerve, but Tangela knew how to cut her down to size. "After Khari's car accident, you were ready to write Marshall off, but I encouraged you to work things out, remember? Why can't you do the same for me?"

"Because Marshall and Warrick are two different people."

"Thank God for that," Tangela mumbled, hugging a cushion to her chest. Where did Sage get off? Just because she was sporting a gargantuan wedding ring didn't make her a relationship expert. "I don't know why we're even having this conversation. It's my heart and my decision."

Plate stacked high with waffles, Cashmere joined Tangela on the sofa. "But what about your mission? I thought you wanted to be hitched by your thirtieth birthday?"

"Yeah, what about it, Tangela? Has Warrick popped the question yet?" Sage spat the words out through clenched teeth, mocking her. "I'm disappointed in you. I thought you were so much smarter than this.…"

Tangela's eyes remained glued to the screen. She was doing everything in her power to keep her composure, but when Sage started yelling at her, she switched off the TV and stood up. "Let yourselves out when you're ready. I'm going to take a shower."

"Don't you get it? Winning you back was nothing more than a game. You're nothing more than an accessory to him. Someone young and pretty who looks good on his arm when he's schmoozing with his millionaire clients."

"That's not true. Warrick loves me," she argued. "You guys are entitled to your opinion, but frankly I don't care what you think. I don't need your approval."

"Are you forgetting who put you up the last time he broke your heart?"

Scalding-hot tears formed in her eyes, but Tangela blinked them away.

Cashmere stopped eating long enough to say, "We love you,

girl, and we don't want to see you get hurt again. Sage is right, Tangela. You deserve to be with someone who thinks the world of you. Don't settle. Be patient. You'll find the right guy."

Tangela raised her chin. Their negativity didn't dampen her spirits. If anything, it gave her more hope for the future. This time, she and Warrick were going to work. "I know what I'm doing. Nothing's going to happen that I can't handle."

"Fine, but don't come crying to me when he breaks your heart again." Sage grabbed her purse and motioned toward the foyer. "Come on, Cashmere, we're out of here."

Hours later, Tangela was still thinking about what Sage had said. Hurling a block of molded cheese into the garbage bin, she replayed their conversation in her mind. *Where does Sage get off calling me desperate?* she fumed, wiping furiously at the ketchup stains inside the fridge door. Warrick wasn't a saint, but he was the right man for her. No one fascinated her like he did and every time he kissed her she melted. *Exquisite* didn't begin to describe how she felt when he touched her. Absent from their previous relationship was genuine intimacy, but this time around, there had been no shortage of smiles, laughs and kisses.

Dropping the sponge into the bucket, Tangela stepped back and surveyed her work. The fridge looked brand-new. Pleased, she closed the door and moved on to the freezer. Within minutes, frozen dinners, chicken wings and pizza pops lined the granite countertop.

"Honey, where are you?" Warrick came around the corner, a wide, crooked grin on his lips. Coming in close, they entwined fingers and met in the middle of the kitchen for a kiss.

Body pulsing with excitement, eyes shining with desire, she shook off her feelings of self-pity and pressed herself hard against him. The tension in her shoulders receded under his loving caress. Dating him was a dream, but becoming Mrs. Warrick James Carver was— Whoa! Where did *that* come from? she thought, striking the idea from her mind. It was much too soon to be thinking about marriage. They'd only been back together for a few weeks, and they had agreed to take things slow.

"You're not still cleaning, are you?"

"I'm almost done." Tangela picked up a frozen dinner and shook it. "Why do you buy this stuff? They're full of chemicals and high in sodium."

"Well, now that you're here, I don't need them. I have my very own sexy little chef and I'm not sharing you with anyone!"

Laughing, she returned to restocking the shelves.

"Hold up, what's all this stuff?" he asked, picking up one of the cans on the counter.

"Healthy, tasty foods with zero calories and no trans fat."

"But I like trans fat!"

"You mean you *used* to," she corrected, pecking him on the cheek.

He read the label out loud. "No thanks, I'll stick with my frozen dinners."

"All those days of bad eating are over, baby. From now on, we're eating healthy," she said, dumping a bag of Oreos into the trash. "Say goodbye to the junk food, Warrick."

"Does that mean we're having salad again tonight?"

"No."

He visibly relaxed. "Thank God. I'm starving."

"We're having spinach casserole."

"Um, yum," he deadpanned. "Can't wait."

"You haven't even tried it!" Tangela watched him stare longingly at the frozen dinner and laughed. "Have I ever made you something you didn't like?"

"Yeah, that tofu stir-fry was disgusting!"

Feigning anger, she pushed him away. "Just for that, you're not getting any tonight."

"Ah, come on. Don't take that away, too!"

"Warrick, it won't kill you to try eating organic food," she told him.

"Organic food?" He wrinkled his nose. "What happened to your mac and cheese, pasta salad and smothered pork chops? *That's* what I want to eat."

"If I start cooking like that again, we'll both be signing up for Jenny Craig. And you don't want me to put back on all that weight, do you?"

He didn't speak for a moment. "Angie, your weight has never been a problem for me. The truth of it is, I miss your curves." Winking, he added, "And the girls, too."

"You don't think I look better now? Everyone else does."

"Well, make that everyone but me. When I saw your *People* magazine cover I almost passed out. I was convinced they'd airbrushed the hell out of it, until I read the article."

Eyes lowered, she fiddled with her thumb ring. "I don't have a problem with food, and I've never been ashamed of my body."

"But the article said—"

"I know what it said. The editor took bits and pieces of my interview and spun it into a juicer story," she explained. "I'm glad I slimmed down but I'm not going to flip out if I gain some of the weight back. Life's too short to count calories. I want to be in good shape, but I'm not going to obsess over that stupid number on the scale."

His arms closed around her. "You should sue them for writing that crap."

"I know the truth and that's all that matters. Some people think you have to be a size zero to be healthy, but there are lots of thin women with health problems. I'm going to just do me. Who cares what society says? I'm fit and fabulous no matter what size I am!"

"I heard that," he agreed.

"Now, go wash up. Dinner will be ready in twenty minutes."

"Is that right?" Grinning, he slipped a hand under her shirt and stroked a nipple with his finger. "I'm hungry, baby, but not for food!"

Chapter Sixteen

Filled with giddy excitement, Tangela slammed the trunk of her car and hurried into the Metropolis. Inside the elevator, she dropped her bags on the floor and rested her head against the wall. Her flight from Newark had been long and uneventful. Like a mindless robot operating on autopilot, she'd served her passengers, then cleaned the aircraft and filled out the requisite paperwork. Tangela hadn't been to her apartment in five days, but the decision to go to Warrick's place was a no-brainer.

Her body warmed when she thought about the plans she'd made for tonight. Warrick hadn't said anything when they spoke earlier in the day, but she knew he had something special in store for Valentine's Day. But he wasn't the only one plotting and scheming. She had a sexy surprise for her man, too. Something he'd always wanted. Something she'd never been confident enough to do before. Staring down at the fuchsia Discreet Boutique bag, she imagined the look on Warrick's face when she sashayed out of the bathroom in the skimpy nurse's uniform.

Sailing out of the elevator onto the eighteenth floor, she calculated the time it would take her to cook dinner, shower and get dressed. Preoccupied with her thoughts, she unlocked the suite door and stumbled on a stray dress shoe lying in the middle of the foyer.

"Ugh!" she grumbled, smacking on the lights. Shocked into silence, Tangela braced herself against the wall. Plugging her nose with her thumb and index finger, she surveyed the disheveled living room. Sofa cushions were thrown about, newspapers were stacked high on the coffee table and the house smelled like garbage. Crumbs littered the carpet and sunlight illuminated the thick layer of dust on the furniture.

Tangela dropped her bags. There was no question about it. The honeymoon was definitely over. Since getting back together, Warrick had been on his best behavior. He made a conscious effort to clean up after himself and didn't leave things lying around. Tangela had known his Molly Maid routine wasn't going to last forever, but she hadn't expected to come home to find the laundry basket higher than the Leaning Tower of Pisa. If he could keep his office clean, why couldn't he make the bed or sweep the floor? Tangela wished he'd swallow his pride and hire a cleaning lady, because she was getting sick and tired of picking up after him.

The state of the kitchen was worse than the living room. Eyes narrowed, lips puckered, she waved a hand in front of her face. It smelled like…feet. Disgusted, she wheeled around and fled the room as if the garbage bin would sprout legs at any moment and chase after her.

When they were living together, she'd had no choice but to clean up after him. But now she had her own place and although the fridge was empty, it was cleaner than this. Before she could decide what to do one way or another, her cell phone rang. "Hello?"

"Welcome home, baby. How was your flight?"

"Fine."

"Everything okay?"

"Uh-huh."

"What's with all the one-word answers?"

Silence infected the line.

"I don't have ESP, Angie. I can't fix things if you don't tell me what's wrong."

Feeling guilty for being short with him, she sighed deeply, and said, "How's work?"

"I didn't call to talk about business. I called to see how you were doing." His voice was touched with concern and Tangela could picture him behind his enormous desk, smiling that easy, comfortable smile. "I'm glad you're home."

"Why, so I can clean up after you?"

"Is that why you're angry, because the place is a little messy?"

"A little messy? It looks like a college frat house in here!"

"You're exaggerating. It's not that bad." Warrick paused and spoke to someone in the room before returning to the phone. "Things have been—"

"Crazy around here," she finished, sighing in frustration. "I know, you keep telling me."

Tangela knew the situation with Lyndon was stressful, and she sympathized with him, but she was sick of his excuses. "Things have been crazy for me, too, but I still clean up after myself and stay on top of everything in the house."

"I was going to clean when I got home last night, but I ended up pulling an all-nighter."

She frowned. "That's the second one this week."

"The presentation in London is turning out to be more work than I thought. Actually, that's why I'm calling. I'm working late and I don't know when I'll be home."

"But it's Valentine's Day."

"I'll make it up to you once I close this deal. I promise."

Tangela didn't want to make an issue of it, but she was bummed that she was going to spend the most romantic day of the year alone. They hadn't seen each other in nine days and she'd been looking forward to a nice, quiet evening with her man. No phones, no television, no distractions. But now he was canceling on her. Again. Thinking back on all the promises he'd broken in the past increased her frustration. "I guess I'll see you tomorrow, then."

"I'll try and be home by eleven. Wait up for me, okay? I really want to see you."

Not bothering to say goodbye, she hung up and wandered into the family room. Suddenly exhausted, she slumped down on the couch and reclined against the cushions. What was she going to do for the rest of the night? Cleaning wasn't an option and neither was cooking. Tangela contemplated calling Sage, but remembered that Marshall had rented them a suite at the Bellagio. Maybe she'd go see a movie. *Brooklyn's Finest* was playing and she still hadn't seen it.

After checking the showtimes on the computer, she logged into her e-mail account. Remembering that Carmen was in town, she flipped open her cell phone and dialed. "I didn't expect you to be home," she said when Carmen answered. "What are you doing?"

"Cutting up Hugo's favorite pair of jeans."

"Again? Didn't you shred his boxer shorts just last week?" Laughing, Tangela cradled the phone to her ear. Signing into TruCommunity, she wondered if any of her friends would be online. The chat rooms, which were usually buzzing with conversation, were silent. "What did he do this time? I thought you guys were working things out."

"It's more like what he *didn't* do. We were supposed to have dinner at Bistro 360, but he forgot to make the reservation."

Feeling the need to vent, Tangela told her girlfriend about her conversation with Warrick. "I know he's under a lot of pressure, but so am I. It's hard being on my feet for hours and catering to a hundred and fifty people at any given time."

"You know what we should do? Get dressed and take our fine-ass selves out to dinner."

"I don't know, Carmen. It's Valentine's Day. The wait time is going to be brutal tonight."

"Do you have anything better to do?"

"Well, no," Tangela conceded, getting up from the computer. "But I don't want to waste the whole night waiting in line to get in somewhere."

"Girl, trust me. I know just the place."

"Where?"

"Don't worry your pretty little head," she said, giggling. "Just be ready in an hour!"

Warrick paced the length of the living-room floor. Mind racing, body fraught with tension, he swallowed the hard lump in his throat. The wall clock chimed and his head snapped up. Three o'clock. He had an early-morning meeting, but instead of reviewing the revised contracts, he was pacing like an expectant father in a hospital waiting room. If Tangela had answered her cell or returned his text messages, he wouldn't be on edge, but not knowing where she was was infuriating.

Ever since he'd seen Tangela on the cover of *People* magazine, his life had been turned upside-down. Keeping his mind on his work and off his girlfriend had never been more difficult and ever since he'd spoke to Rachael yesterday, he couldn't get her words of warning out of her head. "Lose her or commit," she'd admonished, her voice stern. "You're never going to find someone who loves you more than Tangela does."

It was true. Tangela was sensitive of his needs and feelings, deeply caring and a calming presence in his life. Her drug-addicted mother had never been lucid enough to cook dinner or clean the house, but Tangela took great pride in their home. He came home to an immaculate home, a hot meal and a passionate kiss that gave him an instant erection.

No one took care of him like Tangela. When he'd awakened last Saturday with a fever, she'd fed him soup, cuddled with him in bed and read him the comics. By the end of the day, she'd nursed him back to health. Later, he'd popped in a jazz CD, dimmed the lights and when the music drifted out from the speakers, they'd danced. Swaying her body in time to the music, she very leisurely peeled off one article of clothing at a time. Her blouse was the first to go, then the skirt. He'd reclined on the couch and when she lowered herself onto his lap, he'd released a deep groan. After making love, he must have dozed off, because when he woke up the next morning, there was a blanket thrown over him and Tangela was in the kitchen whipping up breakfast.

Rachael had given him something to think about. Three weeks ago, he never would have imagined proposing so soon. He didn't feel the need to formalize their relationship with marriage, but he wanted to prove his commitment. Tangela was the one. His love, his destiny, his life. And once he finished the project he was working on, he'd devote all his time and energy to planning the perfect proposal.

His eyes strayed to the clock—3:17 a.m. Where the hell was she? She couldn't be with one of her old boyfriends, could she? Hell, it was Valentine's Day. The most romantic day of the year. And since their breakup she'd dated a long list of successful men. Tangela could be with one of them. Stroking his jaw, names turning over in his mind like a Ferris wheel, he tried to break free of his raging thoughts.

Warrick stalked out of the living room. He needed a drink. A cold, stiff one. Something with forty-percent alcohol or more. No sooner had he entered the kitchen then he heard the front door open and close. Bent on confronting her, he marched down the hall, rounded the corner and slapped on the lights in the foyer. "Do you know what time it is?"

Face drenched with relief, hands pressed flat against her chest, she let out a long, deep breath. "What are you trying to do, give me a heart attack? You scared me half to death, babe."

Eyes narrowed, he scrutinized her appearance. Tousled hair. Labored breathing. The subtle scent of men's cologne on her skin. And there was no mistaking her exotic vibe.

"How was work?" she asked, slipping off her shoes. "Did you finish what you were—"

"Where have you been?"

"Carmen and I went to the Boa Steakhouse for dinner."

Warrick pointed at his watch. "It closes at midnight."

"I know. We went to Tryst after."

"What for?"

"What do you mean, 'what for?' It's a club. We danced and drank and danced some more!" Giggling, she sashayed into the kitchen. "Baby, you should have seen me. I was on fire tonight! The DJ played 'Get Down on It' and I had everyone up in there doing the bump."

"I bet you did," he grumbled.

Tangela yanked open the fridge, grabbed a bottle of mineral water and leaned against the counter. Chatting amicably about the music, and some of the people she'd met, she unzipped her jacket, dropped it on the chair and fanned a hand over her face. "I can't remember the last time I had so much fun. Carmen and I had a blast. We got free drinks, and…"

Arms folded rigidly across his chest, Warrick noted the thinness of her clingy white dress. Where was the rest of it? The short, jagged hem drew his gaze to her legs and reminded him of something he'd once seen a contestant wear on *Dancing with the Stars*. Under the light, form-hugging material, he saw the visible outline of her braless breasts. "Did one of your old boyfriends meet you there? Is that why you're coming in so late?"

"Yeah, Marcello stopped by, and oh, Leonard was there, too." Rolling her eyes, she took another swig from her water bottle. "You were at work and I had nothing to do, so I went out. Why do you care, anyway? You were at the office all night."

"I came home early. I thought we could have a late dinner or something."

"Baby, if you had told me I would have waited—"

"Who's Jamal Henderson?"

Her eyes opened wide.

"Were you guys lovers?"

"No, he's just a friend."

"A friend you used to date." Warrick checked her reaction. She wasn't fidgeting or stumbling over her words, but that didn't mean she was telling him the truth. "How long were the two of you an item?"

"We only went on a few dates. Where is all this coming from?"

"You forgot to sign out of your e-mail again." He forged on before she could change the subject. "Why haven't you canceled your memberships to all those online dating sites?"

"I haven't gotten around to it."

"What do you mean you haven't gotten around to it? We've been back together for weeks. What are you waiting for?"

"I'll do it tomorrow."

"Have you been seeing other guys behind my back?"

Her face crumbled. "Of course not. I would never do something like that. I'm not that kind of person, Warrick, you know that."

Warrick snorted, the deep, guttural noise akin to that of a hedgehog. The injured sound of her voice made him rethink his argument, but in the end, his emotions won out. "I have a right to know if you've been seeing someone else."

She looked both annoyed and puzzled. "Am I missing something?"

"I don't know, you tell me." His eyes flickered over her chest. "It's obvious you weren't thinking about me when you went out tonight. Look at what you're wearing."

Tangela glanced down at her outfit. "What's wrong with my outfit?"

"Nothing, if you don't mind guys mistaking you for a—"

"Don't you dare." Slamming her water bottle down on the counter, she glared at him with righteous indignation. "I wore this dress the night you took me dancing in New Orleans. As I recall, you said I looked sexy but classy."

Squinting, he scratched the middle of his head, trying to

remember the night in question. Warrick didn't recall saying that, and even if he had, that was then and this was now. It was bad enough she'd dated more guys than the Bachelorette, he didn't want men ogling her or touching her when he wasn't around. And her outfit said "Go on, cop a feel!" He didn't mind when she went with her friends or coworkers for the occasional drink, but these days it was a regular occurrence. After being single for two years, Warrick liked having someone to come home to. Wanting to prove to Tangela he'd changed, he'd quit hitting the clubs and even though the guys clowned him for being "whupped," he preferred being home with her, making love.

"My mom used to say, 'If you don't have anything nice to say, then keep your big mouth shut.'" Her voice climbed, cuing him that he'd hurt her feelings. "*You* should take her advice."

Warrick started to speak, faltered over his words and decided not to share his thoughts. He watched her for a few moments. Truth be told, he missed the old Tangela. She used to be content hanging out at home, waiting for him to return from work, but now she had spin class, girls' nights out and Spanish classes. In the past, he'd never really appreciated the sacrifices she'd made for him, and he missed the days when he was the most important person in her life. Now he had to compete with her career, her girlfriends and those stupid online chat rooms. *Damn,* he thought, *where does that leave me?*

"Why didn't you answer your cell? I called twice."

"I didn't take it with me."

He strained to hear her. "Why not?"

"Because it wouldn't fit into my purse."

"You could've left a note." Feeling bad about what he'd said earlier, he took a step forward, closing the distance and bridging the emotional gap he'd caused. Losing Tangela again terrified him. No one loved him like she did, and he'd be a fool to mess up what they had going. "I didn't know where you were and when I couldn't get hold of you, I got worried."

"Well, you have a funny way of showing it. When did calling someone a ho become a term of endearment?" Venting her frustration, she snatched up her bag and fished out her car keys. "Coming here was a mistake. I'm going back to my place."

"I don't want you driving across town at this time of night."

"It's not your decision to make," she snapped, brushing past him. "And frankly, I don't care what you want."

Warrick caught her arm. "I didn't mean what I said. I'm sorry for acting like a jerk. It's been a stressful day. There are still problems with the houses in New Orleans and I...I lost the contract," he confessed, lowering his head. "Mr. Kewasi decided to go with another firm."

"But that doesn't make any sense." Frowning, she shook her head. "He had such a good time at the dinner party you threw last month. I even overheard him telling his assistant that signing with Maxim Designs and Architects was a done deal."

"I guess he got a better offer."

"There'll be other contracts, better, more lucrative contracts." His dad had said the same thing, but hearing it the second time didn't alleviate his feelings of disappointment. It was the first contract he'd lost since becoming interim president and nothing—not Tangela's kisses or caresses—could coax him out of his funk. The only thing that would placate him would be landing another rich client. And he would, even if it meant working harder. Once he straightened out this mess with Lyndon and signed another million-dollar contract, then he'd propose to Tangela.

Chapter Seventeen

Perched on the edge of her wooden desk, relaying an amusing tale about her three-year-old granddaughter, Ines Vargas kept the students in the intermediate Spanish class so entertained no one noticed the class was over. No one except Tangela.

Observing her classmates, she noted the amused expressions on their faces. Hoping to alleviate the tension in her shoulders, she massaged the painful spot with the balls of her hands. Tangela was sitting in Room 234 at the Language Institute, but her mind was on Warrick. And thinking about the argument they'd had that morning annoyed her afresh.

"Organic cereal?" he'd asked, frowning at the box. "What happened to the Froot Loops cereal?"

"I dumped them. I bought you Kashi cereal instead. It has seven whole grains, soy protein—"

"Tangela, you don't decide what I eat. *I* do. I can take care of myself. Got it?"

Thoroughly annoyed, she'd watched him stomp around the kitchen, yanking open drawers and cupboards like a madman. "Let's get something straight. You're my girlfriend. Not my mother, not my dietician and not my wife."

Her spoon slipped from her fingers. "Is that right? Then why am I picking up after you, cooking your meals and sleeping here at your request?"

That had shut him up, but Tangela was on a roll, and she just couldn't stop. "You want all the privileges of being married but without the commitment. It doesn't work that way, Warrick."

"I don't want to argue with you. Leave my stuff and we'll be fine."

Irked by his tone, she shot him a cold, seething look that she hoped conveyed her disgust. "I'm not your personal maid and it's time you stopped treating me like one."

"What are you talking about? I cleared the dishes last night and I even vacuumed."

Head tilted triumphantly to the side, she clapped her hands together in mock approval. "So, you turned on the dishwasher! Big deal. Do you expect me to give you a prize every time you do something around the house?"

"I'm not the only one reaping the rewards in this relationship. You'd still be driving around in that bucket you called a car if I hadn't cosigned for you to get your Lexus luxury sedan. And I didn't hear you complaining when I paid off your Visa credit card, either."

Later that day, their argument was still playing in her mind. Angry that he'd given her the cold shoulder this morning when she'd tried to kiss him goodbye, she wondered how long it would take before things blew over. Was he punishing her because she'd argued with him? Or because she'd made plans to go away this weekend with her girlfriends? Whatever the reason, he was acting distant, and she was sick of it.

At times Warrick was moody and short-tempered, but she was perceptive enough to know his frustrations had nothing to do with her. They stemmed from his problems at work. After a fairy-tale-like climb to the top, he'd received one setback after another since returning to New Orleans. First, Mr. Kewasi had signed with another firm, then he'd discovered Lyndon wasn't paying his workers and now his deal with a Paris-based company was in jeopardy. Another trip to France was in the works, and although Tangela only had a short break between flights, she was going to join him. It was a long trip for five days, but she had a feeling Warrick would need some cheering up.

When class ended, Tangela decided to stop in at Krueger's. Her quest for health and wellness was a personal decision and she had no right to cram her opinions or her flax-seed bread down Warrick's throat. Her boyfriend was a really great guy. Better than most, she admitted to herself, grabbing a cart and pushing it into the frozen-food section. He made her feel safe, and for a girl with no parents, no roots and no history, that was an incredible feeling. She could search the whole world, from the streets of Montreal to Mozambique, and she'd never find a man who loved her like Warrick did. Despite his youth, he typified grace, charm and what it meant to be a gentleman in this screwed-up, crazy world. He opened doors, picked up the check and held out chairs. Not because it was expected of him or because that's how he'd been taught, but because he wanted her to feel special, cherished, wholly and thoroughly adored.

Hustling down the aisles, humming along with the Ashanti song playing, Tangela wondered if she'd have enough time to whip up a pot of gumbo when she got home. Warrick was working late, but she wanted to have a good, hearty meal waiting for him when he got in.

As she exited the grocery store, carrying a load of plastic bags, she spotted Sage's sleek Lexus pull up to the curb. Tangela felt her shoulders tense. Things had been strained between them ever since Sage and Cashmere barged into her apartment.

Cell phone pressed to her ear, her beloved hobo bag dangling from her slender wrist, Sage emerged from the car with the elegance of Grace Kelly. Her tweed suit and red pumps gave her star-power. Slapping the phone shut, she waved and came around the car. "I didn't even know you were in town. Where've you been hiding?"

"I had a three-day layover in Miami. I got back on Friday."

"The gang came over last night. Why didn't you come?"

"I had other plans."

"Oh, okay. I thought maybe you were still mad at me. Are you?"

Tangela forced herself to answer the question. "I was, but I'm not anymore."

"Do you want to stop in at Heaven Sent and share a dessert?" Sage asked, motioning with a finger to the bakery up the street. "There's something I've been meaning to talk to you about and I have a serious craving for rum cake."

Deciding to take advantage of the balmy weather, they selected a table on the patio, placed their orders and chatted about their jobs while they waited for their dessert. The scent of freshly baked apple pie carried on the breeze and Tangela's mouth watered. Ignoring her sudden hunger pangs, she said, "So, what did you want to talk to me about?"

"It's about Warrick."

"Not this again," she groaned, shaking her head. "I'm sick of—"

"Girl, I'm sorry. I had no right to say what I did. I shouldn't have said those things about Warrick or called you desperate. I was just scared you'd get hurt again."

Tangela felt her mouth fall open. Sage—her opinionated, tell-it-like-it-is best friend was being supportive? Convinced lightning was about to strike, she glanced up at the sky. Not a cloud in sight. "What brought on this sudden change of heart?"

"We all make mistakes, and I'm no different. I wasn't exactly honest about who I was when I met Marshall, but he found it in his heart to forgive me. I wanted to say something sooner, but let's face it, you're not the easiest person to talk to."

"Why do you say things like that?" she asked, glancing around the patio to ensure no one was listening. "I have high standards and there's nothing wrong with that. I expect people to be honest and trustworthy and if they're not it's—"

"'Arrivederci,' right?" Sage took a long sip of her drink

before she continued. "As soon as someone messes up, you show them the door. In your perfect little world there's no room for error. But no one's infallible, Tangela. Everyone screws up. Some more than others. Look at all the famous, high-powered executives going to jail. Do you think they set out to ruin their families' lives? They didn't. They're just like us. Good people who made some bad choices."

Tangela remained mute. Was Sage right? Could she be sabotaging her relationships by having unrealistic expectations?

"You'll never believe what I heard Warrick say last night. I was in the laundry room sorting the clothes after dinner, and I overheard him tell the guys he couldn't go to Tijuana over the May long weekend. When they ribbed him about being on a short leash, he said he wasn't going to screw things up with you this time. Warrick truly loves you, girl, and he doesn't want to lose you again."

"You really think so?"

"That man would dive under a plane for you," Sage said with an easy laugh.

"I don't know about all that. All we seem to do these days is fight."

"Tangela, you've got it in your mind that relationships are all flowers and candy and twenty-four hours of romance, but love is hard work. Over time, the initial excitement of falling in love wears off, but the sense of being in a close, nurturing relationship is a far more powerful feeling. Marshall drives me crazy sometimes, and the Lord knows he's tight with his money, but there's no one in this world I'd rather be married to."

"But we've been back together for months and he hasn't once mentioned getting engaged. What's he waiting for?"

"You can't expect Warrick to do things on your schedule. Love doesn't work that way."

Now more than ever, Tangela needed her best friend to give it to her straight, but Sage was preaching love, forgiveness, patience. Three months ago, getting back with Warrick had seemed like the right thing to do, but now that the excitement had worn off and reality had set in, she wasn't so sure. Being Mrs. Warrick Carver was a dream she'd had for the last seven-plus years. It wasn't the money, or the penthouse or even the title that she coveted. It was going to bed and waking up every morning knowing that she was part of a family, knowing that for the rest of his life she'd have Warrick's love and the love of their children.

Tangela considered asking him point-blank about their future. She'd done that once before, back when they were living together and things had turned ugly. Three years later, and she still remembered the fury in his eyes and the sharp timbre of his voice. "How's Cashmere?" she asked. "She called me a few weeks ago, but I haven't gotten around to calling her back."

"We should all go for mani-pedis tomorrow. Cashmere's in wedding mode, but I think I can convince her to put away the checklist long enough to hang out with her girls."

"What? Cashmere's engaged? To who?"

"Theo, of course."

"But they haven't been together long. Has it even been six months?"

Two of her coworkers had shown up to work last week sporting diamond rings and now Cashmere was engaged to a man she'd met four months ago. Hearing the news of her friend's sudden engagement made Tangela jealous. Tasting her hot chocolate, she decided in her heart that before the week was over, she was going to talk to Warrick about their future.

Hands clasped, buoyant smiles on their faces, Tangela and Warrick exited the balcony and followed the throng of theater lovers into the lobby. Intent on seeing, *Lord, Why Me?* Tangela had called Warrick at work and asked him to meet her at the Charleston Cultural Center. The soul-stirring music and the over-the-top antics of the characters had kept the sold-out audience entertained and Warrick had laughed louder than anyone else. "Aren't you glad I convinced you to come? The play is so funny!"

"Yeah, that grandfather is a trip. I almost fell over when he started doing the Cupid Shuffle! I'm having a nice time, Tangela. After the week I've had, I needed a good laugh." Pecking her cheek, he worked his hand over her shoulders, then rested it casually on her lower back. "Would you like something from the concession stand?" he asked, moving his lips across her ear. "They have those veggie burgers you like so much."

Giggling, she tried to pull away. "Okay, I'll have one with a diet soda and some—"

"Warrick, is that you?"

Squeezing her boyfriend's waist, Tangela turned to see who the haughty female voice belonged to. The smile fell from her lips. Mrs. Verda Harris. Although Quinten and Warrick had been friends for years, Tangela didn't like the obnoxious management consultant and cared even less for his mother.

"Mrs. Harris, it's nice seeing you again," Warrick greeted, kissing her plump cheek. "You remember Tangela, don't you?"

Mrs. Harris gave a curt nod in her direction. "I heard the two of you had gotten back together. So when's the big day?"

Tangela straightened her spine. She had choice words for the meddlesome old biddy, but before she could speak, Warrick chuckled and said, "We're not rushing into anything this time around. We're taking things slow."

Dropping his hand, she turned, studying his side profile. *Is that what we're doing?* Where was she when they'd had *that* discussion? She'd thought they were on the fast track to the altar. Or at the very least getting engaged before the end of this year. And what was with the laugh?

"You're living together?" Verda probed, her penciled eyebrows raised in disdain. "Again?"

Smiling down at Tangela, Warrick tightened his hold,

bringing her back to his side. "No, not yet, but I definitely want my baby back home with me where she belongs."

"Next in line, please," the teen behind the counter said, beckoning with her hands.

Warrick stepped forward, leaving Tangela alone with Mrs. Harris.

"I understand that your mother was in and out of your life." Verda wore a grim expression. "I can only imagine how traumatic your childhood must have been."

Tangela didn't want to think about the pain, didn't want to remember all the times she'd gone to bed hungry, cold and alone, but it was impossible to erase the memories of her past. Her mother had suffered from a laundry list of emotional problems and children's services had finally removed her from the home when she was nine. Her foster mom, Mrs. Claxton, was no better. Dealing with the nurse's erratic behavior on a daily basis had taught Tangela how to reason, how to negotiate and how to remain calm. And those traits served her well now.

"Tangela, just because you weren't raised in a loving home doesn't mean you should live off a man. In my day and age, a woman would never demean herself by shacking up with someone. Don't lower your standards for anyone and for God's sake, have some pride."

"I tell Quinten that all the time," Tangela quipped, looking Mrs. Harris dead in the eye. "I understand men have needs, but strip clubs are just plain nasty."

Mrs. Harris's jaw sagged.

"We'd better return to our seats," Warrick said, approaching them. "Intermission's almost over and I don't want to miss any of the show."

"Bye, Mrs. Harris." Waving, a sickly sweet smile on her lips, Tangela forced herself not to laugh in the woman's face. Mrs. Harris stood like a statue, a lost, befuddled look in her eyes. It felt good giving the old biddy a spoonful of her own medicine, but when Tangela sat down in her seat minutes later, she felt her eyes burn with tears.

Chapter Eighteen

"Baby, what's the matter? You haven't said a word since we left the theater." Warrick pulled into his designated parking space and shut off the engine. Turning to look at her, his face concerned, he put a hand on her leg and squeezed affectionately. "Talk to me, honey. I want to know what's wrong."

Tangela stared out the windshield. How could she tell him that what Mrs. Harris said had gotten under her skin? He wouldn't understand. And if Warrick knew what she'd said to Quinten's mother, he'd be furious at her. "I'm just tired. Let's go inside."

In the kitchen, while Tangela waited for the kettle to boil, she thought about her conversation with Sage three days earlier. Asking Warrick where he saw their relationship headed shouldn't be so stressful, but every day she put it off, the harder it was to broach the subject. But she couldn't go on living like this. She had a great apartment that she hardly saw, and although she had the run of the house, her name wasn't on the lease and she couldn't decorate the way she would if they were married.

Deciding the tea could wait, she opened the fridge and grabbed a beer from the shelf. Tangela twisted off the cap, poured the cold liquid into Warrick's favorite glass and started down the hall. She wanted to know what her boyfriend was thinking and now was as good a time as any to discuss their future.

"Warrick, I was hoping we could talk."

He stopped flipping channels with the remote. "Uh-oh. What did I do now?"

Sitting down between his legs, a hand draped casually over his knee, she stared up at him for several moments. It didn't matter how long they'd been together, she was always awed by his good looks. The depth of his eyes and his killer physique got to her every time. Remaining focused, she parted her lips and forced the question turning in her mind out of her mouth. "Warrick, do we have a future together?"

"Angie, I wouldn't be with you if I wasn't thinking long-term."

"I was hoping you'd say that. I feel the same way."

He smoothed a hand over her hair. "Good, we're on the same page."

"I love you, Warrick, and I want to marry you." When his face broke out into a smile, her heart surged with hope. Encouraged, she continued. "How do you feel about getting engaged this year? My birthday isn't for a few more months, but I was thinking we could have a little party for our friends and family and announce our engagement then."

Warrick shifted in his chair. "Do we have to have this conversation now? Lou Dobbs is about to start, and President Obama's going to be discussing his stimulus plan for corporations."

Crossing her arms, she slanted her head to the right, studying him with dark, narrowed eyes. He was kidding, right? Watching CNN was more important than discussing their relationship? Instead of going off on him, she replied calmly, surprising herself. "Our future is important to me, Warrick and I want to know where we stand. Is marriage part of our—"

"Babe, we've only been back together for a few months.

What happened to spending time together and just enjoying each other's company? Those were your words, remember?"

"Don't you want to get married?"

"Of course I do, Tangela. You know how much I want to marry you."

"When, Warrick? When?"

"Soon. Once things quiet down at the office—"

"I've heard *that* one before," she quipped, rolling her eyes.

"I wouldn't say it if I didn't mean it."

Clutching the sides of the chair, she pushed herself to her feet. "I'm beginning to wonder why we even got back together," she mumbled, shaking her head. "We want different things and there's just no getting around it. I wish I'd been smart enough to realize that earlier, instead of letting you talk me into something I knew wasn't going to work."

"But I love you."

"Sometimes love isn't enough."

The silence was so loud, Tangela couldn't hear herself think.

"Let's discuss this another time. You're upset, I'm tired and it's late."

Water swam in Tangela's eyes. Her ears ached, but she could hear the irritation in his tone. She was having déjà vu. No, it wasn't a feeling. They *had* had this conversation before. Sorry she'd ever said anything, but committed to seeing the conversation through, Tangela asked why he was scared of settling down. "What are you so afraid of, Warrick?"

"I'm not scared of anything, but while we're on the subject, did you know that eighty percent of couples who get married before the age of thirty-six are divorced within three years?" He had the nerve to look pleased with himself. "There are a lot of benefits to waiting."

"You expect me to wait around for the next five years?" The thought was absurd. She wanted to have kids—lots of kids, and at twenty-nine, time was starting to run out. Celebrities could pop babies out at forty, but she knew from talking to her physician that most women couldn't. From the beginning, she'd been open and honest about what she wanted. Marriage, children and family mattered more to her than anything, and she wasn't prepared to take any more chances. All she'd ever wanted to be was a wife and mother, and now Warrick was taking that away from her—again. She was hanging on to a dream, a fantasy, a hopeless aspiration of becoming his wife, and it was time she woke up. "Why did you pursue me if you weren't ready to get married? You know how much having a family means to me."

"I don't like being bullied into things, Tangela. And in case you forgot, I'm the man in this relationship. Not you." His acrimonious words pierced her flesh. "You don't get to call the shots and dictate what I can and can't do."

Tangela frowned. That wasn't Warrick talking. It sounded like something that jerk Quinten would say. Had the boozing womanizer been poisoning Warrick's mind? Never married, and wary of long-term relationships, Quinten shared useless statistics and quotes he read in girlie magazines and encouraged his friends to play the field. Was that what this was about? The guys had ribbed Warrick about being "whupped" and now he was exerting his control and independence. *As if I don't have enough problems,* she thought, annoyed. *Now I have to contend with his pride and ego.*

"Next you'll be asking me to trade in my sports car for a minivan," he said with a snort.

"And what's wrong with that?" Gesturing with her hands around the artfully decorated living room, she glared at him. "You don't expect to raise children here, do you? A penthouse isn't a suitable place for kids, Warrick. Eventually, we'd have to move."

For a long moment, he didn't speak. "Let's not argue. We had a great evening and—"

"Are we getting engaged this year or not?" she demanded,

cutting him off. Refusing to be sucked in by the tender expression on his face and his dreamy voice, she pursed her lips together to keep from yelling at him. "I'm not issuing an ultimatum, or making demands. I just want to know the truth. Where is our relationship going?"

"Move in with me," he proposed, leaning forward in his seat. "I love having you here, and we're practically living together already."

"You'll live with me, but you won't marry me."

"I'm not pressuring you, Tangela. If you don't want to move in, I can respect that."

"And marriage?"

"Let's give it some more time. We'll discuss this again in a few weeks, I promise." He shrugged. "For now, that's the best I can do."

"That's the best you can do?" she parroted. "Warrick, this isn't another one of your business deals. This is my life you're talking about!"

Taken by surprise by her outburst, Warrick sat there quietly, watching her. Pride kept him rooted to his chair. He felt a mournful sinking in his heart as he watched the woman he loved. He wanted to go to her, wanted to comfort her, but he didn't have the courage to admit that he was scared. Scared their marriage would fail, scared she'd walk out on him again. Tangela was his life, but he wasn't going to propose because she'd ordered him to. He would do it his way, in his time. "I'm beat," he began, trying to defuse the situation. "This weekend, when we have clearer heads and more time, we'll discuss—"

"Why won't you commit? Don't you love me?"

"More than you will ever know."

"Then what's the problem?"

After killing himself at the office for ten hours and spending the last three hours at the theater, he was in no mood to get into a verbal sparring match with her. "Tangela, let's be real. You're not ready to get married. You want to wear skimpy outfits, stay out all night with your friends and flirt with other guys."

"I'm having fun, Warrick. I'm not going home with anybody or compromising myself, either." Her voice faltered, but she recovered. "I know what this is about. You're jealous. My life used to revolve around you and now I have hobbies and interests and you can't handle it."

He scratched his cheek. "That's ridiculous."

"Is it? Then why do you get angry every time I go dancing with my girlfriends? You don't hear me complaining when you're out with the guys."

"That's because you're busy trying to make a love connection on those stupid dating Web sites." It was a boneheaded thing to say, but Warrick didn't realize his error until he saw her eyes fill with tears. Her bottom lip quivered, and when Tangela snatched up her jacket, he noticed her hands were shaking. "I…I shouldn't have said that. I didn't mean it."

Sniffling, she glanced frantically around the room. "I can't do this anymore. I can't pretend I'm happy living with you without the permanency of marriage."

"Where are you going?"

"I'm leaving before I say something I'll regret."

"It's too late, Tangela. You already have." Spotting her purse under the table, he picked it up and chucked it on the sofa. "Go ahead, run out of here like you always do."

"I'm not a child, Warrick. I'm not going to stand here and let you berate me."

Glaring at her, his heart beating out of his chest, he rose to his feet. "Every time we argue, you run off to Sage's house and blab about what I did wrong. You know how that makes me feel? Like a joke, that's what." Impenitent about his strong language, he continued. "You want a fifty-thousand-dollar wedding with all the fixings, but you won't invest time into improving our relationship. It's one day, Tangela. One day. What about the next thirty years? Are you prepared for the challenges and hardships that might come down the road? That's what matters. Not, some overpriced designer gown."

"Don't you dare attack me for wanting to have a beautiful wedding!" Lips trembling, she wiped at the tears streaming down her cheeks. "Finally! Finally, I have people in my life who truly care about me. People who have been there for me when I needed them most. I just want everyone I love to be there on my big day. What's so wrong with that?"

Warrick watched her for a long moment. "How am I supposed to believe you're in this for the long haul when you bail at the first sign of trouble?"

Her eyes iced over. This time around, she wasn't going to break down or slink away in the middle of the night. She'd leave with her emotions in check, her head high and her pride intact. "Warrick, you'll never have to worry about my commitment to this relationship, because I *won't* be back." Her vision hazy, she stumbled down the darkened hallway, threw open the front door and rushed into the waiting elevator.

Chapter Nineteen

The Boeing 747 was at its cruising altitude, and passengers were watching the romantic comedy playing on the overhead screens. In an hour, the plane would touch down in San Diego and Tangela would officially be off the clock. Back sore and muscles tight, she dropped onto a seat at the rear of the plane. Thankful for the darkness of the cabin, she stretched out tired legs, crossing them at the ankles.

In these quiet, uninterrupted moments, Tangela couldn't help thinking about Warrick. Their ill-fated relationship hadn't even lasted six months this time around. It was spring, her favorite time of the year, the time when Warrick usually surprised her with a romantic trip to a warm, exotic locale. A sharp, crippling pain racked her body as his words reverberated in her mind. *How am I supposed to believe you're in this for the long haul when you bail at the first sign of trouble?*

Trying to channel her thoughts, Tangela searched the pocket of the seat in front of her for a magazine. Nothing but the flight-safety card. Her study notes were in the bottom of her tote bag, but she didn't feel like reviewing the test questions anymore. Her interview was next week, but she'd been studying nonstop since applying for the Flight Operations position at the end of last month, and she desperately needed a break.

Tangela closed her eyes and tried to wipe out the memory

of Warrick's kiss from her mind. Shivering, her body breaking out into a cold sweat, she felt his moist lips and tongue gliding up and across the back of her neck. It was easier to pretend that Warrick hadn't touched a piece of her soul than to admit she'd lost the only man she'd ever loved—again.

She was fast losing control; tears dribbled down her cheeks like the raindrops streaming down the side window. She'd gone into this relationship with her eyes wide open. Warrick didn't force her into anything. She'd willingly given her heart to him, and although his rejection stung, she wouldn't blame him. The news of Cashmere and Theo's engagement, Mrs. Harris's spiteful comments and her own insecurities had gotten the best of her and instead of taking a step back and assessing her true motives, she'd gone off half-cocked and demanded he marry her.

"This must be my lucky day," a husky male voice said.

Opening her eyes, she shot bolt upright in her seat. Hoping the businessman didn't see her tearstained cheeks, she wiped her face, then adjusted her uniform. "Mr. Kewasi? I didn't know you were on this flight."

"I came on late. I was held up at customs," he explained, chuckling lightly. "I travel a lot for business, which always raises suspicion with security. How is Warrick doing?"

Tangela lowered her gaze to her hands. It had been twelve days since they'd broken up, but she hadn't told anyone yet. Not even Sage. The less people who knew the better. And since it was easier to lie than tell Mr. Kewasi the truth she said, "He's fine. Work's been keeping him real busy." She couldn't resist saying, "I probably shouldn't be telling you this, but Warrick was really disappointed when you signed on with another firm. He was really looking forward to working with you on that condominium project."

Mr. Kewasi leaned against the seat. "I was all set to sign with Maxim Designs and Architects, and then one of my business associates in New Orleans told me that Warrick employs second-tier construction companies."

"That's a lie," she argued, shaking her head. "You know Warrick. He's a meticulous, hardworking architect who expects excellence from all his employees and staff."

"Yes, that's the impression I had of him, too, but once I heard about his involvement in the Urban Development project and all of the complaints from unsatisfied home owners, I—"

"Complaints? What complaints?" The plane pitched to the right and Tangela gripped the headrest to keep from falling over. The seat-belt light popped on and the pilot's soothing voice flowed over the intercom.

"We're passing through some heavy wind," First Officer Andrews explained. "We're asking that everyone remain seated until the seat-belt light is turned off. Thank you."

"I'd better use the lavatory before I get tossed to the floor!" Mr. Kewasi chuckled heartedly. "It was nice seeing you again, Tangela. Please give Warrick my best. I think he's a fine young man who's destined for greatness."

He is great, isn't he? she agreed, wishing things had turned out differently between them. Warrick was an accomplished businessman, too cute for words and had an amazing capacity to love. They wanted the same things out of life, so why had their relationship failed a second time?

Reflecting on what Mr. Kewasi had said earlier, Tangela wondered if Warrick knew the harm Lyndon had caused. He deserved to know what was being said about him. For a split second, she considered calling him. Before she could warm to the idea, reason kicked in. They were through. And though she longed to hear his voice, she couldn't call him, no matter how much she was hurting inside.

"Tangela, quick! Turn on the TV!"

Crawling out from under her blanket, Tangela pressed the cordless phone to her ear and patted back a yawn. Sage had the day off work and had insisted they meet at the Rejuve Spa. "A girls' day of pampering," she'd announced when they'd spoken yesterday. "We'll get beautiful, then have brunch at the House of Blues. It's karaoke night!"

While Sage had jabbered on about her new pain-in-the-ass client, Tangela thought back to that chilly morning in November. The morning she and Warrick had gone to the gospel brunch. Could their date have been any better? They'd laughed, danced and sung along with the choir. Weeks later, she still remembered how nervous she'd felt when he'd taken her into his arms. God, he'd smelled good. A combination of patchouli, musk and grapefruit, a scent both soothing and invigorating. And a perfect depiction of Warrick James Carver.

Sage's voice drew her attention back to the present. "Put it to channel eight. Hurry!"

Bending her arms like a pretzel, she swung her legs out in front of her, yawning as though she hadn't slept in weeks. Her interview wasn't until three o'clock, but it wouldn't hurt to review her employee handbook again. "Sage, I don't have time to watch Spotlight Tinseltown, and for the fifth time, I don't care who George Clooney's sleeping with."

"This is serious, Tangela. A roof collapsed in New Orleans!"

Her tongue went numb.

"Warrick's name has been all over the news. Apparently, Maxim Designs and Architects were hired to design the building four years ago and…"

Mouth dry, her heart racing with dread, she hit the power button on the remote. CNN was on commercial break, but the local news was carrying the story of the horrific building collapse in New Orleans. Thirty-five people had been taken to hospital and half of the victims were small children. Live footage of the Truman Enterprises building was followed by video of Jacob Carver's limousine speeding down the driveway of his lavish Seven Hills mansion.

"When did this happen?"

Sage relayed what she'd heard on Fox News. "Apparently members at Bethesda Gospel Tabernacle were getting their praise on when the ceiling started to crumble. Seconds later, larger, bigger pieces of concrete fell to the ground." Her voice was laced with awe. "Talk about bringing the house down, huh?"

"It's a wonder more people didn't get hurt."

"As you can expect, pandemonium broke out. Most of the injuries occurred as people raced to get out of the church, not from falling concrete."

"I can't believe this is happening." Bethesda Gospel Tabernacle was a refuge for abused women and children and Tangela adored Reverend Massey and his kindhearted congregation.

"The investigation hasn't even begun, but the media has already determined that Warrick and his father are to blame."

"Warrick's team designed the building, but they didn't build it. Lyndon's construction company did."

"And everyone knows what a cheap bastard he is."

"The Carver family has done exceptional work in New Orleans, but no one's come forward to defend them. It's awful. They've pumped more money into the Lower Ninth Ward than any other company and even—"

Tangela jumped up. She had to do something. Warrick wasn't to blame for the building collapse. They weren't a couple anymore and they hadn't spoken since their breakup, but she couldn't sit back and let reporters drag his family's good name through the mud.

Pulling on a white V-neck sweater and jeans, Tangela glanced around the bedroom for her keys. She knew the truth and it was up to her to make the world listen. Warrick and his dad cared about those families and she'd sooner die than stand back and let the media crucify him.

"Warrick needs me," she said, more to herself than Sage. "I'm heading down there."

"To New Orleans? But what about your interview? Tangela, I know you love Warrick, but you can't blow off the most important interview of your career."

"I'll call my supervisor, tell her what happened and hope that she understands why I have to reschedule. Either way, I'm leaving on the next available flight." After a substantial pause, she broke the silence. "Sage, I was there when they laid the foundation of Bethesda Gospel Tabernacle. No one worked harder or put in more time at the construction site than Warrick did. He's not responsible for the collapse and I intend to prove it."

"Girl, are you sure about this? You and Warrick aren't even speaking."

"We're just going through a rough time." The lie tumbled out of her mouth. "We're fine, really. We just had a lover's spat. It was nothing."

"Warrick told Marshall you were over for good."

Inside the closet, she grabbed her suitcase. She was going to New Orleans and there was nothing Sage could say to change her mind. It was the right thing to do. The only thing to do. "I have to run if I'm going to make that flight. I'll call you when I get there."

"I have a bad feeling about this, Tangela. Warrick's not going to welcome you with open arms. You really hurt him."

Her heart rattled around her chest. "He said that?" Realizing she wasn't fooling her best friend, she told the truth. Tangela craved a family more than anything, and she didn't want anyone but Warrick. They thirsted after the same things, and he was the kindest, sincerest man she'd ever met. He was her love, her destiny, the person she'd been searching for her entire life. And since the day she'd walked out on him, she'd been beating herself up. What she wouldn't do to be home with him, sharing a bottle of wine, curled up on the couch in his strong arms. "I have to go down to New Orleans. Warrick needs me now more than ever."

"Tangela, you can't keep playing these mind games. Either you want to be with Warrick or you don't. How many more times are you going to break up and get back together?"

"What are you talking about?" she spat, gripping the receiver. "I love Warrick and I want to marry him. That's what I've always wanted."

"Then why did you walk out on him?" The silence was long and painful. "Love is hard, Tangela. You have to work at it every single day. Happiness doesn't come in a can, and if you're serious about getting married, you have to show Warrick that you're a hundred-percent committed to him and your relationship. You can't leave every time you get into an argument or come hide out in my guest room, either. Warrick needs to know that he can trust you. That you're not going to leave him again."

When Tangela hung up the phone five minutes later, she flopped back into the unmade bed and closed her eyes. Sage was right. Going to New Orleans was a bad idea. Warrick wasn't talking to her, and after the way she'd treated him, she knew his family wouldn't welcome her with open arms, either.

Turning toward the wall, her gaze fell across the digital clock on the side table. *Should I go to my interview or down to New Orleans?* Rescheduling might cost her the Flight Operations position. And someone with more experience could get the job—her job, the one she'd wanted ever since she started her flight-attendant career.

Up on her feet, she went into the closet and took out her favorite Christian Dior designer suit. Holding the fitted jacket at arm's length, Tangela inspected the outfit for stains. Forget Warrick. This time, she'd put her career first. She was going to march into that conference room and impress the American Airlines executives with her knowledge of the company's standards, policies and procedures.

Entering the bathroom, she turned the water on full-blast. Steam rose from the jet tub and Tangela felt her eyes water. Swallowing the lump in her throat, she slowly undressed. If going to the interview was the right decision, then why was she filled with an overwhelming sense of despair at the thought of not being with Warrick when he needed her most?

Chapter Twenty

Residents, city officials and journalists crammed into the recreational facility in the Lower Ninth Ward at seven o'clock on Monday night for a town hall meeting for community development. From her seat at the back of the auditorium, Tangela scrutinized the faces of the people in attendance. His face bruised and swollen, Lyndon sat in the front row, his thick, meaty arms plopped across his burly chest.

He needs a fat lip to go with that black eye, Tangela thought, sucking her teeth. Word on the street was that Lyndon had decked Warrick in the hospital parking lot. According to eye-witness accounts, it had taken three large security guards to separate them. Warrick was too cultured, too refined to get into a street brawl, but when Tangela saw Lyndon's swollen jaw, she knew the rumors were true. She only hoped Warrick didn't look as banged-up as his opponent.

Her eyes landed on Warrick's grandmother. The family took up three rows of seats and although Rachael had invited her to sit with them she'd declined. Though it hurt to admit it, she wasn't a part of the Carver family and she knew Warrick wouldn't want her there. He'd made that perfectly clear when she'd called him that afternoon. After repeated attempts, she'd finally heard his voice answer his cell phone, and when it flowed over the line, she'd forgotten her well-planned speech and stumbled over her words.

"Warrick, it's…Tangela. I heard what happened. If there's anything I can d—"

That's as far as she'd got. He'd interrupted and the harshness of his tone had shocked her.

"I don't need your help. I can handle it."

"Oh, okay…I just wanted you to know that I'm here if you need me. Even if it's just to talk. I'm staying at the—"

"Another call is coming in. I have to go." He'd hung up abruptly and she'd sat with the phone to her ear for several seconds, thinking about the trouble she'd caused. Wasn't she the one who'd told Warrick to cut Lyndon and his men some slack? If it wasn't for her, he would have fired the construction foreman months ago and his family name wouldn't have been dragged through the mud. Lyndon Siegel was bad news, just as Warrick had said, and now the community was paying the price for the foreman's erroneous mistakes.

A hush fell over the crowd as Warrick, the mayor and three suited men took the stage. Thumbs pointed down, eyes tapered in disgust, the crowd broke into boos, jeers and hisses. Wads of paper rained on the stage, narrowly missing Mayor Robinson's close-cropped hair.

Tangela's gaze zeroed in on Warrick. The man was a perfect ten. His crisp black suit was complemented by a white-striped tie. The situation was devastating, but Warrick was the picture of cool. Head erect, back straight, hands clasped in front of him. She was a nervous mess, but Warrick was his usual calm self. Over the years, she'd seen Warrick in some pretty stressful situations, but nothing had ever ruffled his composure. He had always been the type of person to tackle problems head-on and this was no exception. How many other CEOs would have willingly jumped right into the fire? Most would have flown to a secluded island and kept a low profile until the whole matter blew over. Not Warrick. He was here in New Orleans, putting the community's fears to rest.

"Citizens of New Orleans, residents of the Lower Ninth Ward and community members, I'm Warrick Carver, president and chief architect at Maxim Designs and Architects."

The crowd booed so loudly, the children seated in front of Tangela covered their ears.

"I'm not here to lay blame, or point fingers. I take complete responsibility for what happened last night at Bethesda Gospel Tabernacle and I'm going to do everything in my power to resolve this situation. I'm going to see to it that nothing like this ever happens again."

There was a smattering of applause.

"Our thoughts and prayers are with all of the victims and everyone else who has been touched by this traumatic event."

Unflappable in the midst of adversity, he spoke in a firm, self-assured way, not a trace of anxiety in his voice. Tangela had always admired his quiet diplomacy and as she listened to him, her heart flooded with pride. Though financially devastated, Warrick was handling the situation with class, and she hoped his equanimity would rub off on the belligerent crowd.

"We are praying for a swift recovery for the victims. My family and I visited with all of them this afternoon, and they were in very good spirits. All of their medical expenses will be covered by Maxim Designs and Architects and every member of Bethesda Gospel Tabernacle will be fully compensated for their pain and suffering."

The crowd fell silent.

"This is messed up," said a harsh, raspy voice. A teen in an orange bomber jacket popped up in the crowd. "First Katrina, then Gustav and now this. I'm packing my stuff and gettin' the hell out of here. It ain't safe around here no mo'!"

"I'm sorry you feel that way, young man, but I've been spending the summers down here since I was a kid and I love this city." Warrick's gaze panned the audience. "I have a house in the Bay Shore area and I plan to raise my children here one day."

Tangela's ears perked up. Had she heard him right? That had always been *her* dream, not his. Las Vegas had been her home for the past ten years and although she loved the lights, billion-dollar properties and meeting people from all over the world, she appreciated the slower, quieter pace of New Orleans. Filled with hope, but conscious of the tension circulating around the room, Tangela took hold of her emotions before she got carried away. For all she knew, Warrick was just trying to win favor with the crowd. Feeling guilty, she struck the thought from her mind. No, he'd never do something like that. If Warrick said it, it was true.

"Maybe the media's right. Maybe New Orleans *is* cursed."

"Don't go anywhere, young blood," advised a silver-haired man. "There's nothing wrong with our fine city. It's these money-hungry corporations that are to blame. They pay peanuts, make cutbacks and expect construction workers to perform miracles."

Is that what Lyndon was telling people? That Maxim Designs and Architects had short-changed him? It was hard for Tangela to sit there and be quiet. Lyndon had orchestrated this town hall meeting and had obviously worked his magic on the crowd. Infuriated that the audience was turning on Warrick, while Lyndon remained unscathed, she clamped her lips together to keep from screaming out in protest.

"You people make me sick." A plus-size woman stood and pointed a finger at Warrick. "Maybe you should spend less time in your fancy downtown office and more time on-site."

Tangela didn't realize she'd jumped up until she saw the wide, inquisitive expressions of the people sitting in front of her. Twisting around, they stared up at her, their lips clamped together in suppressed anger.

"I was here when the foundation of the church was laid," she began, her voice firm and strong. "I volunteered three months after Katrina hit and have been back since, most recently this past Christmas. I've worked closely with the Urban Development project and can unequivocally say Maxim Designs and Architects is not responsible for the roof collapse at Bethesda Tabernacle."

"Y'all don't know Mr. Carver like we do," interrupted a teen wearing a green do-rag. "He cares about us and this community. He's a slave driver, y'all!"

Laughter broke out.

The kid continued. "He cornered me and my crew on Lamanche Street and asked us to help paint the community center. We made a deal. He gave us driving lessons every day for a week and we painted our butts off!"

One by one, volunteers, staff and employees jumped up in Warrick's defense, and as Tangela listened to each heartfelt story, she felt herself sinking lower into her seat. *What have I done?* Not only had she walked out on him, she'd yelled at him and said cruel, spiteful things. Things she'd do anything to take back.

When the town hall meeting wrapped up ninety minutes later, Tangela was still thinking about Warrick and their future. Talking to one of the Bethesda Tabernacle members, but discreetly watching Warrick in her peripheral vision, she wondered what business he had with the attractive brunette in the designer suit. She considered going over, but lost her nerve when she saw the mayor join them.

"Tangela!" Face alive with excitement, Rachael rushed over and threw her arms around her shoulders. "You were incredible! I thought they were going to burn Warrick at the stake, but what you said turned the whole meeting around."

"It was nothing. All I did was tell the truth." Her eyes scanned the crowd for Warrick. He was talking to the teen who'd spoken earlier.

"He's right in front of you, Tangela." Rachael nudged her forward. "Go get him."

"I can't. We had a fight and I was really nasty to him," she confessed, head lowered. "Warrick's never going to forgive me. He probably hates me."

"That's impossible. My brother loves you. He's *always* loved you." Glancing around, she drew Tangela to a quiet, unoccupied corner. "A few weeks ago when you were away, Warrick came by to hang out with the boys. We took the kids to the mall to buy soccer cleats and stopped in at Cartier." She pressed a hand to Tangela's shoulder. "He didn't buy anything, but he asked what I thought of him proposing on your birthday."

Her eyes were saucers. Tangela didn't think she could feel any worse, but she did. Warrick had been contemplating proposing, but she'd messed things up by running her big mouth. When was she going to learn that she couldn't force him to do what she wanted? Hadn't she learned anything the first time around? Warrick was his own person, his own man and she couldn't control him any more than she could a wild bull in the Gap clothing store.

Her gaze drifted back across the room. A female reporter thrust a microphone in Warrick's face, and, though taken off guard, he turned to the camera. Begging him to take her back would look desperate and although she was, she didn't want the whole world to know. "I'm going to go over there and say hi."

"Child, please, you have to say a lot more than that."

Gathering her courage, she straightened her blouse and maneuvered her way through the crowd. She carried herself with poise, but when Warrick lifted his head and their eyes met, diffidence crept up on her. It was too late to change her mind, and besides, he was watching her. How would it look if she whipped around and ran in the opposite direction?

"I'm surprised to see you here," he said as she approached.

"I wanted to help out. I have friends at Bethesda and I was worried about them."

They remained quiet for a time.

"Your speech was great," she told him. "What you said really hit home."

"How did your interview go? It was this afternoon, wasn't it?"

"I rescheduled it."

A strange, unreadable expression came over his face. "Why?"

"I wanted to be here to show my support."

"But you've been prepping for this interview for weeks."

But I've loved you for years. Her throat swelled shut. Her thoughts were hazy and when she saw his mouth draw tight, her confidence fizzled. Now was not the time to discuss their breakup. She detected a hint of disappointment in his tone and his tense posture spoke of his unease. Camouflaging her sadness, she tried not to notice him searching the crowd.

"I have a long day of meetings ahead of me," he began, gesturing to the men standing beside his father. "I guess I'll see you around."

Stunned into silence, she stood mutely, watching him. *I guess I'll see you around?* That was it? After seven years of loving and caring for each other that's all he had to say? There were hard feelings on both sides, but his coldness shocked her. "Warrick, I'm sorry for—"

"I have to run. The mayor wants us to sit down with CNN."

Crushed, but bent on preserving her dignity, she nodded absently, wishing she'd stayed on the other side of the room. Her face was void of emotion, but she was falling apart on the inside. Compassion was one of Warrick's greatest attributes, except when it came to her. He could visit the victims in the hospital and invest thousands of dollars in the community, but he couldn't give her ten more minutes of his time?

"Take care of yourself, Tangela."

Battling tears, she lowered her head, refusing to meet the eyes she loved so much. "You, too." With a heavy heart, she watched him walk away. It was hard to believe this was the same man whose body used to make her hit notes higher than Mariah Carey could. Had it really been weeks since they'd shared a bed? Images reeled through her mind. It had been a quiet, uneventful night. After they'd cleared the table and stacked the dishes into the dishwasher, they'd climbed into bed to watch *House of Payne*. During a commercial break, she'd returned to the kitchen to fix a snack and he'd sneaked up behind her. His hands had explored her body, stroking, fondling, affecting. The sitcom forgotten, they'd kissed passionately, breathlessly, with such intensity she'd knocked her bowl of fat-free ice cream to the floor.

Picking her up with relative ease, he'd set her down on the counter, unbuckled his pants and drove into her like a man possessed. They'd never done anything like that before. Turned on by the thought of doing something so off-limits, she'd looped a leg around his waist and squeezed her pelvic muscles, tightening her hold on his shaft. Sly and teasing, she'd nipped playfully at his right earlobe. In her mind's eye, she saw them laughing, undressing, stumbling back into the bedroom and making love until the sheets were wet with perspiration.

Unable to pull her eyes away, she gave herself permission to watch Warrick a moment longer. His perspicacity for business and modern architecture was second to none. His innate intelligence helped him make wise decisions and there was no question the company would rebound from this disaster. Tangela only hoped she would, too. Thinking back on happier times made her heart ache. Cooking for one was depressing. Strolling through downtown held no appeal. And without Warrick, St. Croix was just another tourist hot spot.

He turned, caught her gaze and for a moment they just stared. Then, the corners of his mouth slowly rose. His half smile knocked her senseless. As she studied him, images and memories and snapshots of their relationship surfaced. And when he wet his lips in a sly, seductive gesture, Tangela felt a glimmer of hope. Maybe he wasn't as angry as she'd thought. If he was mad at her, he wouldn't be checking her out, and he most certainly was. Excitement rushed through her. She still had a chance. Albeit a tiny one, but a chance nonetheless.

To mask his true feelings, he was being a tough guy, but Tangela wasn't buying it. She knew him better than anyone. He was a sweetheart. A deeply caring, affectionate man. And beyond the facade was a guy who respected women, worked tirelessly to be at the top of his field and held firm to his values. Warrick treasured her and she adored him for being patient with her.

Heading through the community-center doors, she turned and cast a final look at Warrick. He was standing at the front of the room with the rest of the Carver clan. In her heart, she knew their love was inviolable, and it had been ridiculous to think she could pick up the pieces and move on. Fine dining, expense accounts and all the other perks that came with dating a successful architect didn't matter to her. They had never mattered. All Tangela wanted was her man back. Warrick James Carver was her heart, her love, everything she'd ever wanted in a partner, and she was going to bring him home where he belonged.

Chapter Twenty-One

Drowning his sorrows in Bacardi Gold rum wouldn't eradicate Tangela from his thoughts, but the cold liquid made Warrick temporarily forget his problems. Three victims of the building collapse still remained in the hospital, but he'd had to return to Las Vegas yesterday to chair a budget meeting. Media attention had shifted to the tribulations on Wall Street and he'd sighed in relief when he pulled up to Truman Enterprises and there were no camera crews in sight.

Seated between Quinten and DeAndre, he stared at his haggard expression in the mirror behind the elongated bar. The Hot Spot, a restaurant lounge just off the Strip, had a warm, casual charm. Slate-colored floors, mellow lights and fine wood paneling created a relaxing atmosphere to drink, eat and dance. Quinten was keeping a running commentary of the hottest women in the bar, and DeAndre was dividing his attention between one of the female bartenders and the Mariners game on the big screen.

Warrick's thoughts returned to New Orleans. The investigation would take up to a year to complete, but Lyndon's business license had been suspended and he was being indicted on two counts of fraud. Warrick didn't have to give his sworn affidavit until the end of the month, and although he wasn't legally responsible for what Lyndon had done, he wouldn't be able to sleep until the remaining victims were at home with their families.

Business had cooled in recent weeks, but that was to be expected. In the past, his forward-thinking ideas had generated million-dollar contracts for his company and once this issue was resolved, he knew Maxim Designs and Architects would be back on top. But was that what he wanted? Wealth and success with no one to share it with?

His head dipped low, he slipped off his glasses and rubbed the soreness from his eyes. Warrick wondered how Tangela was spending her thirtieth birthday. Fighting off another headache, he expelled a deep, raspy breath. How could he have lost the woman he loved not once, but twice? He'd promised himself he wouldn't hurt her. That he'd do right by her and treat her like the queen she was. He'd done anything but.

Closing his eyes, he pinched the bridge of his nose. A picture of Tangela filled his mind. As unpretentious as a beautiful woman could be, she was sweet and nurturing, but had the heart of a lion. Defending him in front of that hostile New Orleans crowd had taken guts. Feelings of hurt and disappointment ran deep, but he'd never ever forget the sacrifices she'd made for him and his family. Where would he ever find another woman like that? Struggling to maintain control of his emotions, he pushed her image—her eyes, her smile, her luscious lips—out of his mind, only to have it return seconds later.

Tomorrow, he'd chastise himself for drinking heavily, but right now alcohol was the perfect tonic for the predicament he was in. And anything that kept his mind off his troubles was a welcome ally. He stared down at his cell phone lying on the granite bar. For the hundredth time that day, he considered calling Tangela. He should have apologized to her at the press conference, but instead of manning up and doing the right thing, he'd scurried off to the other side of the room. Fear had gotten the best of him and now he didn't have a ghost of a chance of getting her back.

The Hawthorne party came to mind. The thought of Tangela marrying someone else petrified him, but that's the road they were headed on if he didn't make a move—pronto. Did it really matter that she'd been the one to broach the subject of marriage? No. They loved each other, so what was he waiting for? He had the ring, a rehearsed speech and a romantic venue that would steal her breath away. Now all he needed was his woman, but after screwing up again, how could he convince her he was for real this time?

"Look at you, man," Quinten quipped, motioning with his head to the mirror. "Shoulders hunched, bottom lip poking out. You're thinking about her, aren't you?"

"No, man, I was—"

"Liar! You have that sad, faraway look in your eyes, like you're about to bust some suds. You're not going to cry, are you, dog?"

Ignoring the jab, Warrick palmed his glass and lifted it to his mouth.

"Leave him alone," DeAndre said, clamping a hand on Warrick's back. "He misses his girl and ain't nothing wrong with that."

"Thanks, D."

"Just don't cry, man. I left the tissues in the truck!"

His friends brayed with laughter.

"You don't really want some female up under you 24/7, do you?" Quinten asked, leaning over. "She's gone, out of your life. Like I've said before, count yourself lucky."

"You've never been in love, so I'm not even going to waste my breath."

Lips curled, Quinten launched into a lengthy diatribe about his issues with black women. "They're always trying to change somebody. I don't need no fixin'. I'm fine just the way I am. And, Warrick, you're my boy and all, but you're whupped, just like Marshall and that sucker Theo." His voice boomed, drawing the attention of a waitress passing by. "Real men don't sulk. They dust themselves off and move on to the next honey."

DeAndre disagreed. "Every woman isn't a ball breaker, Q. Look at Tangela. Not only is she a dime piece, she knows her way around the kitchen. Not like my ex-wife, Rashida. She couldn't crack an egg and the only way I was getting any booty was if I took her shopping. No shoes, no lovin' was her motto!"

Warrick felt the hole in his heart widen. Tangela was a domestic goddess, a beauty and a loving, nurturing spirit all rolled into one. Able to cook, clean and entertain at a moment's notice, she took good care of him and knew how to impress his clients. And she did this trick with her tongue that made his toes curl. But more than their sexual chemistry was the way she took care of him. When he had a problem and wanted to talk, she gave him her full attention, didn't interrupt and offered insightful suggestions. No matter what he was going through, he could always count on Tangela to cheer him up. And to make him a good hearty meal. They shared a oneness that other couples envied. A unique heartfelt bond that could never be broken.

Why couldn't we have made up and had explosive sex like we had that afternoon in my office? His libidinous imagination carried him away. Back to the moment he'd heard Tangela's footsteps in the hall. Strolling in with a turkey sandwich in one hand and a beer in the other, she'd set the food on his drawing board and turned back toward the door. Craving her touch, he'd pulled her down on his lap. For several seconds, they'd eyed each other, their breathing deep and shallow, their eyes locked in an intense gaze. Forgetting the blinds were drawn, they'd gone at it in front of the windows, like a pair of sex addicts who'd fallen off the wagon. The possibility of being seen by his neighbors had increased his pleasure.

"An apple martini with a dash of calvados and three mara-schino cherries," the waiter announced, placing the cocktail glass on a napkin. "Courtesy of the beauty at the end of the bar."

Leaning forward, Warrick glanced to the right. His tongue seemed too big for his mouth, and all he could do was stare. Tangela. Bewildered, he rubbed a hand over his face, fully expecting her to disappear. But when he looked up, she was still there. Her eyes were hotter than the searing heat of the desert, and her smile made his heart surge.

Getting off the stool with inherent grace, she moved carefully toward the stage and climbed the steps. He could tell she was feeling confident by the sexy way she walked. Her movements had plenty of rhythm, sway and bounce. Examining her outfit, he licked his lips, nodding appreciatively. Tangela wowed in a white one-piece jumpsuit, and her pretty auburn curls kissed her bare shoulders. Copping an eyeful of her cleavage, he rubbed his damp palms over his knees. The collar of his shirt and the accompanying tie were suddenly stifling.

Warrick wanted to stand but worried he'd trip over his feet. It wasn't every day Tangela turned up at his favorite after-work bar looking like an erotic piece of eye candy. Feeling anxious, he wheeled around on his stool so he could have a clear view of the stage.

"I know it isn't karaoke night, but I'm good friends with the owner and she told me to come on up here and do my thing. So, here goes." Her eyes found his through the sea of amused faces. "This is dedicated to Warrick, my friend, my lover, the man of my dreams."

Warrick gulped. He loved Tangela more than life itself, but he prayed to God that she wasn't about to sing. She couldn't hold a note. Not one. His mind flashed back to the last time he'd been at the bar on karaoke night. Hecklers had pitched garbage onto the stage and made the Apollo audience seem tame in comparison.

Loosening his tie, he glanced warily around the lounge. He could see it now. Tangela would start singing and the crowd would boo like they'd never booed before. His facial muscles tightened. No one was going to humiliate his woman. He appreciated the gesture, but all that mattered was that Tangela had come to see him. Not how good her pipes were.

Hoping to save her any embarrassment, he grabbed his coat and jumped to his feet. Warrick was only a few feet from the stage when Tangela opened her mouth and belted out the first bar of the Musiq Soulchild smash hit "Don't Change." Mesmerized by the gentle yearning of her voice, he stood in the middle of the lounge transfixed. When she gripped the microphone and hit the high note, he knew she was lip-synching. *That* was not her voice.

Grinning, he watched the woman he loved sing smoothly, swaying seductively to the music and engaging the mostly male crowd. Everyone cheered, Warrick the loudest of all, and when their eyes locked, he made his move. He was up on the stage, pulling her into his arms, before the song finished playing. Amid cheers, whistles and applause, they reunited in a long lusty kiss, holding each other in a fierce grip.

Mindful of their surroundings, he released his hold and led her backstage. It was dark, but the light streaming in from the lounge illuminated the twinkle in her eyes. "Angie, baby, you were amazing out there. I loved it!"

"No, you loved that I wasn't the one singing!"

"What are you doing here?" he asked, gently stroking her shoulders. "It's your birthday. You should be out somewhere celebrating with your friends."

"Warrick, the only person I want to be with tonight is you."

"Then why do you keep running away?"

The light in her eyes went out. There was so much to say, so much to explain, she didn't know where to begin. "One thing I vividly remember from my childhood was my parents fighting a lot. They didn't talk, they screamed and cursed and pushed each other around. I don't know why, but when things get heated between us, my first inclination has always been to run.

"Warrick, that's always been my way of coping, and I never realized the damage I was doing to our relationship every time I walked out. But, baby, I'm tired of running. I want to be with you forever. I've loved you from the second we met and despite everything we've been through I've never stopped."

Holding the back of her head in his hands, he swept his lips over her mouth. "I want the same thing, Angie. It's not going to happen overnight, but I'm going to work at it. That includes being home in time for dinner and helping out around the house, too. We're a team and I have to start carrying my weight." Grinning ruefully, he winked. "Or at the very least, hire a maid."

Thrown off course by his response, Tangela took a moment to put her thoughts in order. She didn't want Warrick to think she didn't love him, but living together again was definitely out of the question. Before she could protest, he spoke.

"I've never failed at anything, but marriage is one of those things you just can't prepare for. People change, circumstances divide the most loving of couples and the first time around I didn't think we'd make it. I was scared we were too young for a commitment of that magnitude."

Forcing herself to meet his gaze, she touched a hand to his cheek, hoping to convey what was in her heart through her gentle caress. They had a solid relationship built on trust, respect and love, and there was no question in her mind that they'd have a beautiful life together.

"Before Sage and Marshall got hitched, I didn't know anyone who was happily married," he explained. "All of my friends and uncles were miserable and complained about how controlling their wives were. You and I had a great thing going and I didn't want to mess that up.

"I want to get married once, and I want it to last forever, but we'll never work if you walk out whenever there's a problem."

Watching her, he took her hands and held them in his. "There's no such thing as a perfect relationship, Angie. We're going to have ups and downs like every other couple, but if we're open and honest about our feelings, we can survive anything."

Allowing his words to sink in, she nodded slowly, then spoke to his fears. "Warrick, I promise to be more understanding of the pressures you are under and give you the space you need."

His eyebrows were raised in a quizzical slant. "So, you're not going to flip out when I kick it with the boys or drive up to L.A. to play golf for the weekend?"

"Just because we're married doesn't mean we have to do everything together. I like hanging out with the girls, too, you know!"

Tangela laughed. "I want a life with you, Warrick, and I'm willing to do whatever it takes to make us work. And from now on, what happens between us stays between us."

"Well, not everything. I like when you brag to your friends about how good I am in bed!"

"I do not!" Face twisted into a frown, she poked him hard in the chest. "You're lying."

"Am not. I hear you sometimes. Oohh, sister child," he mimicked, his voice a high feminine pitch, his eyes filled with mischief, "my man put it on me last night—"

"You little eavesdropper! What did you do, tap the phones?"

He pointed to his temple. "I'm always a step ahead of everybody else. That's why the company pays me the big bucks!"

Deeply grateful that he'd given her another chance, she folded her arms around his waist and rested her head on his chest. "Our friends are going to flip out when they find out we're back together, especially Quinten."

"I know. That's why we're going to hide out at your place for the rest of the week. We're going to be making up all night," he announced, grinding himself against her. "Baby, this has been the longest month of my life and I need you *bad*."

His touch incited a purr. Her body trembled at the thought of them being in bed for the next twenty-four hours. "Don't you have a presentation to get ready for or an out-of-town client to entertain at one of those girly bars?"

"Nope." They stared at each other for a long moment. Lovingly stroking her shoulders, he sprinkled kisses along the slope of her neck. Hungry for her, he brushed her hair off her face and kissed her passionately, deeply, with everything he had. When he nuzzled his chin against her shoulder, she cooed.

"Angie, I don't care what anyone has to say about us getting back together. I love you more than anything, and nothing will ever change how I feel about you."

"Te quiero, Warrick. Yo no nunca parare adorarte," she whispered, her face flushed with happiness. "I love you, baby. Heart, mind and soul."

Chapter Twenty-Two

"Good evening." The female clerk at Aspen's Sky Hotel wore a bright smile. "It's good to see you again, Ms. Howard. How was your flight?"

Wonderful, since it's the last time I'll ever wear this flight-attendant uniform, Tangela thought. "Fine thanks." As she signed the credit-card slip, she wondered if the Human Resources director had couriered the contracts to her apartment as promised. On Monday, she'd be starting her new job as a flight operations manager, and she still couldn't believe that she'd been offered the executive position at the end of her interview.

Glancing at her watch, Tangela realized she only had thirty minutes to shower and change. The crew insisted on taking her out for a celebratory dinner at her favorite seafood restaurant, and she was looking forward to hanging out with her coworkers one last time.

"You've been upgraded to the deluxe king suite," the clerk announced, handing her a white key card. "Enjoy your stay, Ms. Howard, and if there's anything we can do to make your time at the Sky Hotel more pleasant, please don't hesitate to…"

Having heard the spiel before, she smiled, then turned and hurried through the plush lobby. Set in the heart of downtown Aspen, the Sky Hotel oozed with serenity and charm. Beyond the revolving door, the evening sky was bathed in a patchwork of pastel colors and the light breeze flowing in through the sliding-glass doors was cool.

On the third floor, Tangela stepped off the elevator. Having stayed in the deluxe suite before, she knew to make a left turn at the first corner. As she remembered the last time she'd spent the night at the Sky Hotel, her thoughts turned to Warrick. A smile filled her lips. For the last two weeks, they'd been in their own private world. They relished every moment they had together, and if not for his board meeting that afternoon, they'd still be lounging in bed.

As Tangela approached suite three seventy-two, she noticed a small pink envelope taped to the door. Her name was typed in a bold dark font. Curious, she tore it off, opened it and read the single handwritten sentence. *Tonight is your night.*

Frowning, she returned the card to the envelope. Only God knew what Carmen and the crew had in store for her tonight. *I hope they're not taking me to some nasty strip club,* she thought, sliding the key card into the slot.

Stepping inside the darkened room, Tangela flipped on the lights. Slack-jawed, she cupped a hand over her gaping mouth. Balloons—hundreds of heart-shaped balloons—covered the living-room floor. Showy pink tulips sat in slim, cylindrical vases, and the jumbo candles along the mantel created a warm ambient glow. Glass bowls overflowed with dark chocolate and Tangela's mouth watered at the enticing scent.

As Tangela made her way into the suite, she was stunned to see eight-by-twelve pictures of her and Warrick hanging on the cream walls. Stopping, she reached out and drew her finger along one of the expensive silver frames. It held the picture they'd taken at the end of their first date. Beside it was a photo of them snorkeling in St. Croix. Each photograph, arranged in chronological order, touched her deeply. And when Tangela saw the last picture in the row everything clicked. *Seven pictures, seven years,* she thought, smiling when she saw the overblown *People* magazine cover. *I can't believe Warrick would do something like this!*

Another pink envelope was taped to the bedroom door. "Take a shower, put on the dress and meet me in the living room at eight o'clock," she read out loud. Confused, she rushed inside. The room was decorated lavishly, and there were more crystal vases filled with tulips. Three white boxes fitted with enormous red bows were on the satin-draped bed.

Breathing deeply, slowly, Tangela ripped open the envelope on top of the smallest box. Inside, she read, *To my love, my future, my everything.* Closing her eyes, she clutched the card to her chest. A deep sense of peace filled her. Warrick loved her completely, fully, without condition. He accepted her, validated her feelings, and for as long as she lived, she'd never forget how loved and cherished she felt today.

The tissue paper inside the box was quickly discarded. The tiny diamonds on the pearl bracelet glittered when Tangela lifted it out of its case. A pair of designer shoes were in the second box and a chiffon, one-shoulder dress occupied the third. Feeling like a real-live princess, Tangela held the Oscar de la Renta designer gown up to her body and examined herself in the mirror.

Tears filled her eyes and ran down her cheeks, but she brushed them away. She didn't want Warrick to come in and see her crying. Not after he'd gone to all of this trouble for her. Tangela had no idea what other surprises her boyfriend had in store for her, but she was anxious to find out. Humming the "Wedding March," she floated into the bathroom, wearing a wide, radiant smile.

Forty minutes later, Tangela was bathed, lotioned and dressed. The gown fitted like a dream, and she'd never felt more beautiful. In light of the occasion, she'd taken extra care in fixing her hair and makeup. Mascara thickened her lashes and chocolate-brown lipstick gave her lips extra shine. Desiring a glamorous look, she'd twisted her hair into a bun, secured the knot with a pair of wooden hair sticks and added some jewels throughout.

Slipping on her shoes, she carefully lowered herself onto the bed. Her stomach was heavy with butterflies and her hands were shaking so hard she couldn't secure the ankle strap on the high heels. Absorbed in her task, she didn't notice Warrick watching her from the bedroom door.

"Well, good evening, Ms. Howard."

Warrick had planned to start the night off with a six-course meal and wine, but when he saw Tangela's drop-dead-gorgeous look, he was overtaken by desire, a voracious hunger that couldn't be tamed or quenched. His eyes ran down her hips. To keep from losing his footing, he braced himself against the door frame. Blown away by her beauty, he stared as if he was seeing her for the first time. Warrick had known Tangela would look stunning in the custom-made gown, but he hadn't expected to be knocked off his feet.

Executing the perfect proposal was all about planning, creativity and timing, and Warrick wasn't about to let this moment pass him by. Hadn't he waited long enough? Didn't the woman he loved deserve to finally have her fairy-tale ending? Retrieving the velvet pouch from his suit pocket, he clutched it in his palm and entered the room.

"Even after all these years, you still take my breath away," he whispered, reaching for her. Tangela stood, and when Warrick saw the love reflected in her eyes, he felt himself get choked up. Clearing his throat, he brushed at the curls crowding her face. "This dress was made for you, baby. No one could wear it better."

"I thought you had an emergency board meeting in New York." The sly smile on his lips made her giggle. "When did you become so sneaky?"

"When I saw you at the Hawthorne party in that leather catwoman costume. The second I saw you, I knew I had to find a way to get you back!"

"Warrick, I love everything. The suite, the tulips, this outfit. And when I saw the picture frames, I almost burst out crying."

Glad he'd pleased her, he reached for her hand. Tangela was

his world, and he was going to spend the rest of his life making her happy or die trying. "Baby, I want to spend all of my days and nights with you. You're my destiny, my hope, my future and no one else makes me feel the way you do."

Water filled her eyes.

"Baby, don't cry," he admonished, embracing her and pecking her check. "You're finally going to have the wedding day you've always dreamed of. I'm sorry that it's taken me so long to get my act together, but I'm here now, asking for your hand in marriage. I absolutely want to marry you, and I will…"

Sniffling, Tangela dabbed at her face with her fingertips. Warrick spoke with such passion, with such conviction, she could feel herself beginning to unravel. Her mouth was dry and she felt light-headed, but she forced her herself to stay in the moment.

"The time we spent apart made me want you even more, and I'm never going to let you go again." With care and deliberate slowness, Warrick untied the velvet pouch and took out the pink oval-shaped ring. Speechless, Tangela closed her open mouth. It was the ring Warrick had given her the first time he proposed. It was five and a half carats of perfection. A brilliant Harry Winston diamond that had once made her the envy of all of her girlfriends. *He's been holding on to it for all these years?*

"I'd always planned on marrying you, Angie, and there was never any doubt in my mind that one day we'd get back together. You're the perfect woman for me, the *only* woman for me, and I'd be honored to call you my wife. Will you marry me?"

Overjoyed, tears spilling from her eyes, Tangela kissed Warrick so hard he staggered back onto the bed. Desperate for him, she pushed his suit jacket over his shoulders. Savoring the taste of his lips, she ran her hands over his wide, muscular chest. Like a pair of sixth graders crouched under the bleachers, they pawed and stroked each other, until they were inflamed with desire.

Warrick had planned every minute of the night and making love was the last item on his list, but as they shed their designer clothes, he couldn't think of a better way to start the evening. He'd cued the stereo to play "their" song, and when he heard the distant sound of "Don't Change," he pulled back, staring deeply, intensely into his Tangela's beautiful brown eyes.

"The way we are is how it's gonna be, just as long as your love don't change," he sang, showering her face with kisses.

More tears filled Tangela's eyes. Not only did Warrick love her unconditionally, he made her feel good about herself, and that was a serious turn-on. Skin-to-skin, the warmth of his lips exciting her, she trembled at the spark of electricity tearing through her core. Erect and longing to be touched, she cupped her breasts and lifted her nipples to his open mouth. He ran his tongue around one, all the while kneading and plucking the other. When he jerked off her panties, she sucked in a quick, sudden breath.

Warrick could tell by the way Tangela lifted her hips up off the bed that she was ready for more. Her skin was warm, her body responsive and her lips as sweet as caramel. Granting her unspoken desire, he parted her legs and eased his index finger inside her wetness. The more he stroked her, probing her sex with his long fingers, the harder it was for Tangela to breathe.

To heighten her pleasure, Warrick slowly massaged her clitoris, sliding his finger back and forth, in and out. His heart was thumping, and when she sucked his earlobe into her mouth, a shiver tore down his spine. Starting at his collarbone, Tangela kissed down his chest, sending him over the edge with each flick of her tongue. She dragged her long fingernails down his back while her lips worked their magic.

Touching her softness with the tip of his erection, he palmed her breasts fervently. Entering her, he moved in deep, fluid strokes. Gazes locked, they moved together as one. One body, one soul, one mind. They were lovers, soul mates, and one day they'd be joined forever as husband and wife. As Warrick loved her, he held her tightly in his arms, caressing her, kissing her, stroking her tenderly.

A crippling orgasm tore through her. One after another, deep, mind-numbing, paralyzing spasms filled her. Her mouth was dry, her body damp and weak. Numb and dazzled, she felt herself go limp in his strong arms. She'd never come that fast before, and when Warrick teased her for finishing first, she laughed out loud.

Clutching her hips in his palms, he deepened his penetration. Warrick felt a wave of heat and pressure settling in his groin. Rocked by the intensity of his impending orgasm, he grabbed the headboard for support. He increased his thrusts until he was gulping furiously for air.

Spent, Warrick collapsed onto his back and pulled the woman he loved to his side. Planting kisses on her cheek, he quietly hummed the refrain of "Don't Change." "You know, you never did answer my question," he teased, rubbing his chin against her bare shoulder. "Are you finally going to let me make an honest woman of you?"

He expected her to laugh, and when she didn't, he pulled back so he could see her face. Love was reflected in her eyes, her cheeks were flushed and her smile was the most beautiful thing he'd ever seen.

"I've dreamed of marrying you and starting a family for almost a decade. Warrick, baby, I love you more than you'll ever know, more than words can express. And I'll never stop."

Fingering the bracelet dangling from her wrist, he tightened his hold around her, swallowing the space separating their bodies. "I'd marry you in a heartbeat, baby. Anytime, anywhere, anyplace."

Staring up at him, a plan formulating in her mind, she felt a slow indulgent smile cross her lips. "In that case, what are you doing May long weekend?"

Chapter Twenty-Three

Sparrows tittered, the sun shone and the wind ruffled the trees shielding Warrick's grandparents' North Shore mansion. Overflowing with multicolored flowers, the fragrance rising from the garden aroused the appetites of the eighty guests. Following the sound of children's laughter, Sage and Marshall strolled into the backyard, hand in hand.

"Some barbecue," Sage said, as her husband led her to the gazebo. "This is incredible."

"I'd say." Shaking his head in awe, he released a slow whistle. "Check out the water fountain, and all the rose petals in the pond. I've been to a lot of parties, but I've never seen anything like this."

"I know. Mrs. Carver went all out. It looks like a wedding reception up in…" The sentence died on her lips. Mouth agape, her gaze slowly circled the backyard. She stood in perfect silence, fevered thoughts whipping through her brain. For several moments, she eyed the floor vases packed with gardenias, then the folding chairs positioned on either side of the aisle and finally the white blossoms adrift in the pool. "Sweet mother of Joseph! This isn't a barbecue. It's a wedding reception!"

It wasn't until Sage felt her husband's hand over her mouth

that she realized *she* was the one screaming. "Oh my God! Warrick and Tangela are getting married!"

"Sage, calm down," he whispered. "Everyone's staring at us."

Prying his fingers from her mouth, she said, "I can't believe her! Best friend my ass. I went shopping with Tangela yesterday and she didn't say a word about this."

Wearing a sympathetic smile, Marshall put a comforting hand on her shoulder. "You're disappointed about not being her maid of honor, huh? You two are practically sisters, and I know it's going to be hard to watch her get married—"

"That's not it," she insisted, cutting him off. "If I had known this was a wedding reception, I would have dressed up. I can't take pictures in a tank top and capri pants."

"Honey, you look fine."

"But I don't want *fine*. I want elegant, chic, sophisticated."

Marshall took a swig of his drink. After waiting an hour for his wife to get dressed, then sitting in traffic for another thirty minutes, his frustration level was in the red zone, and all he wanted now was something to eat. Hungry, thirsty and anxious to kick back and celebrate the holiday the way God intended, he told her to try and relax. "There's nothing we can do about it now," he told her. "We're already here, so you're going to have to make the most of it."

"Like hell I am! It's my best friend's wedding, Marshall. Not one of your mother's down-home cookouts." Gripping his hand, she spun on her heels and hurried back up the cobble walkway. "Come on, baby. We're going to make a quick run to Boulevard Mall!"

The French doors opened and Tangela stepped out onto the red satin carpet sprinkled with white tulips. Bedazzled with jewels across the bodice, her ivory-colored strapless gown had lace trim along the neckline and a beaded bustline. Diamonds sprinkled the length of the dress and the sweeping train flowed around her long legs like an elegant whirlpool.

Turning her face toward the sky, she soaked up the warmth of the sun and drew serenity from the gentle rustling of palm trees and the melody of humming sparrows.

Tightening her grip on her bouquet, she smiled brightly, moving gracefully toward the man she loved. They'd pulled off the surprise of the century and even from several feet away she could see the stunned looks on people's faces. Three weeks was hardly enough time to plan a wedding, but after talking things over with his grandparents, they'd decided to go for it. Leaving the planning in Mrs. Carver's very capable hands, they'd concentrated on securing a wedding license, moving Tangela's things into the penthouse and choosing a honeymoon destination. The night he'd proposed, they'd lain in bed for hours discussing their wedding, and realized early on that they didn't want something large, extravagant and flashy. They wanted their special day to encompass all the things they loved—good food, good music and good friends.

Beside Reverend Massey, Warrick stood calmly, his hands clasped in front of him, his eyes alight with excitement. In a traditional black Armani designer tux, buffed shoes and a wide megawatt smile, her husband-to-be deserved his own *People* magazine cover.

Tangela couldn't imagine a more perfect day for a wedding, and, as Warrick stepped forward and took her hand, her heart pulsed with joy. His aftershave smelled divine and a rush of pleasure overtook her. On an extended high from their romantic afternoon at the couples' spa yesterday, she stole a quick look at their friends and family seated behind them and smiled.

People grinned, waved and snapped pictures. Her legs wobbled, and for a moment Tangela thought she might lose her balance, but she straightened her back and dug her heels into the grass. Nothing was going to go wrong. This was the moment she'd been waiting for, the moment she'd been dreaming of since she was a little girl. Today, she would marry her best friend, her lover, her soul mate, the man created and designed especially for her. And nothing, not even a serious case of the nerves, was going to stand in her way.

"Friends, family, well-wishers, we are gathered here this afternoon to join this man and this woman in holy matrimony." A prayer followed, and then Reverend Massey spoke briefly about the beauty and significance of marriage and their roles as husband and wife. "The couple has written their own vows and I invite them to share them now."

Eyes radiating with pride, Warrick brought a hand to Tangela's cheek and gently caressed her face. "My God, Angie, you're exquisite. Absolutely perfect in every way."

Blinking incessantly, she willed herself not to cry. Tangela cleared the emotion from her throat and tried to focus her gaze on her fiancé's face. Crying would ruin her makeup and she didn't want to look a mess in their wedding pictures.

"I've loved you from the moment I saw you and despite all the challenges we've faced, I knew you'd be my wife one day. From this day forward and for the rest of our lives, I will honor you, cherish you and respect you. There'll be real good days and some hard times, but when I mess up, I promise to buy you a gift from Harry Winston!"

Guests tittered. When the laughter died down, he said, "This is my solemn vow," and sealed his declaration with a chaste kiss. "We're going to have an amazing life together, Tangela. A life we're going to live to the fullest."

Tangela's eyes grew cloudy again. She'd promised herself—and her makeup artist—that she wouldn't break down, but she couldn't hold her feelings in any longer. Like a tide overrunning a dam, tears gushed down her cheeks. And when Warrick brushed them away, she cried even harder. The loving gesture wasn't lost on their guests, either. Behind her, someone wept, and soon, the air was inundated with sniffles, whimpers and hushed sobs.

Steeling herself against her emotions, she straightened her back, lifted her chin and returned Warrick's tender smile. She was minutes away from becoming Mrs. Warrick Carver and she didn't want to miss a single moment of the ceremony. His broad grin testified to how relaxed he was and Tangela wished she had a fifth of his confidence. Just another one of the characteristics she loved about her husband-to-be. A man of action, with a no-holds-barred approach to life, he was calm, composed and unruffled, no matter the occasion or forum.

Reverend Massey nodded at Tangela, cueing her that it was her turn to speak.

Scared her nerves would get the best of her, she'd copied her vows on the tiny piece of paper stuck to her palm. Glancing down now, she expelled a nervous breath, blocked out the distant sound of a wailing baby and spoke from the heart.

"Today, I marry my best friend. The man I was destined to marry, the man fated to be my partner, my lover and, more important, my husband. And I can say that with complete assurance, because over the years I dated a lot of frogs."

Smiling knowingly, the female guests in attendance nodded empathically.

Emboldened by the strength of her voice, and the peace that had settled over her, she continued. "Warrick, my love for you is real, never-ending, absolute. I will cherish our love forever, and I promise never to take you for granted. Nothing can, or ever will change my feelings for you. This is my solemn vow."

Reverend Massey asked for the rings, blessed them, then asked Tangela to repeat after him. "Take this ring as a seal upon the marriage vows I have spoken, and as you wear it, may it be a reminder of how much I love you, not only on this precious day, but every single day of your life. You are truly the only man I want."

"Tangela, five years ago, I gave you this ring as a symbol of my love, my faith in our strength together and my covenant to learn and grow with you. I gave this ring as my gift to you. Wear it and think of me and know that I love you."

"Now that you have exchanged these rings and these vows, and have agreed to be married according to the beliefs of the church and the laws of the state of Nevada, it gives me great pleasure to pronounce you husband and wife. Warrick, you may kiss your bride."

Shaping his lips into a wide, broad-faced grin, he cupped her face in his palm and kissed her with such wild unrestraint, Tangela held on to him so she wouldn't topple over into the bushes. Lightly stroking the back of his head, she inclined her head and coaxed his tongue out of his mouth. It was a passionate, spiritual moment, one she'd never forget. It was burned inside her brain forever and Tangela couldn't ever remember being this happy.

Smiling good-naturedly, Reverend Massey leaned forward and whispered, "All right, you two. There'll be plenty of time for kissing later. People are hungry, y'all!"

Hands clasped, eyes shimmering with delight, they reluctantly broke off the kiss. Tangela gripped her husband's forearm. They'd done it. It was official. She'd spend the rest of her life living with and loving the man of her dreams, her first and only love, a gracious, compassionate soul who treated her with the utmost respect.

Facing their esteemed guests, she searched the crowd for Sage. The decision not to have a bridal party had caused Tangela many sleepless nights, but when she saw the buoyant expression on her best friend's face, she knew there were no hard feelings. Sage and Marshall were dressed to the nines and their formal attire made Tangela wonder if they'd known what was up all along. Tangela never could keep a secret and it was obvious Sage had seen right through her charade.

Clutching the leather-bound Bible to his chest, Reverend Massey gestured for the audience to stand. "Ladies and gentlemen, it is my pleasure to introduce for the very first time Mr. and Mrs. Warrick Carver."

The cheers and applause were thunderous.

"This is the beginning of the rest of our lives," Warrick whispered, turning toward his new bride. "Are you ready, Mrs. Tangela Carver?"

Gazing up at her husband, she squeezed his hand and took the first step toward the rest of their lives, confident their days would be filled with love, joy and laughter.

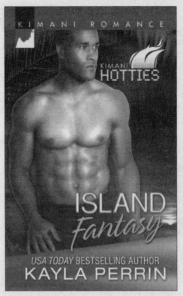

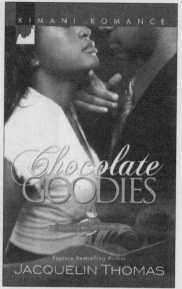

REQUEST YOUR FREE BOOKS!

2 FREE NOVELS
PLUS 2 *FREE GIFTS!*

KIMANI™
ROMANCE

Love's ultimate destination!

YES! Please send me 2 FREE Kimani™ Romance novels and my 2 FREE gifts (gifts are worth about $10). After receiving them, if I don't wish to receive any more books, I can return the shipping statement marked "cancel." If I don't cancel, I will receive 4 brand-new novels every month and be billed just $4.69 per book in the U.S. or $5.24 per book in Canada. That's a saving of over 20% off the cover price. It's quite a bargain! Shipping and handling is just 50¢ per book in the U.S. and 75¢ per book in Canada.* I understand that accepting the 2 free books and gifts places me under no obligation to buy anything. I can always return a shipment and cancel at any time. Even if I never buy another book from Kimani Press, the two free books and gifts are mine to keep forever.

168 XDN E4CA   368 XDN E4CM

Name	(PLEASE PRINT)

Address	Apt. #

City	State/Prov.	Zip/Postal Code

Signature (if under 18, a parent or guardian must sign)

Mail to **The Reader Service:**
IN U.S.A.: P.O. Box 1867, Buffalo, NY 14240-1867
IN CANADA: P.O. Box 609, Fort Erie, Ontario L2A 5X3

Not valid for current subscribers to Kimani Romance books.

Want to try two free books from another line?
Call 1-800-873-8635 or visit www.morefreebooks.com.

* Terms and prices subject to change without notice. Prices do not include applicable taxes. N.Y. residents add applicable sales tax. Canadian residents will be charged applicable provincial taxes and GST. Offer not valid in Quebec. This offer is limited to one order per household. All orders subject to approval. Credit or debit balances in a customer's account(s) may be offset by any other outstanding balance owed by or to the customer. Please allow 4 to 6 weeks for delivery. Offer available while quantities last.

Your Privacy: Kimani Press is committed to protecting your privacy. Our Privacy Policy is available online at www.eHarlequin.com or upon request from the Reader Service. From time to time we make our lists of customers available to reputable third parties who may have a product or service of interest to you. If you would prefer we not share your name and address, please check here. ☐

Help us get it right—We strive for accurate, respectful and relevant communications. To clarify or modify your communication preferences, visit us at www.ReaderService.com/consumerchoice.

KROM10